The Green Man's Dark Secret

Ruler's Wit

"Do not trust the words and writings of these authors, who have used their mischief and wiles to create a fiction within these unspeakable pages."

Matthew Hopkins

Prologue

March 1993

Joe Marshall sighed and looked around the busy market square; his back ached and he wanted to go home. The early starts were taking their toll and he allowed his mind to wander, dreaming of some time off. Brenda, one of their regulars, waved at him as she approached, and shrugging off his daydream he smiled in response.

'How's the world with you, ma duck?'

'Hello, Brenda. Can't complain – the sun's shining and spring is most definitely in the air. Now, what can I get for you?'

'I'll have half a pound of carrots, some sprouts – you know how my Stan loves sprouts – two onions, a cabbage, for me bubble and squeak the day after ...'

Joe half listened as Brenda repeated, almost word for word, what she usually had from his fruit and veg stalls. He looked around as he selected the produce. Still no sign of his wife, Maud, and he wondered how long the relative peace would last. He had long since learned to hold his tongue at her outbursts, and any attempt at reason fell on deaf ears. Their life, she angrily told him, was not enough, but she had no intention of doing anything about it.

'So, that'll be all and I'll see you again next week,' Brenda said as she handed over the money for her goods. 'You look after yourself and say hello to Maud for me.'

Joe chuckled to himself as he turned to the stall and tidied the veg, covering the gaps left by the items he'd sold. If only you knew what she said to your back, he thought.

'What're you laughing at, you great lump?'

The smile vanished as his wife strode over, snatching the money apron from him and tying it around her ever-increasing waist – a fact Maud was determined to refute by telling anyone who would listen that she rarely ate, and never a cream cake, consuming only the smallest portions of the fresh products that she sold. In her hand was a brown paper bag and Joe knew without looking that it contained a cream horn. The same every week – she never asked him what he might have liked. This was never discussed. She'd have denied it with her dying breath, and most probably have swiped at him for his impertinence, so he never mentioned it.

'Now, why don't you go off for a walk and keep out of my way for half an hour or so,' she said, placing the brown paper bag on the foldaway table where they kept their flasks of tea. 'And don't you dare go into that over-priced fancy-pants coffee shop again,' she hissed. 'Now go! I need some peace.'

Joe watched his wife turn her back on him before making his way across the square. A short walk around the park would help to clear his head, but he needed to make a quick stop first. Patting the front of his jacket he felt the long thin cigarette nestled inside the lining and sent a silent thank you to the customer who'd dropped it earlier. He'd have loved a coffee to go with it, but Maud had screamed at him when he'd stupidly revealed the cost of a cup of coffee he'd bought a few months ago. He loved coffee but their flasks always contained tea because that's what Maud drank. She'd have none of that bitter tasting rubbish in their house.

Glancing around to make sure no one was watching, Joe

ducked into the alleyway, surprised to see Fenella, one of the other stallholders, in front of him. The bright red of her hair shone despite the shadows of the alley and Joe wondered where she was heading at such a fast pace.

'Fenella. Wait up, will you?' he called to her retreating back. She turned and smiled at him before disappearing

Joe closed his eyes, took a deep breath and counted to ten. It was a habit he'd adopted during Maud's screaming sessions. 'When I open my eyes, Fenella will be standing right where she was, she will not have disappeared and she will be waiting for me,' he reasoned.

He opened his eyes.

'Bugger! Not. Standing. There. Right, where on earth has she gone then?'

Approaching the spot where Fenella had stood Joe looked around. Behind him, the alley was empty and in shadow, but as he turned back Joe felt a tingling sensation down his back and his head felt like jelly, bending and squashing in a very odd sensation. He felt hot, hotter than he'd ever felt and he could hear muttering, but in no language he'd ever heard before. Bright orange and yellow sparks flew in front of his face as the alleyway began to spin and then everything went black.

Part One

Chapter 1

The Codex Gigas, Present Day

Matthew Hopkins sank into his window seat and looked out onto Arlanda's wet tarmac. Stockholm had been welcoming and, to his great satisfaction, very successful. The plane soon filled up and doors were closed ready for take-off. Cabin crew took their seats and the KLM flight to Schiphol began to move onto the runway. He sat back and closed his eyes enjoying the sensation as the plane rose, leaving behind Sweden's landscape and cold weather.

He'd seen it! With his own eyes, he'd seen it! There in the Treasury in Humlegården, was the Codex Gigas – The Devil's Book! It was huge – thirty-six inches tall, twenty wide, and eight-and-a-half thick, so the woman in the library had told him. She'd also said that it weighed more than she did at a hundred and sixty-five pounds, which didn't surprise him as it was reputedly written on vellum from a hundred and sixty donkeys. That he did doubt, more like calfskin, he thought, but that wasn't his concern. What was his concern was that he was able to confirm that ten pages were indeed missing – originally three hundred and twenty, now only three hundred and ten pages continued to exist, although the images of three excised pages remained just visible and that could only mean one thing – that witch didn't have them all yet.

Relieved that no one had taken the seat next to him, he refused an in-flight drink and pulled out a book to read on the two-hour flight. Having to change at Amsterdam was an irritation he could well do without but there were no direct flights to East Midlands Airport. The scheduling worked well, however, affording him enough time to navigate Schipol Airport and then it was just an eighty-minute hop to East Midlands. He would pick up his hire-car and drive to the police station in Loughborough and his meeting with a Sergeant Boyle and a detective inspector who had been brought in to investigate some cold missing persons cases. Another irritation he could do without. He did feel smug though when he thought of his role as a specialist policing consultant – they would probably think he was counter terrorism. He smiled and picked up the book; his ancestor's book: The Discovery of Witches by Matthew Hopkins. A picture on the front cover showed a man in seventeenth century clothing and underneath it read: The Witchfinder General. His great, great – he'd forgotten how many greats – grandfather had begun the quest and now it was up to him to complete it. He opened the book and his father's letter fell onto his lap. When his father had departed this world for the next he had left Matthew the letter along with one of the 'missing' pages, Jerome's letter to Paulinus 'Frater Ambrosius. Matthew felt an anger rising within him. Until he could trade the correct number of souls for the rest of the pages, they wouldn't be his to fulfil not only his father's greatest wish, and that he'd died without finding the pages, but to now gain the promise he ultimately desired.

He picked up the letter and opened it out. He'd read it a hundred times but read it again to remind himself of his mission. Then he carefully refolded it and slipped it back into the book.

Chapter 2

Loughborough Market, 1663

The market was alive, bustling and vibrant, captivating Hooke's attention. Robert Hooke had a lively mind that flitted from one idea to another, and a keen interest in people, in life. He walked with a bouncing step, his gait mirroring the atmosphere in the marketplace of Loughborough where he had come to visit from London, his place of residence and work. It was his approach to the world that had made his former tutor keep track of him. Unlike the older man, whose greying hair came just below his ears and was tousled in appearance under its hat, Robert's dark hair was coiffed and held back neatly with a ribbon. They both wore breeches and boots, but Hall matched his with the requisite long black frogged coat and white cravat. Robert's flounced white shirt protruded stylishly from below his coloured waist jacket; a jaunty look matching his character. Robert had visited Hall before at his family seat in the north but this was his first time in the Midlands' town.

'I had not expected such busyness away from the capital, Hall! 'Tis a veritable feast of entertainment!' Robert turned to his companion, the Reverend Nicholas Hall, and patted his arm in an enthusiastic gesture. They were on their way to the guildhall to meet with Lord Hastings. All three were well acquainted with each other, having met at Oxford University, and been involved in studies together, Robert as a student of the others. The newly restored Hall had invited Hooke to stay at the rectory once he had settled his family back into their home and ousted that rake, Bromskill. He'd told Hooke that he was trying to ignore the fact that Bromskill had repaired to new lodgings a matter of yards away. Hooke had been secretly fascinated by the gossip that Friends were holding meetings, essentially challenging the re-establishment of the true church.

'Oh, aye, 'tis that all right! I didst think you might find it diverting, my friend. There are all sorts here, even from as far as France. 'Tis the wool that brings them. No doubt there'll be a few Frenchies in the guildhall.' Hall gestured to the building on the other side of the market square. 'But we can take some time to peruse what is on offer, should you wish.'

'I wouldst indeed,' came the answer.

'And perhaps we might partake of a sup of chocolate, in yonder coffeehouse?'

'That would be a fine thing, Hall. There are many such houses in London town at present but I do not have the time or the facility to enjoy them, I'm afraid.'

He looked across the busy market where like produce were grouped together and signs displaying trades were on show. The guildhall was prominent on the opposite side of the market from where they stood. At the head of the square a simple stone cross was raised on granite steps. To the side of this a man was in the stocks, and several people aimed rotten produce at him.

'Another hooker, I dare say,' Hall observed, looking at the victim whose clothes, underneath all the vegetable deitrus, were passably fit. 'Hooking clothes through windows seems to be on the increase nowadays.'

Robert selected the least slimy looking brassica from a box, pitched it at the man and wiped his hand down his breeches.

Hooke noticed the disapproval in Hall's glance and felt his hand on his shoulder.

'Leave that to these folk,' Hall said, as his touch guided Robert past the regular stallholders grouped in the Shambles, who had set out an array of meats. Robert's mouth watered at the bacon, tripe and trotters. Animal skins came next. They strode quickly past the fish and the cheese stalls with their pungent smells competing against each other. Street sellers mingled with the crowds, some singing and calling, others selling or handing out leaflets, adding to his delight. Robert stopped to appreciate the fresh produce – the colourful displays of carrots, beets, spinach, onions and radishes on offer from the more transient hucksters and higlers. There were dried beans and cereals: corn, wheat and oats that must have been stored over winter. There were women hawking woollen garments, shawls and stockings that most of the women clearly wore.

Some stalls sold tobacco and pipes, another luxury he had so far avoided, though the aroma was captivating.

'This way, my boy,' Hall advised, leading Robert towards the stationer's area where stalls held all kinds of chapbooks, as well as quills and inks.

'I wouldst make a purchase, Hall,' he said, eyeing the quills. 'May I?' he asked the stallholder, raising his voice over the hubbub, and picking up a fine feather. He flexed it and noted its tip, cut to a point.

'I must show you my latest glass,' he said to his friend, with the quill still in his hand. 'Looking through it at matter like this, is truly another world.' He felt for his leather purse, hidden within his waistcoat, which contained several groats and silver pennies.

'Take it later, perhaps, Robert,' Hall suggested. 'Look at this pamphlet.' His face was colouring up. 'That upstart, Bromskill, is boldly advertising his meetings now, and George Fox to attend! He has no shame,' he blustered.

'Mr Fox is speaking yonder,' said the young pamphleteer. Through the melee Robert could see someone standing a head above the onlookers, although he couldn't be heard clearly because of the increasing clamour.

'Let's get a look at him, Hall.' Robert headed towards the speaker with his tutor in tow.

'Must we, dear boy? Now, look, Hastings and his wife have come out of the guildhall. And something is wrong.' He was almost shouting over what was now a real commotion.

For the moment, Robert only had eyes for Fox, a man in his late thirties. He was standing on a wooden box, dressed in black, not unlike Hall, with a cravat at his neck and a flat, wide-brimmed black hat. Fox was pointing in the direction of the noise. In a crisp, commanding voice he called over the crowd, ignoring the approaching discord as well as he could.

'There is an ocean of darkness and death spreading the world, but hear me! An ocean of light and love flows over that darkness if you'll let it.'

Robert heard Hall's outraged splutter: ''Tis a charavaris mocking Hastings! 'Tis too much.'

They watched as a gaggle of outlandishly dressed people creating an untuned racket by banging pots and other strange instruments, danced and leapt around a mock horse. The rider was wearing an ornate hat and a notice was pinned to his front labelling him a hustler. People watching were being knocked aside, a sort of wave of movement rippling through the bystanders.

'Art thou a child of the Light? And have you walked into the Light?' Fox shouted to the people, as the force of motion caused Robert to lurch forward. His shoulder barged the younger of two women who had been standing close by causing her to stumble.

The older woman stood back and gasped. 'Ellen, are you all right?'

The younger girl had her hands over her ears and her eyes tightly shut. When she opened them she seemed transfixed.

'Oh, Jayne, I just want to go home,' Robert heard her whisper. He watched as she slipped an oblong object of smooth grey material from her pocket. She held it up as he might have done with his glass. A pink light enveloped all three, the girl, Robert and Fox, and the market as Robert knew it, disappeared.

Chapter 3

The Incident Room, Present Day

The incident room was rammed and it was only ten thirty. Florence Carter watched as a thick-set man fired demands across a table, while simultaneously talking into the phone he held to his ear. On the other side of the table sat three people. Two of them held notebooks and were scribbling furiously, while the third kept nodding as he jabbed away at the iPad on his lap.

Each bank of desks, and Florence counted six, had at least four police officers around it. The volume of noise suggested that most of the staff were on the phone.

At the front of the room was an enormous white board. The entire left side was covered in photographs, while the right side had an array of different coloured writing. Red lines ran across the board – connecting photographs to single words, phrases, even entire sentences.

The general buzz took Florence back. It had been more than twenty years since she'd stood in this room as a police constable on secondment to CID, but the years slid sideways placing her there as if yesterday. They had all been so sure of an arrest. There had been a number of theories, explanations and suspects, but the case had collapsed around their ears. Hundreds of man hours, including phone calls, house-to-house, arrests and interviews had got them nowhere. It still left Florence with a sense of unease. Every corner had been searched, every rational explanation explored, but the missing people had remained missing, no sightings reported and the only connection had been between the Green Man and the marketplace.

The door opened and Sergeant Harriet Boyle poked her head in. Gesturing frantically, she beckoned Florence over.

'Ah, there you are, Carter. I told Fred to show you to the Duty Inspector's office,' Boyle said, as they made their way into the corridor and away from the noise. The door swished shut and the silence was instant. 'Come on, we'll go there now. Can't hear yourself scream in this place. You do remember Fred, don't you? He was here back in the day. Anyway,' she continued, 'the Inspector is out at a council meeting and won't be back for a couple of hours, so it will be quiet – not like this place.'

'That man was Fred Sands? I thought I knew his face and he certainly knew me. He was going for promotion when I left and I heard he'd made sergeant. He was in the intake before me. Good God, he's got erm, well ...'

'Fat. Yes, I know. He got caught up in a struggle on the High Street five years ago. We'd had a report of a missing person and Fred thought he'd spotted her. Turned out he was mistaken and the woman reacted badly. Knocked his confidence and when the desk sergeant position arose, well he jumped at it and pretty much stopped caring about himself. His wife left him last year. Yes, I know, we were all shocked too. Still,' Boyle said, 'good to see you haven't let yourself go. I hear you made Firearms. Does that make you the force's first female on that unit?'

Florence grinned. 'I was, but there are two of us now and she's every bit as determined as I am.'

'Fantastic. Always good to hear there are more women like us. Very well done to you. Now, we must get on, so follow me and we will get a coffee on the way.'

Florence smiled as Boyle turned away and began to walk

along the corridor. Following behind she noted the changes in the older woman. Boyle's shorter hairstyle was new, as were the stylish glasses that had replaced the black thick-rimmed frames she'd worn twenty years before, but the energy was still there, crackling out of her.

The team they'd worked on had viewed Boyle as eccentric; a personality trait that had made her remarkably difficult to pigeon hole, both in and out of work, but Florence had seen the conscientious and driven side of the older woman. Impressed and inspired, Florence had been one of the few permitted to see the out-of-uniform Boyle, and with respect had come friendship.

In fact, they had even shed a tear or two together over the occasional death they'd attended, and Boyle could always be relied upon in a fight. 'Maybe that was why we worked so well together,' Florence mused, noting as they passed, the drab yellow colour on the walls that each police station corridor seemed to be cursed with.

Florence had never known her to have a partner; she wondered now if that had changed.

'It's been a long time, Harriet, how are you?' Florence asked.

'I'm well thank you, Carter. Ah, Perkins,' Boyle broke off to address the young police constable who had met them in the corridor, 'there you are. Please can you ...'

'Morning, Sarge. Morning ..?'

'Detective Constable Perkins, this is Police Constable Carter'.

Florence nodded at the young man who smiled in return.

'As I was saying, can you grab us a couple of coffees and meet me in the usual office.' This wasn't a question, and Florence watched with a smile as the officer scampered away to do Boyle's bidding.

Florence followed Boyle past several doors and down

one flight of stairs before stopping at a door marked Duty Inspector where Boyle input some numbers into the entry code before the door whooshed open.

'Thought it best if there were no recording devices for this meeting,' Boyle said, as she pushed it closed behind them. 'There, now we won't get disturbed and can get down to business.'

Florence took the chair Boyle pointed to and sat down. The office was standard size, but the walls were an attractive shade of green; the effect calming and tranquil. There was a huge potted palm in the corner and the vertical blinds on both windows were a shade darker than that on the walls. There were two large bookcases on the wall to the left and a couple of comfortable-looking chairs in the far corner; the sort people buy from Ikea, along with a footstool each. The room was dominated by the desk in the centre, upon which sat a large black briefcase. She watched as Boyle spun the case round, thumbed the keylock and popped open the latches. The lid stayed firmly closed.

'Nice office,' Florence commented, sitting back in the unusually snug office chair on the other side of the desk.

'Ah, yes. This is the lair of Chief Inspector Pearson. Not the sort to mess about and she certainly has flair – point blank refused the office the last inspector vacated upon retirement. Insisted on windows, new carpet and a decorating job. It makes a nice change though. We all get tired of that bloody yellow colour.'

'A new carpet? Jesus Christ! I thought the main rule of police stations was to keep the same ones, mouldy, staple-ridden – not forgetting the revolting coarseness of them – for at least fifty years!' Florence laughed at the smiling expression on Boyle's face. The years melted away and they were again two young women just trying to get through a shift.

'You remember that night we found that car upside down in a ditch and both shit ourselves 'cause there was a body on the back seat?'

Boyle spluttered and reached for the box of tissues on the desk. 'Oh God, yes. I'll never forget your bravery as you volunteered to crawl under the hedge and into that cold water. It was so dark and we only had our mag lights. I suggested paper, rock, scissors, but before we started, I decided I couldn't let you go alone so we both got onto all fours and started crawling.'

'I was so scared,' Florence recalled with a chuckle. 'I'd only been out of training school a month or so and was so relieved when you came with me.'

'I just remember scrambling down that bank and through the slimy water and you shouting "hello, can you hear me? It's the police. Are you hurt? I'm Florence and this is Sergeant Boyle."'

'I didn't know your first name then.' Florence put her hand to her mouth.

'I'd got to the driver's door before you appeared on the opposite side and will never, ever forget your face as we crouched on either side of the car and realisation crossed your face,' Boyle managed before dissolving into laughter.

'A bloody blow-up doll!' Florence gasped, reaching for a tissue as tears formed in her eyes.

'With enormous boobs, red lips and that ridiculous expression of shock on its face.'

All control lost, both women crumpled into heaving laughter, clutching their stomachs as tears flowed down their cheeks.

'I've never understood that expression. I mean, why would any bloke relish a look of shock from a woman when in a bedroom scenario?' Boyle asked, one eyebrow raised.

Florence wiped her face and looked across the desk. 'Erm, Harriet,' she said, deadpan, 'why do you think?'

Confusion momentarily shot across Boyle's face before realisation dawned, which resulted in more laughter, on both sides.

'Anyway,' Boyle cleared her throat and blew her nose. 'Back to business. You remember the missing people in ninety-three that we never found?'

'Yes of course I do,' Florence replied, dabbing her eyes, 'you know I do. That's why I'm here, and why I'm meeting that DI later. Did you get what time he can meet?'

'Ah, yes. DI Sandbach. He just said to arrange it with you and let him know.' Boyle leant back and grabbed a file from the windowsill, before passing it across the table. 'Odd chap, but comes highly recommended for this kind of thing. He's had great success with some cases where the answer, erm, maybe isn't the most obvious one. Inside that file is all the info he will need regarding the past mispers, so let him get up to date properly first.'

'Okay, he sounds perfect for our mystery then.' Florence laughed and pulled the file across the table. 'I'm going into Loughborough town once I've left here. I want to get a feel for the old place again.'

'I'll get him to meet you in Costa then shall I? Two p.m. okay?'

'Yes, I suppose. So, back to those mispers. You and I both felt there was something more; something other than very unhappy people disappearing from their equally unhappy lives. All those people and simply no sign of them.' Florence stopped talking suddenly as there was a gentle knock on the door.

'Hold on to that thought,' Boyle said, as she went to open the door.

'Your drinks, Sarg,' Perkins said as he entered the room carrying a tray with two mugs of coffee, a jug and some sachets of sugar.

'Thank you, Perkins.' Boyle took the tray and placed it on the desk. 'That'll be all. Back to your desk and chase up the last sighting we had in 1993 of that market-stall holder, Joe Marshall.'

'But Sarg, don't you think it's all just a bit ...' Perkins

trailed off and Florence watched as he shifted his weight from his right leg to his left.

'I know it'll be a waste of time, but we have to show willingness.'

'Right,' she said, returning to her seat as the door closed behind Perkins, 'where were we? Ah, yes. Well, to put it succinctly, there was something more. Indeed, there is something more.'

Florence stared at Boyle. Her eyes shone behind the lenses of her glasses and she was the most excited Florence had ever seen her.

'Are you telling me that more people have gone missing, Harriet?'

'Oh, indeed yes. Three more, well recently, three more that we know of, in and around the marketplace, but the stories of missing people have been circulating for ages.'

'Okay, so what's the thinking this time? Is there a new gaffer on board with a mind slightly more open than a sealed-up cave, buried beneath three hundred tons of rock, soil and other debris?'

'Not exactly.' Boyle grinned as she pulled the briefcase across the desk so that it was between them. 'You and I always agreed that there was something more – something hidden from us. Well, it took some searching, but by God I found it.' Their eyes met and Florence watched in fascination as Boyle slowly opened the case.

This was so unlike the Harriet Boyle that Florence remembered from twenty years before. Then Boyle was controlled, reserved, not one for unnecessary drama or fuss, but this Boyle – well, she had Florence all but salivating.

A commotion outside the door made Florence jump to her feet. The door crashed open and Perkins careered into the room. Boyle slammed the lid to the briefcase shut and flicked the keys with her fingers to lock it.

'Sarg, you've got to come. Superintendent Davey has had the papers on the phone and she's demanding you go see her.' Perkins drew a deep breath. 'She's serious 'cos she threatened to nail my balls to the wall if I didn't return with you forthwith.'

Florence watched as Boyle stood up. 'I can come back, or maybe I could wait here,' Florence suggested hopefully, glancing at the briefcase.

'Or, you could simply come with me,' Boyle said with a grimace as she walked towards the door. 'Come on, we can endure the wrath of Maleficent together and then we will discuss the contents of this case. It's too important to leave it any longer. Lead the way, young Perkins,' Boyle exclaimed as she held the door open for Perkins to precede her, 'and you too can come and witness how not to lead a team of exemplary officers.'

'Maleficent? Are you serious?' Florence muttered, as she grabbed the file and her own bag before following them from the room and back along the corridor.

'Yes, I know,' Boyle said with a chuckle as Florence fell into step alongside her, 'but believe me, when you meet her you will totally understand.'

'What on earth happened to Thompson?'

'He retired on medical grounds and we were very lucky that Superintendent Davey was able to join us here. Or so she has told us. Repeatedly.'

'What's the deal with her then and why the nickname?'

'There is something of the night about her and I'm not wholly convinced she's of this earth. Hates people, kids – even animals,' Boyle explained, with a shake of her head.

'Well, okay. I mean, I get the first two, but animals, really? – who hates animals for God's sake?'

'Maleficent does, although she puts on a good show for the top brass and the media. Oh, sorry, sir,' Boyle apologised as they all but walked into two men rounding the corner.

'Have a care, Boyle,' the man wearing Inspector pips on

his shoulders said, before addressing the man at his side. 'I do apologise, Mr Hopkins. Please, let's continue.'

Florence was startled to see the man addressed as Mr Hopkins staring at her. A scowl darkened his otherwise handsome face and his eyes, well, they burnt the oddest colour. If she'd been asked she'd have sworn they had amber centres, with the strangest orange glow. His gaze raked over her body – the effect of which left her breathless – before nodding briefly and striding away.

'Jesus Christ, who the hell was that?' Florence gasped to an equally stunned Boyle.

'Mr Hopkins, although I obviously wasn't worth an introduction from Inspector Edwards. Have you seen him before, Perkins?'

'No, Sarg.' Perkins shrugged and gave a shy smile at Florence.

'Those eyes,' Florence murmured.

'What's that about his eyes?' Boyle asked. 'Come on, you two. We've kept her Highness waiting long enough.

Florence simply shook her head as she followed them both along the corridor.

Chapter 4

Loughborough Market, Present Day

The crash, which sounded like pot smashing at a Grecian festival, echoed throughout the stalls that lined the marketplace. A man rushed past, almost knocking Paige from her feet.

'Well, he's certainly in a hurry,' Paige said, and went to pick up her hat that had been dislodged in the collision.

'I'm sorry.' The man, who had stopped running, turned and bent down. He scooped up the hat and offered it to her. As Paige took it she noticed that his right hand had two fingers missing.

'Thank you, er ...' she said, and smiled.

'Pete,' the man answered and winked, which caused a scar down his right cheek to appear. 'My pleasure – must dash.'

Paige put her hat back on and linked her arm through Wesley's.

'I wonder what all that commotion was,' Wesley said. 'Come along, this could be interesting.'

Paige resignedly shook her head and walked with Wesley as he made his way towards the disturbance that had occurred. The sight that met them was one of shambles and confusion. Two stalls were tipped on their sides; crockery was smashed on the flags of the marketplace and a miscellany of fruits and vegetables covered the pavement. Some had rolled into the gutter. They moved in closer and Wesley took out his notepad.

'For goodness' sake,' Paige hissed, 'can't you just let this one go?'

Wesley stepped into the middle of the destruction and raised his right index finger, something he always did when pondering a situation.

'Someone's obviously had a disagreement with the stallholders and caused this. Now can we please go?' Paige insisted.

'Which stallholders?' Wesley asked.

'Well the ones who look after those two,' Paige answered, pointing to the upturned trestles. 'Does it really matter?'

Wesley picked his way over broken pots, carefully avoiding any squashed fruit, and approached a lady whose stall consisted of racks of clothing that were, thankfully, still upright and untouched.

'Excuse me, madam,' Wesley said, and Paige saw the blonde, mini-skirted and very made-up clothes seller, flash a red-lipped smile when she realised Wesley was speaking to her.

'Yes,' she purred. 'How may I help you?'

'Could you tell me who owns these stalls please?' Wesley gave her what Paige called his shamelessly seductive smile.

The woman appeared to shudder and seemed unable to speak. Paige walked over to Wesley and slipped her arm through his.

'Hello,' she greeted. 'What on earth's happened here?'

'How would I know?' The woman cast a furtive sideways glance at Wesley, who cocked his head and winked at her.

Paige moved away a couple of paces to allow Wesley to extract the information he was looking for. She looked across at the overturned stalls and sniffed the air – the smell of apples was almost overpowering. A woman with long red hair was walking away and laughing at one of the stallholders, who shook his fist at her. Paige thought that the woman's green clothes went well with her fiery locks. She turned her attention back to Wesley and the owner of the clothes stall.

'Do you know the owners of the stalls?' she heard Wesley enquire again, his voice insistent.

'Oh. That's John Stearne's,' the blonde lady said, pointing to the smashed crockery. 'Serves him right. He's never got a good word to say to anyone. I'm surprised he sells anything with his attitude.'

'And the fruit and veg?' Wesley coaxed.

'Oh, that's Malcolm's. He's a lovely bloke.'

'And where are they, er, sorry I didn't catch your name?'

'Linda.' She beamed and pushed out her chest. 'That's Stearne over there on the phone,' she told him. Paige followed Linda's indication as she pointed to a bald man with a stomach the size of a space hopper – the same man who had shook his fist at the red head.

'Do you know,' Linda continued, 'he once told a really nice lady who was collecting for charity, to get away from his stall as customers couldn't get near! Miserable git.'

'Which charity was she collecting for?' Wesley asked.

'Oh, a homeless charity. She wasn't selling The Big Issue or anything. It was a tin rattle, not that you can rattle tins anymore. She was just standing nearby. I've never seen her since – he must have upset her badly.'

'And Malcolm? Where is he?'

'I dunno. He was here a while back but I can't see him now.'

Linda had turned pale and sank down onto the ground. Paige rushed over.

'Are you all right, Linda?'

'I'm not sure. I hope Malcolm isn't another one.'

'Another one?' Wesley asked and Paige saw his eyes twinkle at the thought of 'something interesting' occurring.

'Yes. A young homeless woman disappeared not long after Joe. They've never been found. I think folks have forgotten, but I haven't.' Linda pushed herself up again and stood close to Wesley. 'Something's not right,' she whispered, holding on to his arm. 'Joe, the bloke who had that fruit and veg stall before, disappeared over twenty years ago. Then Malcolm took it over and now he's …'

'And were there any other strange happenings back then? Or unusual visitors to the town?' Wesley asked, prising her hand away.

'Are you a policeman?' was her answer.

'No.'

'You're not the market inspector, are you?'

'No, we're just passing through.'

She appeared to visibly soften and replaced her hand on Wesley's arm.

'Not that I can remember, but it was a long time ago. Although we do get a lot of visitors because of the university.'

'Thank you, Linda, but we must be on our way now. Have a good day.' Wesley went to move away and Paige saw a disappointed look wash over Linda's face.

'I like that top,' Paige said, pointing to a shimmery teal-coloured sleeveless blouse.'

'It's lovely, isn't it?' Linda said, lifting the top from its rail. 'I had one like it back in the eighties when we all used to go down the Green Man of a Saturday night. I was only fifteen. A lot of us were underage, but we got away with it.' She giggled, and then became more serious. 'Malcolm used to go too.' She sighed and smiled. 'Those were the days.'

'I'll take it,' Paige said, and handed a large white banknote to Linda.

'What's that?' Linda almost spat her words out.

'Sorry,' Paige said, and quickly took the money back. Wesley smiled and handed her two new ten-pound notes. 'We've been away and I forgot to change my money back,' Paige explained.

Linda pushed the banknotes into her apron pocket and the blouse into a plastic bag.

'And the bag'll be five pence, please,' she said.

'Oh, I don't have any change.' Paige searched her pockets.

'I'm only kidding, you daft 'apeth. Go on, enjoy wearing it.'

'I'll wear it to the Green Man tonight,' Paige said.

'You'll have a job,' Linda told her.

'Why's that?' Wesley asked.

'It's not there anymore. Well it is, but it ain't.'

'Sorry?'

'It closed in March 1993, not long after Joe disappeared come to think of it. It's all still there, just as it was, but it's all sealed up.'

'Interesting,' Wesley said.

'We must go,' Paige insisted.

Wesley thanked Linda and they made their way to the other side of the market and away from the upturned stalls that were being cleared away.

'Oh look,' Paige said, pointing across the square. 'There's a green man over there. He looks as though he's balancing on a drum.'

'Mmm. How ugly,' Wesley said and for no useful reason tripped and stumbled against a market stall. Brown, glass bottles rattled and a number of them fell over.

'Hey, look where you're going.'

Paige, who was about to make her way over to the green figure with the outstretched leg, stopped when she heard the stallholder's rebuke. She saw that the reason for Wesley's misstep was an embossed leather tube that had rolled into his path. He bent and picked it up.

'Give that to me!'

The demand came from the same woman in green with wild Titian hair that Paige had seen earlier. She was holding her hand out towards Wesley.

'I do beg your pardon, that was clumsy of me,' he said, and handed over the leather cylinder.

Paige drew in closer to his side and expected the stallholder's anger to melt with Wesley's apology. Instead, the woman's jaw was set and her green eyes flashed as she snatched away the leather tube and pushed it into a large tapestried bag.

'Sorry to have been a trouble,' Wesley said with a smile and a tilt of his head. He took Paige's elbow and steered her away.

'You're losing your touch,' Paige joked. 'Fenella was most unforgiving.'

'Fenella?'

'Yes, Fenella of Fenella's Philtres and Potions for Your Protection – the frosty stallholder.'

'Maybe.' Wesley seemed pensive.

'Is that legal?' Paige mused and nodded at the sign that adorned the stall with the strange bottles.

'It does sound a little improper, but I think she's only peddling herbal remedies.' Wesley rubbed his hand and sucked in his breath through clenched teeth.

'Are you all right?' Paige asked.

'My hand's stinging,' he said, hoarsely, and shook it.

Paige glanced back towards the stall. Fenella was watching them. She raised her eyebrows, cocked her head slightly and smirked as she watched Wesley's discomfort.

'Let me see,' Paige said, and took his hand. A rash of raised bumps spread over his palm and snaked up to his wrist.

'Oooh, that looks extraordinarily painful,' Paige

remarked. She pressed her cool hand onto Wesley's angry one and immediately pulled it away again.

'Ouch!' she exclaimed, wide-eyed. 'It feels like nettle stings.'

As suddenly as it had appeared, the rash crept back along Wesley's hand and disappeared from his fingertips. Mystified, they looked into each other's eyes. Paige frowned. Wesley kissed her on the forehead, and seemingly dismissing the incident he said: 'Let's take a look at this chap then.' He pointed to the seated statue of a fat, balding man with one socked-leg raised, while the other dangled, sockless, above the ground.

'I wonder if it has a name,' Paige said.

'It's the Sockman, love,' a lady carrying bags full of seemingly battered fruit and vegetables told her. 'He's been here since 1998. Nobody liked him much at first, but nowadays, we all love him. He's part of us now.'

'Of course he is,' Paige said.

'Why don't you touch him, for good luck?' the lady with the bags said over her shoulder as she left them.

Paige reached out and laid her hand on the bronze statue. It felt cool and she realised that the stinging had left her palm. She turned to Wesley, who was looking towards the Philtres and Potions stall.

'I think we should go,' she said. Wesley spun back round and together they moved away and as they did so a man wearing a beige raincoat over his grey suit walked up to the Sockman. He appeared to be talking to himself. Paige stifled a giggle and looked at Wesley who said: 'Come on, it's getting rather weird around here.'

Chapter 5

Sandbach at the Police Station, Present Day

'Ah, Detective Sandwich,' a forthright voice announced behind him, making him jump slightly as he waited by the reception desk.

He spun round to see a well-built but not fat, female police officer approaching him. She had a solid chin held high in the air and short brown hair, cropped at the back and longer at the front. It softened her appearance.

'That's Sandbach,' he corrected her.

'Of course,' she said, without any evident concern. 'Welcome to Loughborough. I'm Sergeant Boyle and this is Constable Perkins.' She waved over her shoulder. Perkins opened his mouth, ready presumably to make a greeting, but he quickly stopped as Sergeant Boyle began to speak. 'Bit of a drive for you was it?'

'Yes, had a bit of trouble with the M1. I believe there was ...'

'Shall we get on with it?' she interrupted. 'You're due to meet our new consultant, Mr Hopkins, in half an hour.'

'Erm yes, why not. I've read the memo, but I'd like to get more of a feel for the basics, first.'

Of course. PC Perkins will be able to fill you in,' she

responded, waving a hand casually in her colleague's general direction. Sergeant Boyle leant forward towards Sandbach. He felt a little uncomfortable about the proximity but presumed there was something important to be shared, so reluctantly leant forward too. 'When this is all written up, you will be showing the local law enforcement officers in a good light I presume?'

'Absolutely,' he replied. 'I've often needed to be creative with my reports.'

'Excellent, then I'll leave you with Perkins.' She nodded satisfactorily to Sandbach, then to Constable Perkins and turned to leave, but not before the smile dropped from her face and she muttered something under her breath.

Sandbach frowned. Could be nothing, but if Sergeant Boyle was hiding something, it could make initial investigation more complicated.

'So, PC Perkins, why don't you fill me in with what's been going on here?'

'Certainly, sir, um, would you like to follow me? This way—. By the way, Detective Sandbach, I, um, I'm an admirer of your work. Very clever, sir.'

'Thank you, Perkins. Can I borrow you for a hearing next week?'

'Sorry, sir?'

'No, nothing. Don't worry. Let's get some background, shall we?'

*

Sandbach sat opposite the consultant in the modern but cluttered meeting room that Perkins had led him to after their sketchy briefing. It all seemed rather mundane. Hardly the sort of case he would usually be called to. An old missing persons case, so Perkins had told him. But then he'd added that there was something more, something about artefacts, which was why there was a consultant here.

The consultant, Hopkins, said nothing and simply stared at Sandbach with strange eyes that he found unnerving. Sandbach initially felt the need to break the awkward silence while they waited, but then decided to join in the game. So much could be gained by studying someone's silence, he felt. People can lie with words, but by observing their silence you can see how confident or aggressive someone is, whether they're hiding something or excited to share, even whether someone is going to be a useful ally or someone who was going to make life difficult. If you knew what to look for, of course. Hopkins, although ostensibly calm and composed, seemed to possess a look of burning drive and fearless determination behind his hawk-like eyes. Sandbach got the feeling that not much got past this person; he looked as if he had the ability to compel those he dealt with to tell him things openly and unwittingly. An interesting person.

The door burst open and Sergeant Boyle walked in followed by the still nervous-looking Constable Perkins, who was carrying a tray of drinks.

'Here we are, coffees all round,' Boyle announced.

'Thank you. I asked for tea,' Sandbach replied.

'Sorry about that. Perkins, fetch a cup of tea, will you?' she said, and then turned to the hawk-eyed consultant with a sickly smile. 'Coffee OK for you, Mr Hopkins?'

'I didn't ask for a drink, thank you,' he replied. Hopkins's accent was southern, not from London though. East Anglia somewhere, Suffolk perhaps?

'We don't have any tea at the moment I'm afraid,' Perkins said apologetically to Sandbach.

'No tea?!' Boyle replied incredulously. 'Go and get some then. We can't leave our guests thirsty.'

'There's no need, coffee will be fine,' Sandbach said to ease the tension.

Perkins mouthed the words 'thank you' to him.

'Good. Let's get started then shall we?' Boyle sat down next to the consultant, then pointed to the chair next to Sandbach for Perkins to take.

Sandbach smiled, took a sip of his drink, and grimaced. He was tempted to send Perkins off to the shops for tea after all.

'What do you know about this case, Detective?' Boyle asked.

'Some missing stallholders, a couple of arguments, nothing out of the ordinary,' Sandbach replied. 'But something's not right. Not quite as it seems. Other than the fact that you called me in on a matter your officers are more than capable of dealing with. No, there's something else going on. People know this and aren't letting on. Something is being covered up or hidden.'

Hopkins smiled and offered a nod of approval in Sandbach's direction. It felt patronising, but he took it.

'Am I getting warm?' Sandbach asked, glancing between the two officers opposite.

'You're right,' Boyle replied. 'There has been some arguments with the stallholders, and it may or may not have anything to do with the reason that you are here. But what we do know is that someone is operating around the area, acquiring stolen goods. We're not talking about laptops, phones, or even gold watches – this is much more …'

'Someone has stolen priceless treasures,' Hopkins interrupted her. 'Pages taken from an ancient bible, hand written and illustrated by Benedictine monks in the thirteenth century. It's value is priceless. The National Library in Sweden – who holds the bible – has tasked me with the recovery of these pages. But I need your help. We have a prime suspect and have been following her closely, but she knows us and our tactics.'

Sandbach sat back, a little surprised. He seemed to get given unusual cases fairly often, but this seemed particularly odd.

'I'm sorry, are you Dan Brown in disguise?' Sandbach

asked, looking down at the floor. 'The theft of holy relics, conspiracy theories. Is the Pope involved?'

Hopkins placed a very thin manilla envelope in front of Sandbach. He opened it and slid out the paperwork within – six sheets of paper in total.

'Is this all?' Sandbach asked, sceptically.

'It's all you need to know for now.'

There was a photograph and a profile on a floaty-looking woman, plus details on a handful of locations. One of them caught his eye. A pub, photographed in the eighties or nineties by the look of it.

'The Green Man?' Sandbach asked.

'That location is no longer of interest,' Hopkins snapped. 'You just need to locate where these pages have been hidden. You do not need to retrieve them – I'll handle that.'

Boyle looked as if she had just remembered something and piped up: 'Oh, and you'll be working with an officer who was involved in the cases, that may or may not be connected to this, from over twenty-five years ago. If there is a connection then her knowledge may be useful, and she knows the locations in question. Her name is Florence Carter. She's already been into the station this morning, but she wanted to get out and reacquaint herself with the town so I suggested you meet her later this afternoon. The Costa coffee shop in town at two o'clock. Any questions?'

'I generally work alone, so not ideal,' Sandbach said. Boyle was taking a liberty with her arrangements, but now was not the time to make waves, and getting into the centre of Loughborough, where these people had been disappearing from, would be useful. 'I do have one nagging question, however. Why me?'

'Is there a problem?' Boyle asked.

'The case looks fairly straightforward, if a little unusual. But I don't understand why you requested me for this specific job here in the East Midlands. Surely you have people locally who could help?'

'So you're not up to the job then?' Boyle said.

'I didn't say that,' Sandbach replied. 'I know that my reputation, such as it is, precedes me. Which is why I usually get called to things like grotesque unexplained murders that frankly no one else wants to deal with. So either you are wasting my time or there's something significant you're not telling me.'

Boyle and Hopkins exchanged an uncomfortable looking glance. Boyle, for a change, seemed at a loss for words. Hopkins, however, leant forward with a look of someone annoyed at having to share their sweets.

'The subject in that report is not all she appears to be,' Hopkins said, his voice menacingly quiet. 'We don't believe her to be dangerous, but a level of extreme discretion, and an appreciation for the unexplainable, is advantageous. If you take my meaning.'

'Is everything I need to know in these notes?' Sandbach asked. 'In relation to my appreciation for the unexplainable?'

'Certainly not.' Boyle cut in, sounding almost offended by the suggestion.

'Then I need to know the whole story with this woman,' Sandbach said, as he glanced at the photograph and print-out.

'For this operation she is to be known as Fenella. I can't tell you everything,' Hopkins replied, 'and anything that is divulged must remain off the record. Our understanding is that you have a certain knack for resolving cases and returning acceptable reports, regardless of the situation.'

Sandbach shrugged, but decided it was probably best not to confirm or deny this.

'We believe,' Hopkins continued, 'that Fenella, is a practitioner in the art of witchcraft, and that she is responsible for the disappearance of at least two of the market's stallholders by means that we don't fully understand.'

'Or maybe she has nothing to do with the disappearances and is just an innocent bystander. I take it you have some evidence?' Sandbach's reply was scathing.

'We found something,' Hopkins said. His face was deadly serious.

Hopkins reached under his chair and pulled out a solid-looking, locked briefcase. He undid the combination locks on each side of the handle and then ran his thumb across the logo in the middle. The case beeped twice and the locks clicked. Hopkins lifted the lid and pulled out a leather tube covered with intricate markings. He slid a sheet of paper from it and replaced the tube in his case. The paper was the colour of pale leather, blackened at the edges. On it was calligraphy handwriting along with fine drawings and diagrams. Odd markings in black and gold ran down one side. Hopkins laid it carefully in front of Sandbach.

'It's very nice. What is it?' Sandbach said, deliberately sounding unimpressed.

'One of the pages that was missing.'

'Excellent, one less to find. Why are you showing it to me?'

Hopkins took a lighter from his pocket, lit it, then held the page over the flame.

'Mr Hopkins! What are you doing?' The pitch of Boyle's voice shot up and Sandbach felt her anxiety as she moved towards the desk.

Hopkins simply glared at her for a moment, stopping her motion, and then turned back to the ancient document he was in the process of setting fire to. Nothing seemed to be happening at first. Then suddenly there was a bright light as the page was engulfed in green flames. It burnt fiercely for a few seconds and then it was gone. Ashes drifted down onto the table, leaving very little evidence that it ever existed in the first place.

'But, but ...' Boyle stammered.

Hopkins shushed her and then held out a hand,

signifying that they should wait. There was a small green flicker of light from one of the specks of ash. It grew slightly. More flickers came from it and the speck grew larger. It continued flickering and growing until Sandbach was able to see the pale leather colour and familiar-looking calligraphic text. It grew, and grew, moving on the table top as it did so until the page was complete again. Every word, diagram and symbol was back to where it had been before.

Sandbach stared at the page, then at Hopkins and then at Boyle, but she was staring at the page herself. Hopkins lifted the page, put it back into the tube, dropped that in the briefcase and locked it again. He placed the case on the floor under his chair and then turned to face Sandbach, his hands clasped in front of him. He looked at Sandbach with raised eyebrows evidently awaiting a response.

'OK,' Sandbach said finally. 'I'm interested.'

Chapter 6

The Green Man, 1993

One moment he had been in the market with his friend, Hall. The next? Well, the next was something quite different. Robert opened his eyes for a second time, keeping them open for longer than the fraction of time the first effort took. He was sitting with his back against a wall that seemed solid enough even if the rest didn't make sense. He'd righted himself with his eyes closed after stumbling and falling at the first shock. His hands had felt the unfamiliar velvety surface, slightly sticky, underneath him. There was a buzz of voices, laughter and chinking of glasses and through it all, a heavy, beating music of a sort he'd never heard before. The smell of food and the maltiness of ale filled his nostrils.

'What is this place?' he whispered, as he endeavoured to make sense of what he saw. Arched vaults and bright lights, seating made of wooden slats, and people. Many people, all talking, guffawing, quaffing. It was clearly some kind of inn.

''Tis a veritable den of iniquity!'

Robert turned his head. 'Fox! You're Fox! You were speaking in the market.'

'Indeed, I was! But pray, where now can we be?' Fox's eyes were round and his eyebrows high. Robert watched his gaze move from one side of their present venue to the other before Fox spoke again.

'I am George Fox. You saw me. You were there, so I dream not. Your name, young man?'

'Hooke, Robert Hooke, sir. I am recently down from Oxford and am visiting Loughborough to reacquaint myself with my tutor, the Reverend Hall, or so I thought ...'

Robert's voice tapered off as two young persons (were they women?) approached. They were both clad in tight blue pantaloons that showed every line of their legs. Their arms and necklines were bare; their flimsy, flouncy tops were only fit for the bedroom. Robert's eyes were drawn to the leading figure who was speaking, her top was the shimmering greenish blue of a butterfly's wing. She had loose, curly hair dressed in cavalier fashion, some of it caught in a band on top of her head, the rest falling over her shoulders. Her companion was more an exotic bird, her short spiky hair had impossible blue streaks and she wore a gold stud in her nose. Large gold hoops dangled from both of their ears. Their faces were painted in the manner of a lady of the night.

'So I said to him: "You've got to be joking. I know I want to travel but I'm not flying off to the other side of the world at the drop of a hat with someone I hardly know yet. I've only just got my stall up and running, and anyway, I'm a good Catholic girl! What would my mum say?"'

'Bloody Hell, Linda! You're in your mid-twenties, not some baby. He was offering to take you to New York for a week. A week! America, for God's sake. You can bunk off for that long, Lin. Tell him you changed your mind. Bugger your mum!'

Robert and Fox both stared at these curious specimens, as they brushed past them with a perfunctory glance down to where they were seated. They watched the look the girls exchanged; one winked, and the other mouthed 'Guy Fawkes!' They both spluttered with laughter. Half-running and tottering they made their way down the hall, small bags on long straps looped over their shoulders. As the one called Linda pushed open a door marked 'Ladies' she said: 'Come on, Sharon! I'm dying for a wazz. And a go of your new lipstick!' The one called Sharon laughed, showing all her teeth – white, straight teeth – and gave her friend a push.

'It takes five weeks for a letter to reach me from the Americas,' Fox commented, staring at the now closed door.

'She does not look as if she is dying,' countered Robert, scrambling to his feet, and offering Fox his hand. 'Let us sit for a moment, at that table.' He indicated the suggested destination with a nod, and seeing what he took for assent, he made his way over and slid onto a bench seat. Fox sat down next to him. They both noticed the mural behind them that seemed to depict medieval scenes of castles and jousting, but neither said anything. Fox lifted an eyebrow at Robert, and they turned their attention to the display in front of them.

'What manner of ale is this?' Fox said, picking up a large dimpled glass that still had an inch or so of a heavy brown liquid in it. He sniffed, drank, then nodded and drained the glass. Robert bent and smelled the silver coloured dish full of crumpled brown and white cylinders and ash.

'Tobacco!' he announced. Next he examined a deposit of screwed up shiny red and white paper that revealed the words 'Walkers crisps' as Robert smoothed it out. The silvery inside held tiny morsels – leftovers of the contents. He licked his finger, touched a crumb and put it in his mouth. 'Salt!'

'Some kind of broadsheet,' Fox speculated, reaching over to pull towards him the folded newspaper that was discarded on the chair next to him. He pushed the glasses away and opened the paper flat. It was printed in an even, slightly strange script, but they could both read the heading: Loughborough Echo followed by, 'Market Trader Goes Missing.'

Fox gasped and Robert watched him tap down at a line

of smaller print that had caught his eye. He pushed the paper towards Robert and they both read: 7th March 1993.

They sat in silence for a few moments, both of them scanning the strange room with a more bold attention than previously.

''Tis the date of publishing.' Robert spoke, his eyes taking in the people eating, drinking, and two speaking while holding rectangular objects (of the like he'd seen a short while ago in the hands of that young girl in the market) to their ears. 'We seem to have moved forward in time.'

'Pah! Nonsense! Only one marked with the devil would suggest such a preposterous idea.'

'I am a student of science, sir. And I can assure you I am fully in my right mind. At least I was but thirty minutes ago. We have to accept, I believe, that we are not, at present, where we were, or when we were.'

'And I am a simple man of God. I have travelled afar and spoken with many. But this! I just don't know. That creature mentioned Guy Fawkes, did she not? Surely that disproves your theory?' Fox turned, making as if to get up. 'I must make my way back to my lodgings and take advice from my fellow Friends.'

'I doubt your lodgings, or any Quakers, will be where you expect,' said Robert, resting his hand on Fox's arm to keep him seated. 'But I agree we will need to move. We must think logically – that is the basis of all science. I am trained to observe. No one is taking much notice of us so far, so let us take a moment to think.'

Chapter 7

The Market, Present Day

Detective Sandbach surveyed the busy marketplace. People were bustling and pushing along, trying to get past each other in a hurry. Expressions of annoyance and head shaking could be seen when someone stopped one of the meandering flows of traffic to admire an imitation Gucci watch or a pair of luminous pink tights. A woman dragging a small snotty child, while pushing a sleeping toddler in a pushchair, clipped his ankle. He moved towards an unusual looking statue in the middle of the pedestrianised street, to try and get out of the busiest traffic. The sculpture was a greenish metal figure sitting on a block and holding one chunky leg out in front of him. On it was the clear shape of a sock. This he understood was locally known as the Sock Man.

Terrence, his imaginary dog, jumped up onto the outstretched leg and began panting frantically.

'I saw a burger van back there, can we get something to eat?' he said excitedly, his wagging tail brushing the toes of the statue.'

Sandbach grimaced at the thought and simply shook his head.

'Eyes on the job please,' Sandbach replied. 'Keep a

lookout for anything unusual. Let's see if we can pick anything up before the local uniform can ruin the scene. Have you spotted anything?'

The dog, a Jack Russell, was untidy even as an imagined companion. He stood up and turned slowly on the spot, eyes darting from one thing to the next. Sandbach followed suit, while sipping a tasteless tea from an insulated cardboard cup.

There were so many sights to take in once he began to look below the surface and take in people's actions, expressions and attitudes to each other. A middle-aged woman in a full-length cream coloured coat was dragging what appeared to be a long-suffering husband with her by the arm. The look of resignation and despair in his eyes suggested he'd given up arguing with her long ago. Three male youths, late teens, were laughing and joking with each other, apparently particularly amused by something that had just happened behind them. One laughed behind his hand, while another yelled something abusive back down the street. The final one glared at Sandbach as they walked past, then spat on the paved ground right in front of his feet, reminding Sandbach that he was actually standing in this scene rather than just observing from a distance.

He turned back to Terrence, who seemed to be staring intently at something. Following the direction, Sandbach could make out an argument in front of one of the stalls. An angry-looking, stocky-built man with a shaved head and faded yellow t-shirt, was shaking his fist in the face of a woman best described as floaty. She had long flowing spiderwebs of auburn hair, a full-length green dress with a striking floral pattern that wafted in the breeze and a general demeanour that seemed to float along in much the same way. She was laughing at the man's ranting, which only seemed to annoy him more.

'Interesting. That looks like the woman Hopkins seemed so concerned about.'

'No time to go after her now, though,' Terrence

reminded him. 'You've got a date waiting in Costa.'

'A date? I suppose you think that's funny,' Sandbach told his canine sidekick. 'But you're right. Ms Florence Carter awaits; time for in-depth investigations later.' He turned towards the cafe and pushed open the door; the strong coffee smell assaulted his nostrils.

Chapter 8

Costa Coffee, Present Day

Gazing out of the window Florence absentmindedly swirled the coffee in her cup. It was literally years since she'd been in Loughborough and so much had changed, the large imposing Costa for a start. Yes, it was lovely and she was sitting in a pleasantly striped comfy chair that was, thankfully, far enough away from the almost deafening noise the coffee machine made, to actually be able to sit back and relax. Placing her hand on the folder in front of her, she glanced at the display on her phone – one-thirty. Half an hour until her meeting with DI Sandbach.

Florence wondered at the probability of it all happening again. More than twenty-five years had passed and yet she could still remember the expression on the team's faces as the DCI had explained that the case they had been diligently working on for over a year was to be passed to the unsolved team, and they were all to be returned to normal duty. Like the rest of her colleagues, she had been shocked that no conclusion had been found to the disappearance of the market traders, and yet, they had all agreed, and away from the disapproving ears of their then hostile gaffer, that something strange had been going on. No witnesses, no sightings, not even a body, which would at least have gone some way in helping to make sense of it all. Instead, she had been left with an uneasy feeling that even now made its presence known.

The door banged open and a red-haired woman walked in, head held high; she was obviously looking for someone. Her attention caught, Florence watched as the woman walked to the sandwich counter, purse in hand. Scanning the room again the woman took a step forward and then stopped, before delving her hand deep into her huge tapestry bag. Florence controlled her need to laugh as the woman's whole arm seemed to disappear. Intrigued as to what items might be lurking in the depths, Florence shifted on her seat in order to survey the woman properly. There was something furtive about her – it was almost as if she was embarrassed. The woman finally made it to the counter, but Florence was too far away to hear her request. She only saw the barista walk to the tap and fill a plastic cup before handing it to the woman, who then went and sat down facing the main door.

With a sigh, Florence straightened her jacket and glanced at the time again. Twenty minutes now until her meeting, so enough time to go through the folder that Boyle had handed her. Pushing her coffee cup away she opened it and started to flick through the pages. The photographs of the missing people danced before her eyes. As far as she knew they'd never been found, dead or alive.

'Excuse me, madam, have you finished with your cup?'

Florence looked up into the eyes of the man who'd been serving behind the counter, and was now standing next to the table. 'No, I haven't finished.' She took a mouthful and grimaced as the cold sludge swirled around her mouth. 'Oh yuk, it's gone cold!'

'Would you like me to bring you another? Americano with hot milk wasn't it?'

'Oh, please, that would be great. Here, let me give you the cash,' Florence said, as she scooped her bag from the chair and took out her purse.

'Thank you. Now, is there anything else you'd like? I've just put out some carrot cake and I can honestly say it's the best.' The waiter coughed. 'Ah well, I guess I'm biased, but it really is so good. Would you like a piece to go with your coffee?'

Florence grinned and looked over at the food cabinet, her tummy rumbling as if on cue. Normally, she hated eating in front of strangers but surely a piece of cake didn't count? 'How did you know my favourite is carrot cake? Yes, please, and thanks for asking. Now, how much do I owe you?'

The cake and coffee paid for, Florence leant back in her chair and looked out of the window, her gaze travelling over the shoppers and passers-by. A tall man wearing a beige coat was standing by the statue of the Sock Man. His actions caught her attention. He was looking down and she could see his mouth moving as if he was talking to someone. There was no one near him and Florence watched transfixed as he looked around, his mouth still moving as if in deep conversation.

'Here you are,' the waiter said, as he placed a plate with an exceptionally large piece of cake on the table. 'I know you said an Americano but I wanted to introduce you to our flat white. It is sensational and goes especially well with cake, but if you don't like it, I will obviously exchange it.'

'Thank you. I will certainly try it.'

As the waiter walked away Florence leant forward and drew her finger across the glistening frosting before sucking her finger clean.

'Oh my,' she muttered to herself as she picked up the steaming mug of coffee. 'Now for the coffee.' Taking a sip she turned and caught the waiter's eye. She put her thumb up and he smiled in response before moving across the busy room. Florence watched him as he approached the lady with red hair. His hands were wide in an almost apologetic manner.

A man laughed behind her and Florence turned back to her table. The cake was perched on a plate, and picking up her fork, Florence cut off a piece and popped it into her mouth. The cake was indeed exceptional, and between sips of the really rather good coffee, Florence finished the heavenly treat with delight.

Chapter 9

Paige and Wesley's Cottage, Present Day

'It's good to be home,' Paige said and kicked off her shoes. 'You really are incorrigible – the look on that letting agent's face, when you told him nineteen Albert Place, was priceless.'

'I do my best,' Wesley replied, and dropped a small bunch of keys down onto the windowsill. 'I thought we should go through the proper channels rather than just move in.'

'He'll probably have a sleepless night thinking he's lost the keys to this place.'

'Mmm. How careless.' Wesley grinned and poured himself a large single malt.

'How's your hand?' Paige asked. Wesley sat down at an oak table in front of the window and looked at his right hand.

'It seems to be all right now. That woman is cause for concern. Fenella did you say?'

'Yes. She did appear rather unapproachable. At least she didn't make us late for the meeting with the letting agent.'

'But that wasn't the rendezvous I think we need to make.' Wesley took a mouthful of whisky and lifted some yellowing papers that had been rolled up on the table.

'Oh, I thought it was. What might our planned meeting be, then?' Paige lifted the glass and sipped the scotch. She wrinkled her nose. 'Far too peaty for me,' she said, and handed it back. 'Islay?'

'Indeed,' Wesley confirmed. 'It looks as though we need to meet with someone who seems to be way out of their century. At least, I assume it's a meeting.'

'I wonder how that happened,' Paige pondered. 'Where shall we meet them?'

Wesley looked down as if consulting a wristwatch, although he didn't wear one. It was the tattoo on his left arm that interested him. The compass held by two cupped hands, which the ink normally showed, had been replaced by a number and a pagan-like image. Paige touched his arm.

'Eugh. What's that?'

'If I'm not mistaken it's a Green Man,' Wesley answered. 'This town supposedly has quite a few images of Green Men. Some are on buildings but I think it is a building, perhaps called the Green Man, that we need to find. Maybe a walk into town after dark might be fruitful.'

'That's the place Linda spoke of,' Paige said.

'Who?'

'Linda! The one who sold me this gorgeous top,' Paige said, and pulled the flimsy blouse from its carrier bag. She held it next to her shoulders and smiled at Wesley.

'Ah, that Linda.'

'Yes, and she fancied you rotten, but you know that don't you, Mr babe-magnet?'

'It's my irresistible charm.'

Ignoring his quip Paige asked: 'Is this town safe with all those pagan figures around? It's quite spooky.'

'You're with me. Of course it's safe,' Wesley said, and took another drink of the smoky amber liquid.

'Oh, the numbers aren't very clear,' Paige remarked and stroked his arm.

'It's a date, for sure, but which one exactly ...'

'It's hard to tell.' Paige examined the image closer. 'The scar from your war-wound has distorted one of the numbers.'

'Mmm. I think it says 1933.'

'Or 1983, or even 1993.'

'If we need to find someone who is way out of their century, then it must be 1933.'

'Man or woman?' Paige asked.

'Man.'

'What makes you so sure?'

'Just a gut feeling.'

Paige stroked Wesley's arm and let her fingers brush over the tattoo. It was slightly raised on the left-hand side.

'A gut feeling?' she asked, tipping her head to one side. 'Of course it is,' she said, mockingly, but he didn't answer, he was smoothing out the discoloured papers that showed maps of the town. After a few minutes of surveying them he said: 'I think we're going to like it here. I must say, this is a convenient spot, look at all these gates – we won't have any problems in travelling to any of those dates if we need to.'

Paige leant into his back and wrapped her arms around his neck.

'Oh my goodness, there are quite a few,' she said. 'As long as you don't go leaving any of them open.'

'Will I never hear the last of that?' Wesley said, and turned his head to kiss her cheek.

'Probably not, but you did almost allow history to be completely altered when you left the one open that allowed Hitler through in 1918.'

'No harm done,' Wesley said, nonchalantly. He was still pouring over the documents.

'Pinfold Gate. I like the sound of that one,' he announced, 'and Church Gate, that must be the one we came here by and will no doubt take us back when we want to leave. Then there's Woodgate, which isn't far from here, and, looking at this map,' he pulled out a really old-looking document, 'High Street was once High Gate.'

'Gata is, I believe, a viking word meaning way or round that later became Gate,' Paige told him, and she moved round the table so that she could better see the maps. She traced her fingers over the gates they'd mentioned. 'But this must have been a Saxon town originally,' she said, 'these gates would have had a wall around them. And the middle one's Baxter Gate, I wonder where that one will take us.'

'Hopefully to the Green Man.' Wesley tilted his head instead of moving the maps.

'Where is it?' Paige asked leaning in closer – his skin smelled delicious. Wesley pulled a different map out from underneath the one they had been studying.

'Aha! It's on Swan Street, according to this,' Wesley said, and took another sip of his drink. 'And Church Gate, not Baxter Gate, therefore, is the nearest, so we'll take that one.' He slid his arm around Paige's waist and pulled her onto his lap. 'But not just yet.'

Chapter 10

Costa Coffee, Present Day

A loud bang drew Florence's attention from the talking man
outside and jumping to her feet she swung round. The red-haired
lady was on her feet, her chair lying on its side – the culprit
responsible for the sudden noise. There was no one with the
woman, but she was clearly agitated, and Florence watched as
the chair was righted and the monstrous bag hauled off the floor
and placed on the table, before the woman sat back down. With a
start, Florence realised that she was staring and the woman was
staring right back. Their eyes locked and Florence had the
distinct impression ...

'Excuse me, are you Florence Carter?'

Florence stood up; her arm outstretched. 'Yes. Detective
Sandbach?' she asked. He nodded.

The man, who she had seen through the window earlier
seemingly talking to the floor, now stood awkwardly in front of
her, hands in his pockets. He looked around.

'Thank you for agreeing to meet me here. Can I get you a
drink? What would you like?' she asked, grabbing her bag.

'Erm, do they do such a thing as a cup of tea? I'm never
quite sure what the rules are in a coffee shop,' Sandbach said. He
pulled a chair back and sat down, wrapping his coat around him.

'Oh yes, tea is allowed. I'm pretty sure you can get a large variety too, should you wish to stray from the norm.'

'Tea. Plain and simple tea, please.'

'Have you eaten? Only I could get you a sandwich or maybe a pastry ...?' Florence stopped as Sandbach jerked his head down and waved his hand at the floor.

'No, no thanks. He is right though – a bacon sandwich would be perfect.' Sandbach laughed; an odd bark of a sound.

'Bacon sandwich? I'm sure they do a pre-packed.' Florence frowned. 'Erm, who's right?'

'No one. I was just thinking out loud.' Sandbach leant forward and picked the file up off the table. 'I take it this is for me to look at?'

'Yes. Sergeant Boyle gave it to me earlier. Is there anything in particular that you would like to focus on or shall we just discuss it all over coffee, or indeed, tea?'

'Give me ten minutes to have a look and then we'll go from there.'

'Okay. Just remind me – did you want anything to eat?'

Flicking open the file he glanced up at her. 'Just tea for me, please.'

Conscious that she was staring again – what was it with this place? – Florence made her way to the counter. Joining the queue, she glanced at the red-haired woman who had her eyes closed while her hands seemed to be hovering over the bag on the table. Florence was closer now and could see that the enormous tapestry bag appeared to be moving, in fact, she could hear the click that the feet of the table made as it rocked from side to side.

'Can I help you?'

Florence swung round to face the barista behind the counter. 'Oh God, yes, I'm sorry, erm, I'd like a pot of tea and another flat white, please. No, no food, thank you.'

'Do you need a hand carrying those back to your table?'

'No thanks, I'm fine.' Florence drew a deep breath and forced her eyes to close. Turning to pick up the tray of drinks she glanced again towards where the red-haired woman had been. The table was empty and Florence just caught sight of her as she passed through the main door and disappeared outside. Mentally shaking herself, Florence picked up the tray and returned to Sandbach, who appeared oblivious to anything but the contents of the folder spread out in front of him.

Taking her seat, Florence placed the tray to the side of the folder.

'Did you want to go through that with me now?' she asked.

'Well, yes – let's talk about those missing people first. Can you tell me about your time on the case, who you worked directly with and what your thoughts were?'

'Okay, well I was new in service and spent a lot of my shifts with Harriet Boyle. You met her earlier. We were drafted in to do some house-to-house, take initial statements and generally provide some police presence to calm the locals.' Florence paused, picked up her coffee and took a sip. She was really rather impressed with the Flat White – her usual choice of Americano with milk had now been shelved. 'It was all so strange,' she continued, 'and the fact that nothing was seen or heard of the missing people again still niggles away at me. You can read for yourself my notes regarding who they were and where they were from.'

'Yes, I see that they all disappeared in and around the market area. Were they all local?'

'Yes – all from Loughborough.'

Florence drank more coffee as Sandbach continued to read her notes.

'So, simply disappeared then. I find that highly unlikely – there must be an explanation of sorts,' Sandbach stated.

Florence laughed. 'Well of course there must be an

explanation – only we didn't find it and any concerns or misgivings we had were ignored by the gaffers.'

'What do you mean by misgivings?'

'Well, Harriet and I were always a bit unsure as to how those people could simply disappear without trace.'

Florence watched as Sandbach flicked through the file again – it looked to her as though he was searching for something.

'People just don't disappear,' Florence said, 'unless someone got hold of the cloak of invisibility prior to JK Rowling using it for Harry Potter.'

Sandbach's expression caused Florence's laugh to die in her throat and erupt from her mouth in a loud snort.

'Oh funny, ha ha,' Florence continued, 'let's bring magic into the equation and pop that report on the super's desk.'

'Actually, it is funny you should say that,' Sandbach replied.

Chapter 11

Outline Costa Coffee, Present Day

Sandbach stepped out of the warm coffee shop into a cool breeze. The sun was bright, however, and he shielded his eyes against it while he got his bearings. He didn't think much of these new-fangled drinking establishments that seemed to be popping up everywhere. Every time a shop closed – one that had been a pillar of the community, managed diligently for generations – it seemed to disappear quietly and without complaint, only to be replaced by yet another coffee shop. How much coffee do we need to drink as a nation?

'And they didn't have any bacon,' Terrence muttered from near his ankle.

'Quite. What kind of place sells seventeen million different types of Danish pastry but no bacon?' Sandbach replied. 'This is the beginning of the end, mark my words.'

As he walked he pondered on the conversation with Carter. A nice enough police officer but always the logical mind. Life is not straightforward, although admittedly, there was usually a straightforward explanation. He had seen a spark of excitement when he'd told her about the burnt page regenerating itself. He doubted very much that she'd open her mind enough to fully engage with this investigation. Maybe she'd surprise him.

'Come on then, let's see if we can find something of this missing pub before we get a proper –– Ow!'

Sandbach had been surveying the area to get his bearings when something heavy struck his leg. He turned to see the floaty woman from the market stall earlier, her long fiery-red hair billowing in the breeze. She had also been in the coffee shop just a couple of tables away. She ignored him and pushed past with an enormous bag. It appeared to be very heavy too.

'No that's fine. Don't worry about me,' he said aloud. 'My day's been great so far, so thanks for bashing my leg!' She didn't respond, instead she pushed her way through the busy shoppers apparently oblivious of her actions. An old man was knocked against a wall and a small child had to leap out of the way. Sandbach almost laughed at her behaviour, at least it wasn't personal, but he was intrigued.

Terrence growled and then trotted along after her. Sandbach rubbed his shin and followed. She kept close to the shop fronts as she headed away from the Sock Man statue and down towards what he thought was the main road through town. A woman with two large bags of shopping was about to step out of yet another coffee shop further down, but managed to catch herself before she collided with the bag-wielding menace. Terrence dodged past the shopping bag lady and was almost on the heel of the floaty woman when she turned sharp left into an alleyway, so inconspicuous that he probably wouldn't have noticed it otherwise. Sandbach jogged in an ungainly fashion to catch up – he despised running or any physical exertion if he could avoid it. Terrence arrived at the alleyway first and stopped. He barked at the entrance but didn't go in. When Sandbach finally arrived there was no sign of her. It wasn't a very big alleyway, but he expected he would have still been able to see her.

'Shh, stop it. Where did she go?' Sandbach asked.

'I don't know,' Terrence replied. 'There's no sign of her.'

Chapter 12

Outside Caravelli's, Present Day

Florence turned the key towards her; the car fell silent, the lights switched off – the only sound the gentle ticking as the engine began to cool down. She'd managed to park right in front of Caravelli's, which was really fortunate; no parking for the much-loved restaurant and hotel meant it was usually first there, closest parked.

Reaching across the car she opened her handbag and rooted around for her phone, before locating her friend Caitlin's number and pressing call.

'Hey, it's me,' Florence said when the call connected. 'How are you, but more importantly, how is my gorgeous boy?'

'Hi and charming. Always the bloody cat first! We're fine. Tom's just diving into a bowl of tuna and I've opened the wine. You get there okay?' Caitlin Blake's voice echoed down the line.

'Yes, I'm here. So much has changed. I barely recognised the town centre, but thankfully the Old Manor House is still standing. It's gone up in the world as it's now Caravelli's hotel and restaurant,' Florence said, placing her head back on the car seat and gazing out of the window. 'I've warned you about my cat's tummy and tuna. You'll regret it!'

Florence listened as Caitlin laughed. 'I know, but he

always looks so hungry after that dried crap you insist on.'

'It's not crap. It costs a bloody fortune – grain free, salt free, pea-something free.'

'Taste-free,' Caitlin interrupted.

'Ha ha,' Florence said, chuckling. 'Okay, so the little sod gets tuna. I understand. Aunty Caitlin feels the need to spoil my hard-done-by, bedraggled, rescue cat.'

'So, any of your old pals around to catch up with?'

'Sadly not. They keep retiring! Only Boyle is still here and she's made bloody sergeant.' Florence sighed. 'God, I feel old. I've been brought back for a twenty-five-year-old mystery that appears to have raised its head ...' She faltered as she noticed the red-haired woman from earlier walk through the main doors of Caravelli's. 'The funny thing is,' she continued, 'that the local bods, just like years ago, are really dismissive and the only one taking it remotely seriously is Boyle. She's drafted in a detective inspector from somewhere up north, Crewe, I think, called Sandbach. He's got a reputation for solving the odd and old shit that the police sometimes get called to deal with. I met him earlier and we didn't exactly hit it off. It was a misunderstanding really, but I think he understood what I suspected years ago. Unfortunately, I'd decided to not confide my real thoughts as I haven't discussed this with anyone save Boyle in over two decades. Plus, I thought he'd think I was nuts.'

'Oh for goodness' sake, Florence. When you think how long this case has bothered you, surely the fact that Sandbach has even been seconded must mean that someone is starting to take this seriously!'

'I know. I had just started to relax, despite having drunk two coffees, when he abruptly leans forward, closes the file, asks where I'm staying, says he will see me later before standing up and leaving.' Florence sighed. 'He thinks I'm as closed off as the rest, so I need time to sort that out while trying to offer any assistance I can.'

'How much time have you got?'

'Work has only been sanctioned this week, but if things continue as they have I may stay longer. I'll get home for the weekend though. There's something oddly fascinating about Sandbach and he seems to talk to himself all the time, but ...'

'And this from a woman who cites a cat as her best friend?'

'Yada, yada! You're only jealous of the immense love and respect shown to me from my cat. You may tempt him with tuna, but he will always love me bestest. Tom is my one true love.' Florence took a deep breath and sighed dramatically. She listened as laughter floated down the telephone line.

'You're nuts. But never fear, your boy is safe with me. I know what he means to you. I've been writing today and he's very content to squeeze his furry little ass in-between the desk and my tum.'

'That article coming along well?'

'Yes, very. I'm going to have to visit some old mates next week but that'll keep. Listen, have you found somewhere to stay?'

'Yes, I'm actually staying at Caravelli's. I'm parked right outside now. I'm going to grab some dinner, and if I remember correctly, they also have a rather spectacular wine list.'

Both women sighed appreciatively.

'Right, okay. Like I said, don't worry about Tom. He's eating well and seems very settled. Call when you can and good luck with Sandbach. I'm sure it will all have a very logical explanation in the end.'

Florence said goodbye and ended the call. Getting out of the car she glanced to her left. The church opposite was silent, but attractive – the graveyard illuminated by concealed ground lighting. Florence opened the boot and grabbed her bag before locking the car and heading towards the main doors of Caravelli's.

Chapter 13

The Green Man, 1993

Hooke and Fox both fell quiet, taking in where they were. A woman wearing flowing green-hued robes, her brash red hair falling below her shoulders, brushed past their table on the way to the room into which the girls had disappeared a few moments ago. Robert saw her pause just outside the door marked Ladies and then pull a long cylinder covered in strange markings from the large tapestry bag on her arm.

At that moment, Sharon and Linda tripped back into the corridor. Sharon's lips were the colour of purple grapes; she pursed them into an exaggerated kiss aimed at the red-haired woman, who held the cylinder close to her body as they passed her, laughing together and linking arms. Robert watched as the woman glanced around, apparently to check she was unobserved, and moved the cylinder in a circular motion. Movement, noise, everything around them stopped. Robert looked down and brought the broadsheet towards him as her gaze swept over him. Lifting his eyes slowly, he watched as the woman pulled several more tubes from her bag. She pressed them onto the wall next to the decorative moulding, just above her eye level. She stood back and pointed at it with the cylinder she was holding– and the tubes disappeared.

Robert heard a low gasp. He looked over to Fox, whose mouth dropped open. They both looked on as the woman weaved her way through the throng of stilled folk towards the stairs. She turned and moved the cylinder around her head and dropped it into her bag. Then she disappeared.

'Fie! I know not what to think,' whispered Fox. 'Perhaps I have lost my reason.'

The whole episode had taken but moments. Robert wasn't sure, either, whether the woman had completed her journey up the stairs or was just gone. All life, movement and noise had all returned, however. Perhaps this strange situation had played with his imagination. Robert laid the broadsheet flat on the table. Smoothing it with his hand, he tapped the image in the bottom corner.

'I think we may find many surprising things. Look at this.' He read: 'European Car of the Year: Volkswagen Golf. 0–60 mph in 8.3 seconds.' Mph? Miles per hour? he thought. A nearby article reported, 'Girl Killed by Speeding Car.' The car in question had apparently been doing fifty in a thirty-mph limited area. He held his breath. Where were the horses? Horses couldn't move so swiftly. Could it be possible to travel so fast in that sleek-looking vehicle? Questions about material, power and driver-ship started formulating in his mind. He was distracted from these disturbing but exciting ideas as Fox started speaking again. He tried to concentrate on what Fox was saying.

'That woman went away up those stairs. We should follow her, but we must take care. She seems unnatural.' He paused, as Robert stood up. It was time to move and they would need to blend in.

'I wouldst have that coat, the better to blend in with these folk,' Robert said. 'A fellow left it over his chair and is oft, seemingly dancing. Leastways, he is not attending.'

Fox spluttered. 'Nay, that's stealing. Thou must not,' but Robert was moving towards the nearby chair. He lifted the leather jacket from its resting place and folded it over his arm.

'And leave your hat, sir! 'T'will attract attention.'

'Never! Not even the highest court in the land has managed to part me from this hat.'

'Bring it then, if you must. But carry it.'

Nodding his head, Robert indicated his desired direction and moved through the throng. Fox jammed his hat on his head and followed. They paused halfway up the stairs by mutual agreement and Robert shrugged the coat on. Now they were both wearing leather.

It was the sounds that first met their ears; hooting, screeching, whirring of mechanics. There are times when even if you think you are prepared, the shock of meeting something new takes away all your breath. Both men stopped still when they reached the top of the stairs that led from the tavern. Neither noticed the wet grey paving shimmering with reflected light beneath their feet, or the rain falling softly from the sky, or the cold of the early March evening; they were transfixed by the beacons of light, the intertwining colours and the movement of the spectacle before them.

'Hell's teeth, Hooke! What in Heaven's name is this? We are beset with behemoths,' Fox breathed, his body vibrating.

Robert's eyebrows were doing a dance on his face, as his legs jigged with excitement.

''Tis truly a marvel. Transport of the age, no doubt,' he gasped, eyes following the metal carriages in reds, blues, black and even bright yellow, fronted by bright lights. They propelled themselves past him from right to left, while over some way others went in the opposite direction. He stepped forward, mesmerised by these miracles of mechanics.

'Get back,' Fox shouted, grabbing Robert's leather sleeve, and pulling him away from the carriageway with some force.

'What?' A huge blue object, as large as a ship, came out of the night and pulled in just to the right of them. It had pictures and writing on its side, and two sets of windows, one high and one low. Doors swished open and people stepped down. Others stepped up and disappeared inside, some mounting a stairway, others taking seats on the same level. Their eyes wide, they held each other's arms tightly, as the doors closed and the blue ship started up and passed them by.

'How does it work? How do they not collide?'

'The woman. We were following that unearthly woman,' Fox said, suddenly. 'Where did she go?'

'She was familiar to me in a way that nothing else is here. Her countenance was one I have seen before,' mused Robert, as his gaze worked its way through the traffic to the buildings on the other side of the thoroughfare. The building opposite them was lit up, lights sparkling from all the windows and the word Casablanca across its front, but there was no mistaking its past. People were milling about outside that establishment in much the same manner as those on their side of the street.

''Tis the Guild, Mr Fox! St George's Guild. What has happened to it?'

'Nay, nay,' said Fox, but Robert saw his gaze fix on the building. 'Well, it could well be,' he acceded, stumbling back and grabbing Robert's arm again. 'The timbers are very like. The shape, too. But where, then, is the marketplace?' He turned away from the unfamiliar, yet familiar, building and the moving mechanical behemoths to look back to where their market used to be, to the building from where they had both emerged. 'The Green Man,' he read.

Robert surveyed the huge complex built over the cellar they had been in.

'This is where our market was. It's gone. All gone!' Their eyes met and Robert could see his own disbelief mirrored in his companion's face.

Chapter 14

The Green Man, 1933

'It's enough to freeze the whatsits off a brass monkey,' Paige said, and slipped her arm through Wesley's, as they walked along 1930s Church Gate.

'And there one is,' Wesley said.

Paige looked up and saw three brass balls hanging above Broughton's Pawnbroker's shop.

'I'm sure Mr Broughton would be pleased to know that his are safe this evening,' Wesley joked.

Paige elbowed him and they walked swiftly on.

'Oh, look at all the lovely hats in there,' Paige said, pointing to a double-fronted boutique. 'The Notion Shop – what a curious name.'

They carried along the gate that Wesley had decided would lead them to meeting the man who was 'out of his century' and no doubt in need of help to find his way back.

Wesley held Paige close as they passed the Unicorn; the rabble from within the pub on the corner was loud and bawdy. They hurried past and turned into Swan Street.

'Is that it?' Paige said when she saw the building across the road with a high stepped gable and Offilers' Ales emblazoned beneath the third-story window. To the left was a tobacconist's called Gerald Grudgings and to the right a shop called Tylers, which appeared to sell everything from seeds to ironmongery. The illuminated pub sign that was to the right of the front door did indeed say Green Man. They walked inside and through to the tap room. The air was thick with heavy pungent tobacco smoke, and raucous laughter could be heard coming from a corner near the bar.

'I'll just go through to the other bar and see if I can find the chap. I wish I knew his name,' said Wesley. 'I think you should stay here by the exit.'

'Are you sure we're in the right place?' Paige asked, looking around at the townsfolk, who already seemed to be quite drunk.

'Quite sure,' Wesley answered, before making his way across the grimy room.

Paige sat down on a stool not too far away from the tap room's door. There was a welcome waft of fresh air every time someone entered or left. She wasn't sure it was correct, or even allowed, for her to be in a public bar without a man to chaperone her, but there did seem to be quite a lot of single women in this particular one. She watched a group of them who, one by one, were approached by the men who had been standing by the bar, and then they left, one at a time, with some of them.

'Oi! You can't sit there.' A coarse female voice caused Paige to look up into the face of a woman with lank dark hair and an interestingly painted face. She smelled of stale body odour – the whole pub stank of stale body odour.

'I'm sorry,' Paige said, and rose to her feet. 'Is this your seat?'

'This is my pitch, me and them girls there.' The harlot nodded towards what remained of the small group. 'So you can piss off and find your own.'

'I'm with someone,' Paige told her, but she couldn't see Wesley anywhere. A bony finger stabbed her in the chest and the woman pushed her up against the wall.

'Get out, you la-de-dah bitch.' The woman spat in Paige's face. She had more than one tooth missing and her breath was rank. Paige pushed the hag away and wiped her face. She looked around frantically for Wesley – where the hell was he?

'Come on, Mary, how about giving me a knee-trembler up the cemetery?'

An unlikely rescuer had unknowingly come to Paige's aid – a man who smelled worse than the woman, had a greying beard and clothes that shone with grease. He put an arm around Mary's shoulders and propelled her towards the door. Mary glanced back towards Paige.

'If I ever see you here again, I'll swing for yer,' she rasped and left with her night's prospect.

Paige sat back down on the wooden stool, and as she caught her breath she stared at the filthy floorboards. In her line of vision came a pair of polished black shoes that seemed out of place in a dive like this. She looked up and saw that the owner of the shoes was well-dressed and remarkably handsome. She glanced over to where the whored of prostitutes had been – she didn't want any more trouble – and, relieved that they had all found their take-home-pay for the evening, looked back to the stranger. She felt dizzy as she stared into his eyes, which, even in this light, she discerned were a spellbinding, amber-like colour.

'Are you all right?' he asked in a pleasantly mellow voice. 'You look a little shaken after your altercation with Mucky Mary. Here, take this, it will ease your distress.'

Paige accepted the glass he was offering and took a sip of brandy.

'Thank you.'

'You shouldn't be here alone, it's not safe. My name's Matthew by the way, Matthew Hopkins.'

Instead of replying, Paige took another sip of the brandy. She felt extremely light-headed – she really shouldn't drink on an empty stomach. She sensed a hand under her elbow, encouraging her to stand.

'Come with me and we'll take in some air,' Matthew told her, and he took the empty glass.

'I'm, I'm waiting for ...' Paige felt faint, and was grateful for Matthew's support, but just wanted to sit down again.

'Come on,' Matthew insisted, and he tried again to get her to walk towards the door. He put his arm around her waist and almost dragged her.

'No! Stop!' Paige tried to push him away, but he was too strong. Everywhere seemed to go dim, as if someone had turned all the lights out. She thought she was going to pass out. Her head sank onto his shoulder and she reluctantly clutched Mathew's arm. Through the muzzyness she heard a welcome voice.

'May I be of assistance?' Wesley asked.

Although she was groggy, Paige began to feel stronger as soon as she knew Wesley was close by. Matthew let go and she almost fell to the revolting floor. Wesley caught her and she leant into him. Matthew moved away and as he grew more distant, so her head cleared and she straightened up again as best as she could. The fog cleared from her brain and Paige glimpsed someone, who looked familiar, hastily leaving through the bar, and presumably out of the back door. The woman taking leave had long red hair and seemed to be almost floating – or maybe she was still a little woozy, Paige thought. Matthew Hopkins looked as though he was following the redhead, but he then turned back to Paige and stared at her.

'Next time,' he mouthed.

Paige shuddered. She had no idea why that man had made her feel so uneasy.

'Come on, let's get out of here,' Wesley said and guided her out through the door and into the reviving night air. As they walked back along Church Gate she felt almost back to normal.

'What a horrible man,' she said. 'Do you think he

assumed I was one of the ladies of the night?'

'No, I think he had a different agenda, but I'm not sure what.'

'There was a woman in the bar who looked very much like the one we saw in the market today.'

'Which woman?'

'The one who didn't fancy you.' Paige was definitely feeling all right. 'The one with the strange tube that stung your hand.'

'Maybe it was her mother,' Wesley said.

'I don't know, but that bloke who tried to take me outside was certainly interested in her.'

'Perhaps he was on a promise,' Wesley said, and she felt him pull her in close to him.

'Did you find the person you were looking for?' Paige asked as they headed towards home.

'No, we were in the wrong Green Man.'

Paige wanted to say 'I told you so', but just shook her head in resignation. She took his arm and made sure the gate was firmly closed behind them.

Chapter 15

The Cottage, Present Day

'Well that was weird,' Paige said, and flopped down onto the sofa. Wesley sat down beside her.

'Are you really all right, my love?' he asked and took her hand. She turned to face him.

'I'm fine, thanks to you, but I still can't get over that man. Do you think he is the one you are supposed to meet? He didn't look as though he fitted in.'

'No. Even though he appeared out of place he didn't look out of his century, nor did he speak as though he was.'

'But that doesn't make sense. We went back to 1933, which is in the previous century, and your tattoo doesn't give anything earlier, so it must be the twentieth century that we're to go to.'

'We obviously got it wrong and maybe we should have gone to 1993 as that's only just in the last century.'

Paige took his face in her hands and felt the scratch of his stubble on her palms. She kissed him full on the lips and then whispered, 'I think 1983 would be more fun.'

Wesley gave her a peck on the cheek and, seemingly ignoring her remark, stood up and walked over to the cabinet to get a drink.

'What did you say that man's name was?'

'I think he said it was Matthew, but it's all a bit hazy.'

'Did he have a second name?'

'Yes, but I can't quite remember. King something or other, I think.' Paige stood up, took Wesley's glass from him, and downed his whisky in one. She shuddered at the taste.

'Another?' Wesley asked.

'No, thank you.'

He poured himself a replacement whisky and they both sat down again on the sofa. After a few minutes Paige spoke.

'Hawkins, or Atkins, something like that.'

Wesley nodded and tipped the remaining whisky into his mouth.

'Do you think he's important?' Paige asked.

'No, not at all. I think he was someone to avoid back then. The woman with the red hair probably saw him off.'

'Or he saw her off.'

'Not our problem.'

'Then why are we here?'

'To be honest, I don't really know. A holiday, perhaps?'

'A holiday! In Loughborough, a market town in the middle of the country? In March? You have to be kidding.'

Wesley pulled her in close and stretched his arm out in front of her.

'Of course,' she said, looking down at the tattoo, 'we need to sort out whatever it is that needs sorting out.'

'1993,' Wesley replied.

'Wasn't that when Linda said that market stallholders had disappeared? Do you think we are here because of the missing people?'

'I don't know. It might just be coincidence.'

'That's why you want to go to the Green Man in 1993, isn't it?' She peered closely at the numbers on his arm to see if she could distinguish the date but the scar was not helping. She felt his lips on the back of her neck. 'I still think 1983 would be more fun,' she said and turned to face him. Could she persuade him? She kissed him and stood up. 'I'll just go and get changed into clothes more suitable for the time,' she said, and headed for the stairs knowing that he would soon follow her.

Chapter 16

Caravelli's, Present Day

The bed was made, towels that had been left in the shower tray had been replaced and the refreshments replenished. The guest in this room was a policeman or something. He was tidy, but a few clues lay about. It was a game Ellen played that was a bit like people watching. She could tell a lot from how guests left their rooms. Ellen stood in the doorway of the Lovell room and surveyed her work. It was faultless, she was sure. Anyone would be pleased to stay here. The rooms in Caravelli's were all lovely. The Lovell was the smallest, but it still had a double bed and an en suite. Satisfied, she closed the door to Lovell and moved onto her next room using the large key on her ring. There weren't any mod-con card readers here, although the rooms were all appointed to a high standard. Caravelli's was an old building, dating back to the fourteenth century and there were only five rooms, so it was easy to service. The next one was her favourite.

'Hello, Hastings,' she said in a low voice. Ellen crossed the room, heart pounding. She ran her fingers over the stone lintel and her heart beat even faster. There was always a faint hope. She had never minded chambermaid duties, because she could get into this room with the fireplace and remember how she'd been staying here five years ago with her family. Hastings was her room. That was when her phone had taken her back to 1663.

'Will it ever happen again?' she wondered out loud. She was never quite sure if she wanted it to or not, but she'd had to be nearby. The job was useful money. But it wasn't the money that had really attracted Ellen. What she did wasn't important. Why she did it was though. She had to be here, because maybe, just maybe, being here also meant she could be there, or rather, then. If she was in the right place at the right time. As she mused, Ellen's eyes were drawn to the pictures and photos strewn over the bed.

Ellen sighed. She piled the papers up and made the bed as she had been taught. She hated it when guests left this room in particular in disarray. She picked up the books that were on the bed and on the floor, her eyebrows raising at the titles, and piled them on the bedside table. There were also photos and cuttings lined up neatly, covering the whole surface of the desk. Scissors, tape in a dispenser and various marker pens lay ready. 'It takes all sorts!' Ellen thought, emptying the bin that was full of paper scraps, while trying to put her feelings on hold; guests were entitled to respect and privacy. Still, this was a strange one. She didn't dare move anything so she decided not to dust, but she couldn't help noticing one picture was of a striking red-haired woman who seemed familiar. She vacuumed all round, cleaned the bathroom and then left. She was glad to be done in there today.

'Finished, Ellen?'

Her friend, Izzy, had pulled open Huntingdon's door, trapping it back with her hip, as she manouvered her trolley of cleaning things into the hallway.

They had been working away from each other for half an hour or so, but their conversation continued as if there had been no break. She and Isabella were both students at Loughborough University but in different years and studying different courses –

they'd only really met through this job. Izzy was new but they'd clicked straight away. She was from Italy and her English was great, but colloquialisms often puzzled her. Friday and Saturdays they would both be working as chambermaids in the mornings and then waitressing at lunch times and in the evenings.

'Yeah, all done,' Ellen answered. 'Have you seen the man that's in this room at the mo? He's got some strange books by his bedside. There's Witch Hunt: The Persecution of Witches in England and a paperback called Codex Gigas: Discover The Devil's Bible.' She didn't mention the pictures or the fact that he also had The Discovery of Witches by Matthew Hopkins, Witchfinder General. It was one step too far, something that needed thinking about – people were really scared of the Matthew Hopkins from the 1660s, as she knew, personally. And the bizarre thing was, this guest was called Matthew Hopkins. He was! She'd seen his name in the register when they'd checked which rooms needed doing.

'Ellen, you're not supposed to be touching the guest's things!'

'I wasn't. Honest. They were on the bed and the floor. I had to tidy them to make the bed and hoover. Have you seen him then?'

'Well I did, how you say, get a look at him when he was going out. He's got weird eyes.'

'Weird eyes, eh? So there is something strange about him!'

'Just because a visitor looks different, it doesn't not mean he is up to something, you know.'

'Yeah, I know.'

'What is it the English say, though? Nuts?' Izzy tapped the side of her head and they both laughed.

'Yeah, nutty as a fruitcake!'

'Fruitcake?'

'Cake with lots of fruit and nuts in. It's a play on the word nut.' They both laughed.

'Been up to anything nice since last week?'

'Not much, really. I've been trying to complete an assignment. I don't know how you have managed to work and study, but I'm doing my best. I need the money. To study in England is not, how you say? Cheap?'

'It helps, for sure. I've just got used to it. I've been working here part-time for five years now, since I was fourteen. Washing up, chambermaiding, waitressing and bar work since I was eighteen. It's only a small place so we all muck in.'

'Muck in? What is that?'

'Help each other out with anything that's going.'

As they were talking Ellen was aware of footsteps on the stairs. A head appeared and they both fell quiet, realising it was the man they'd been talking about, the man she knew was called Matthew Hopkins. Ellen's heart was beating fast and she felt as if her breath was stuck in her throat. He looked from one to the other. His eyes were compelling. He had the same jawline as the sixteenth century Matthew Hopkins. With straggly hair, rather than the neat cut this one wore, and a pointy hat, he would look remarkably similar.

'Have either of you been in my room?' he demanded.

'Yes, sir, it's all ti––'

'Well stay out of it in future! No one is to go in there again while I'm staying here.' He was almost spitting. 'Is that understood? No one!'

'Yes. Of course, sir.' Ellen's mouth had dried up, but she managed to get her words out. 'I'll make sure the message is passed on.'

She was still speaking as he opened the door to his room, stepped inside and slammed the door in her face.

'Whoa, what was that about?' she directed at Izzy. Izzy shrugged her shoulders and snorted with suppressed laughter.

'You shoulda seen your face,' she teased as she

disappeared into Despenser.

Later, Ellen went into the staff room. She slipped her overall off and tied on her frilly white pinny. Doing this always reminded her of the times she spent as a kitchen maid over the road in the rectory back in 1663. She had mucked in with Jayne, all right. No choice when you're dumped in another century.

'You in there, Ellen?'

'Yeah, won't be a mo. Ready for the onslaught, Izz?'

It was hard holding two worlds in your head at once. Having the phone with her back in the past had been such a risk, she thought, peering into the mirror over the basin in the staff loo and picking a bit of mascara from her eyelid. She was always worried about being caught, accused of being a witch or something. It was strange to think that the people she had known then really believed that magic and malevolent forces could be responsible for everyday occurrences. Ridiculous! It should be ridiculous and yet she had gone there, and lived there, a couple of times. It'd been a weird period. She'd never been sure, when she was then, in 1662 or 3, or whenever it was – the flipping Gregorian calendar had caused continual confusion with dates – whether she'd be able to get back to now. No, not now, then, five years ago. That was then now, not then then. For goodness' sake! Time travel was so confusing.

Ellen watched the door push open in the mirror, and Izzy's head appeared. 'Come on, Noodle,' she said. 'It's time.'

Having someone chivvy her up like that could momentarily whip her back in time. Jayne, her first friend in 1663, had hurried her along the first day they'd met. Of course, she hadn't known that Ellen was acting so muddleheaded because she'd just been transported more than three centuries back in time. Claybrain was what Jayne had called Ellen on the stairs of what was now the Old Rectory Museum.

'Keep your hair on! I'm on my way.' Ellen followed Izzy downstairs and into the restaurant.

'Ah, girls. Here you are.' Massimo, one of the two owners and their boss, was waiting in front of the doorway ready to open up; it was Luigi's night off. 'Ellen, would you help Isabella to set up and then check the tables, please? Cutlery, napkins, you know whata to do.'

'Yes, Bossimo,' Ellen said, directing a smile at him. 'Come on, then, Izzy!'

Chapter 17

Caravelli's, Present Day

Sandbach walked down the stairs and through into the bar area. The smell of Italian food cooking in the kitchen was already making his stomach grumble.

'I think that's pancetta,' Terrence said, running alongside him.

'You could be right,' Sandbach replied.

Massimo was handing a glass of wine to a lady at the bar; he looked up and smiled towards Sandbach.

'Ah, Mr Sandbag, you like your room?'

'It's beautiful thank you, Massimo,' Sandbach replied with a beaming smile.

'Excellent. I have a table for you. Is just for one, yes?'

Sandbach nodded and followed him through into the restaurant, where he was guided towards a small table with two chairs that was tucked just behind a pillar. Presumably they generally expected couples or larger groups.

'Here you go, table for one, for now, eh?'

Sandbach frowned back at him. Massimo handed Sandbach the menu and then grinned and held his hands up in defeat.

'Can I get you a drink? The house red is especially good.'

'Just tea, please – milk no sugar,' Sandbach said, placing a serviette carefully across his lap.

'Certainly. We have Earl Grey, Lapsang Souchong, Darjeeling, Oolong, Matcha …'

'Erm, PG?'

Massimo rolled his eyes and then walked off shaking his head and muttering something.

Although he was pleased to be tucked away from the other restaurant guests, he didn't like having his back towards them. He got up and switched to the seat opposite so that his back was towards the window. He felt much more comfortable now he could see what was going on. A young waitress walked in and placed a cup of tea in front of him. He started looking through the menu, mentally crossing off everything he knew was out of the running. He didn't do starters and he didn't want a dessert – that narrowed it to just main courses. Nothing with fish, nothing with olives, nothing with cream. There! Chicken and bacon in a tomato sauce with pasta. Hmm. He glanced up and caught the attention of a second waitress, who came promptly.

'Are you ready to order, sir?'

'Ah, Isabella,' Sandbach replied having spotted her name badge, 'OK, can I have one of these, but can I swap the pasta for chips?' Sandbach asked, pointing to the item on the menu.

Isabella looked at him with what could only be described as pity.

'There is a fish and chip shop down the road.'

Sandbach mulled the thought over in his head. It would be cheaper, but he suspected they wouldn't let him back into Caravelli's until he'd finished.

'Chips, not pasta, please!'

'Fine. We can switch for the chips. You want anything else?'

Sandbach shook his head and blissfully sipped his familiar-tasting tea. He looked up to see the first young waitress stare at him again as she walked past, but was a little taken aback by the sudden change in her expression as she saw two guests being shown to their table, apparently just the other side of the pillar to where he was sitting. She had stopped and was staring wide-eyed at one of them, biting her lip. Massimo walked over and said something quietly. She blushed and quickly walked off.

Massimo shook his head and moved back to the bar.

Terrence jumped up onto the table, he turned his nose up at a small bowl of olives that had been placed there but sat next to them anyway.

'Well this is nice isn't it?' Terrence said. 'Table for one man and his dog.'

'Isn't it just?' Sandbach replied.

'The natives could prove interesting tonight though.'

'What do you mean?'

Terrence nodded towards the door.

Sandbach turned to see the woman of interest, Fenella. Her long flowing red hair wafted outwards and narrowly missed other guests at their tables. She was still clutching her big bag, but it didn't look as heavy as before. Massimo escorted her over towards them, arriving at the small table set right next to the one they were at. She didn't seem to have noticed him yet, but Sandbach felt the need for anonymity and began studying the wine list intently.

'I don't think you're meant to climb inside those things,' Terrence said.

Sandbach shushed him and immediately regretted it.

'Mr Sandbag,' Massimo said, 'you want a glass of wine after all?'

'Erm, maybe,' he replied in an unnecessarily high-pitched voice.

Terrence made a noise like a snort, that could have been laughter, and Sandbach shushed him again.

'Yes, why not?' Sandbach said aloud, trying to sound

more natural but still hiding behind the wine list. 'A glass of the house red would be lovely, thank you.'

'Yes, OK.' Massimo replied. 'I serve this lovely lady first though.'

Sandbach nodded without looking up.

'What can I get you, madam?' Massimo could be heard asking Fenella.

'Just a water, thank you,' she replied. 'I need to use the ladies' room if you don't mind?'

'Certainly.'

Massimo left, followed shortly by Fenella. Sandbach lowered the menu and sighed.

'International man of mystery aren't you?' Terrence whispered.

'Thank you very much,' Sandbach muttered under his breath.

'Ooh, she's left her bag though,' Terrence announced.

Sandbach glanced around the room. The restaurant staff seemed busy elsewhere, so he bent down and undid his shoe laces.

'Oh you're not doing that trick are you?' Terrence asked.

'If you're not going to help, you can at least be quiet. Why don't you keep an eye out in case we have company?' Still with his head tucked down low, he reached over to the bag and slid it quickly under his own table. He undid it, slowly, but Terrence gave a short bark. He quickly sat up just as the first waitress walked past, scowling at him. He smiled and nodded back at her, then took a sip of tea. When she was out of sight and busy speaking to another customer, he ducked under the table to take a proper look in the bag. It was made of fabric and well-worn, but it felt strong and surprisingly inflexible. The stitched rose pattern on the bright-green background was eye-catching and strangely hypnotic. Sandbach found himself following the lines of stitching from one flower to the next. The pattern flowed and swooshed, making him feel slightly dizzy.

'It matches your eyes,' Terrence said, snapping him out of his stupor.

'Ah, yes. Thank you for that,' Sandbach replied, feeling a little embarrassed.

There was no zip to the bag; it had a pull-cord and toggle that when loosened allowed the top flap to be lifted so he could see the contents. It was empty apart from a tissue, a car park ticket and loose change. If the bag were more solid it would probably echo.

'Well done, you,' Terrence said, sarcastically.

Sandbach was about to close the bag up again, then spotted a pocket inside the lining, only visible due to something bulging inside it. He reached in and slid out an old-looking, worn-but-sturdy, leather tube. It had symbols or runes on it; nothing he recognised seeing before.

Sandbach glanced back up just in time to see Fenella returning. He panicked, shoved the tube back into the pocket and pulled the cord tight on the top of the bag, but there was no way he could get it back under her table without her seeing.

'Ahem.' Terrence gave a fake cough.

His trusty pooch was sitting back on the table. Terrence nodded first to the cutlery in front of Sandbach, then onto the floor to the other side of Fenella's table. Sandbach smiled. He gave a ridiculously fake cough, and then clumsily swiped his cutlery off the table and onto the floor. It landed with a clatter that caught the attention of most people in the restaurant, so Fenella must have noticed. He made a show of leaning over to pick it up, while carefully pushing the bag back under Fenella's table with his foot. He sat back up holding his knife, fork and spoon, rolled his eyes in mock embarrassment, then mouthed the word 'sorry' to anyone who might be looking. The first waitress walked over, lips pursed, and shaking her head she plonked a glass of red wine on his table. He glanced at her name badge.

'Thank you, Ellen,' he said, trying to keep watch without drawing any more attention to himself.

Fenella sat back down at her table, glaring across at him and clutching her stomach awkwardly. He couldn't be sure whether she remembered him from earlier, or not. He supposed she had no real reason to other than recognising his representation of the law, such as it was.

Ignoring the wine, Sandbach picked up his cup of tea and nodded a silent 'cheers.' Fenella frowned at him and then reached down and slid her bag towards her. She pulled open the toggle and then drew something out from under her cardigan. It looked like the leather-bound tube he'd just seen – old and battered – but she handled it reverently before placing it carefully into the bag.

'Would you like a few more minutes to choose your meal?' Massimo asked, appearing at her table.

'What? No,' she replied, aggressively. 'I'm not hungry.' She jumped to her feet, pulled her bag close and marched quickly out of the restaurant.

'Does she usually do that?' Sandbach asked a rather confused looking Massimo.

'I don't know. I've never seen her before,' he replied, and then his face lit up as the waitress brought over a plate of lovingly arranged French-fry style chips with chicken and bacon bathed in a deep-red tomato sauce and sitting proudly in the centre of the plate. 'Ah, excellent, Izzy. I take it you have your appetite still, Mr Sandbag?'

Sandbach was mesmerised by the marvellous sight and smell, combined with something as wonderfully familiar as chips. All he could do was smile and nod. Terrence sat panting eagerly with his mouth open.

'Oh yes,' Sandbach said, and with a huge smile he tucked in like a man possessed.

Chapter 18

Caravelli's, Present Day

The foyer of Caravelli's was just as Florence remembered. She was greeted at the reception desk by a well-dressed man, whose name badge identified him as Massimo, and a genuine smile.

'Good evening, madam. Do you have a reservation with us?'

'Good evening.' She placed her overnight bag on the floor and her handbag on the counter. 'I called about an hour ago. My name's Florence Carter.'

'Ah, welcome. You are in luck as we are busy tonight. You had the last of our rooms, Miss Carter. I am Massimo and if there is anything I can assist you with during your stay, please do not hesitate to ask. Now, please sign here and then I will take your bag and show you to your room. You are booked into the restaurant for dinner in an hour, but feel free to sit at the bar beforehand.'

'Thank you. Now please tell me you have something wonderfully rich on the menu to go with an outstanding glass of red wine?'

Florence watched as Massimo walked round the counter and picked up her bag. 'Indeed we do,' he said, indicating that she should follow him, 'and as I was saying to another customer earlier this evening, the house red is especially goc

Movement in the mirror above the bar cau
attention and glancing to the right she watched as
woman from the coffee shop walked out of the din
Holding the large bag by her side the woman strode through the
bar and out of the main doors. Despite not having looked directly
at her, Florence was left with the distinct impression that the
woman knew she was there. Picking up her own handbag,
Florence headed for the staircase after Massimo.

'The hotel was built in the fourteenth century,' he said as
she caught him up and they climbed the stairs, 'and as such is a
building of great historical interest. Your room for the night is
the Despenser room, which happens to be my favourite.' Turning,
Massimo winked at her, before continuing, 'as it has oak beams
and is very delightful. All our rooms are en suite.'

Florence hid a grin and watched as he placed her bag on
the bed. 'Thank you. I'm sure I shall be very comfortable. Now,
about that glass of red wine …'

Massimo looked momentarily confused, before smiling
at her. 'Of course, madam has had a long day. Do you wish to
accompany me to the bar, or would you like to come down later?'

'Give me ten minutes and I'll be there. A large glass of
that house red will be just what I need. Thank you,' she called to
his departing back.

Exactly ten minutes later Florence walked into the bar,
happy to see a large glass of red wine waiting for her. She raised
it to take a sip, her gaze drawn to the mirror in front of her.
Sandbach's reflection stared back. With a start, Florence spun
around on the stool.

Thankful that Sandbach hadn't seen her, Florence turned
back to the bar and took an appreciative sip of her wine. Their
conversation earlier had not gone to plan and despite openly
discussing the file on the table between them, she'd been left
annoyed with herself for not getting her point across in a more

ـsitive manner. Twenty-odd years ago the unit she'd been working with had been disbanded and while her colleagues had shared her feelings that all was not as it seemed, the senior officers had been quick to shut the investigation down.

Finishing her wine, Florence waved at Massimo as he approached from the dining room. To her dismay, she realised that Sandbach had noticed her and that he did not look pleased by this fact.

'Your table is ready, Miss Carter. Would you follow me, please?'

Sliding from the bar stool, Florence collected her bag and followed Massimo into the dining room.

'Here we are,' Massimo said, with a wave of his arm as he pulled a chair out for her, 'you shall have a moment to read the menu, before Ellen or Isabella take your order. In the meantime, can I get you another glass of wine?'

'Yes, please.' Florence watched Sandbach rise from his seat, before making his way towards her. Tilting her face up she smiled as he approached.

'Good evening,' Sandbach said. 'I don't wish to intrude, but I suggest that we meet over breakfast and discuss the case. There are a few lines of enquiry I wish to pursue and we can talk more freely after sleep and a cup of tea. Shall we say eight o'clock?'

'Well, yes that sounds great. I have a few leads that we could look into and there must be a couple of the old team knocking about that I can shake the memories from.'

'I'd prefer it if we follow our investigations separately. It's not my thing to work in pairs – makes me think of Morse, or maybe Lewis,' Sandbach said. Florence was amused by the way he stroked his chin while speaking. 'Anyway, we can make a plan and then meet at the station early afternoon and see what progress we've made.'

Florence nodded as Sandbach turned and walked away,

unsure of what else was required of her.

'Oh, no, wait a mo,' she called, realising as she did that other diners had stopped talking and turned to look at her. Florence smiled at them in apology.

Sandbach returned to her. 'Yes?'

'Could you maybe sit for a minute?' she asked. He pulled the opposite chair back, sank into it and dropped the case-file onto the table.

'I just wanted you to know that I think we are, in fact, on the same page and I'm sorry that I didn't make myself clearer in the coffee shop. I thought, as did Boyle and a couple of other colleagues, that there was something else, something unexplainable in this case. There must be a link, but to span a distance of so many years, it hardly seems possible that there is a connection, but ...'

'Of course it's connected,' Sandbach exclaimed, leaning back in his chair and pointing at the folder in front of them, 'how can you possibly think otherwise?'

Florence watched his left hand scratch his neck, while his right hand hung by his side, the fingers splayed – almost as if he was shushing someone. He coughed, and she met his gaze.

'I don't think otherwise. In fact, I think I share some of the same ideas as you, but you don't seem to be listening to anything I've told you.' She stopped and stared as Sandbach picked up her wine glass and took a huge gulp of wine, swallowed and shuddered.

'God, I really don't like wine,' he muttered, pushing the glass away and signalling for the waitress. 'Another pot of tea, please,' he asked, before adding, 'would you like anything?'

'Ahem, yes.' Florence looked up at the waitress whose name badge identified her as Ellen. 'I'll have another glass of red wine, please.'

Sandbach waited until Ellen had retreated and then leant forward, both elbows on the table. 'The fact is, people have been going missing since 1993, and I've no doubt that there are others that were not reported, in and around George Yard. Furthermore, the Green Man pub was closed early 1993, according to your reports,' Sandbach gestured to the folder on the table.

'The Green Man was indeed closed early March 1993 and, as you saw today, there's a shopping centre over the top of it.' Florence flicked open the folder, retrieved two photographs and passed them to Sandbach. 'These show the inside of the Green Man just before it closed.'

Sandbach flipped through the photos showing people with outmoded hairstyles and clothes, against an unremarkable backdrop, as far as she could see. 'Closed when the disappearances started ... hmmm ... all this combined with what I saw after leaving you at that coffee shop ...'

'What did you ...' Florence paused while the waitress placed their drinks on the table in front of them, '... see?' she hissed.

Sandbach was peering at one photo more closely. He tapped it with his finger and pushed it towards Florence. 'Look at that. That woman in the background, could it be ... does she look familiar to you?'

'Yes, the lady in the coffee shop with the humongous bag – she was here earlier too.'

'Fenella. Apparently her name is Fenella,' he interrupted, frowning at her. 'I followed her after our meeting towards George Yard.' He coughed. 'I was just wondering where she was going as she had this really intense look about her and as I turned the corner, she'd, well erm,' he lowered his voice and beckoned her nearer, 'disappeared.'

'What, disappeared, like "poof and then she was gone" disappeared?' Florence sat back in her chair and laughed. 'Come on, you are not seriously expecting me to suspend all common sense and— Oh!' She stopped at the expression on Sandbach's face. 'You are actually suggesting that? Are you also suggesting that she is in this photo,' she lowered her voice and whispered, 'a photo from 1993?'

Sandbach met her gaze. Florence closed her eyes and placed her fingertips on her eyebrows. Opening her eyes she stared at her wineglass – it was empty. Florence frowned at it before turning and signalling to Ellen. 'Another red, please. Oh and Ellen, make it a large one.'

'Right, okay,' she continued with a deep breath, 'let me get this straight. You're suggesting that Fenella is what ... some kind of magician sort of person?'

Sandbach poured milk into his tea, his expression unreadable. 'Not a magician, exactly, more along the lines of a ... witch-type person.'

'Witch? What like "turns you into toads, makes it rain, eats children, dances around a cauldron, four hundred years old" type witch?'

'And there's your childhood storybooks rolled out for all to see.' Sandbach grinned – a weird sight and something he obviously didn't do often. 'Yes, a witch, but not the storybook kind.'

Florence sighed and waited as the waitress placed her glass of red wine on the table. The photo in one hand, she picked the glass up with the other and took a sip, then another and then a third. 'A witch!' Shaking her head she laughed. 'Okay, I'll play. Let's go with this witch theory for a moment. So, are you suggesting that Fenella is in some way responsible for the market traders disappearing? That her witch status allows her to pop off to God knows where whenever she feels like it? Oooh, do you think she has a wand? Only I've always wanted to .... Anyway, you are saying ...' Florence took a breath, 'that she has kidnapped these people to satisfy her own evil ...'

'Oh for God's sake, stop being so dramatic,' Sandbach interrupted.

'Dramatic? Erm, Mr Pot, Mr Kettle's on line three ... I'm

not the one being sodding dramatic. Have you heard yourself? Witches, disappearing through walls? Come on, really?'

'No, I'm not suggesting that. Well, maybe some of it. The bit about her being responsible for the market traders, yes, now that is highly likely, but why and for what purpose?' He looked at the floor and nodded. 'Yes, yes, it does all revolve around Fenella and we just have to find out what exactly that is.'

Florence reached for her glass. It was empty, again.

Chapter 19

The Green Man, 1983

Despite still being March the evening was fairly warm and Paige linked her arm through Wesley's as they made their way across the deserted marketplace. Wesley stopped beside a water fountain.

'What is it?' Paige asked.

'This way,' Wesley said, and strode out again. 'Baxter Gate! let's try that one.'

The streets were quiet and there was hardly anyone about. They came through the gate, turned right and crossed the road.

'Here we are,' Wesley said, and pointed to a sign that said Swan Street. They carried on walking, crossed that street and before long Paige found herself standing in front of a large glass entrance to a public house. Wesley pushed the door open.

'Nineteen eighties' Green Man awaits us,' he said.

Paige's mouth dropped open and she touched the new blouse she'd bought from the blonde lady in the marketplace earlier.

'You did this for me?' she asked.

'I do everything for you, my love,' Wesley said, and kissed her full on the lips.

Paige pulled away and narrowed her gaze.

'As much as I'd like to believe that,' she said and kissed him back, 'I think there's more to this than just a trip back here for me and my new top.'

'Dubiety doesn't suit you,' he said. Taking her hand in his he led her down a staircase that changed direction halfway. They continued through glass doors at the foot of the stairs and turned again; a few steps to the right led them into a room where people were laughing, drinking and smoking.

'It's a basement bar!' Paige said and looked around. Although they were underground it wasn't at all dark, but bright and vibrant. The bar to their left was welcoming and the lady standing behind it smiled at them as they walked past.

Wesley pulled Paige in close, kissed her cheek and said: 'I'll just go and rub shoulders with a few of the locals. You'll be all right, won't you?'

'Of course,' Paige wobbled her head, mockingly, and sat down on a wooden-backed seat.

The bar was shrouded in a smoky mist and it was making Paige's eyes water.

'Hello, do you mind if I sit here?'

Paige looked up and saw a dark-haired young man with a thin moustache and a haircut that was short on top and long at the back.

'No, please do,' she said, and he slid onto the bench next to her. His denim jacket looked as though it was two sizes bigger than he needed.

'I'm Pete, by the way,' he said. 'What's your name?'

'Paige.'

'Can I buy you a drink, Paige?'

She looked across the fuggy room towards Wesley, who was deep in conversation with two women who looked a little older than most of the other clientele. She turned back to Pete and smiled.

'Thank you, that would be lovely.'

'What would you like?'

Paige looked around to see what others were drinking.

'I'll have one of those please,' she said, pointing to a girl with tightly curled hair who was sitting with a group almost opposite.

'Cherry B it is then,' Pete said, and made his way to the curved wooden-fronted bar.

Paige took in her surroundings. There were large, sweeping alcoves around the room – the two at the bottom of the bar had medieval paintings on the walls and one had a castle in the background and showed knights on horseback in the fore. It looked as though a jousting contest was about to begin. Opposite, and along the other walls, blinds covered the panels, as if something precious were being protected.

Pete came back and put a glass down in front of her – it contained a deep-red liquid that smelled of almonds. Paige noticed that two fingers were missing on his right hand.

'Thank you,' she said, and took a sip. It was like drinking cherry velvet. 'Ooh, that's delicious.' She smiled at her drinks-donor, he smiled back and she noticed a scar that ran from temple to jawline.

''Ere, who's your bird, Pete?' a girl with long blonde curls called across.

'Ay up, Linda,' Pete replied. 'Does your dad know you're in here?'

'No, and don't you go telling him either.'

'Paige, this is Linda, she's fifteen and shouldn't be here,' Pete said and shook his head. Paige wanted to say 'I know', but kept silent.

'You mind yer own,' Linda said, 'I ain't the only one.' She turned again to Paige. 'Nice top. It's a bit like mine.'

'So it is,' Paige said. 'I bought it from a lady on the market this afternoon.'

'You've got good taste,' Linda said, and returned to her drink.

'You smell nice.' Pete was sitting a little too close for Paige's liking.

'Oh, thank you. So do you,' Paige told him and looked again towards Wesley who was now surrounded by a group of what Paige would have called ladies with experience. He turned and winked at her, then went back to his conversation. He's enjoying himself, she thought.

'It's Brut,' Pete said, and tapped his cheek.

'Oh, your aftershave. Yes, it's very nice.' Paige pointed to Pete's hand as he lifted his glass. 'If you don't mind me asking, how did you lose your fingers?'

'Same as how I got this,' Pete said, indicating the scar. 'To be honest, I can't remember much about it. It was about ten years ago; I used to help my dad on the market. He sent me to get him some tobacco from Grudgings's and I was going down George Yard when something hit me.'

'George Yard?'

'Yes, it's at the back of here and leads into the marketplace.'

'What happened?'

'As I said, I can't remember much about it except that there was this bloke standing in my way. He was bigger than me and wouldn't let me pass. Then he went for me and all of a sudden something struck my face. I put my hand up to defend myself and then I must have passed out. I woke up in the hospital and found out I'd lost two fingers and had twenty stitches in me face.' He lifted his glass and took a long drink. Paige noticed that beads of sweat had formed on his brow.

'Interesting,' Wesley said, as he slid onto the bench next to Paige, who realised that he'd obviously escaped the cougars.

Pete put his glass down and wiped his mouth with the back of his hand.

'Pete, meet Wesley,' Paige said, and Wesley offered his hand. Pete took it but looked uncomfortable.

'I'd better get back to me mates.' Pete stood up and lifted his dimpled pint glass. 'Nice to meet you.'

'Thank you for the drink,' Paige said. Pete nodded and walked over to the crowd opposite them.

Paige turned to Wesley. 'When did you say this was?' she asked.

'Nineteen eighty-three,' he told her. 'You said you wanted to go to the eighties' Green Man, and here we are. I told you those gates would be useful.'

'So you did. Have you seen anyone who might need our help?' Paige asked, and took another sip of her drink.

'No, I don't think he's here yet. I'll go and take another look round – I think the ladies are missing me.'

Paige watched Wesley walk back to the group of women, who appeared to welcome him back to their conclave with open arms. She pushed her hand down the side of the seat cushion and felt something metallic – a coin, now that could come in handy. She continued to search further round and found a few more pieces of small change that had fallen from pockets and were caught in the upholstery. She turned her attention to the floor – it was certainly cleaner than the other Green Man's spit-and-sawdust. There was a folded piece of paper near her foot. She bent forward and picked it up. It was green with a picture of the Queen alongside the words 'Bank of England' and 'One Pound'. Paige finished her drink and thought that the note could be useful if Wesley didn't return soon. She turned the note over to see Sir Isaac Newton, who was reading a book. Her line of vision strayed to a pair of shiny black shoes before her. The man, who she guessed was in his mid-twenties, moved closer and sat down beside her. He didn't speak and was staring at the door.

'Are you waiting for someone?' Paige asked.

'You could say that,' the man answered. He looked

familiar, but she couldn't see his face properly.

'Don't I know you?' Paige couldn't think where she might have seen him before.

'I don't think so.'

There was a sudden burst of laughter from the group in the opposite seat.

'They're having fun.' Paige laughed with them, but the man didn't.

'Do you know those people?' he asked.

'You'll be asking me if I come here often next.' Paige tried to lighten his mood. He turned and, stone faced, looked straight at her. She stiffened and her laughter faded. Those eyes! She had seen him before – but it couldn't be. He stretched out his arm and laid it along the back of the seat, just brushing her shoulders. She shivered.

'Not cold, are you?' he asked.

'Yes, a little. This top is quite thin,' Paige said, and looked around for Wesley.

'I'll get you a drink, er, sorry I don't know your name.'

'Paige.'

'Brandy, Paige, to warm you?'

'No, thank you,' Paige said, and she stood up. 'I'm sorry, I must go.'

'Of course you must.' His smile was more of a leer.

Paige pushed her way down to the far end of the bar where Wesley was sitting with the ladies. She tipped her head, indicating for him to leave the women and join her. He extracted himself and she drew him into a poorly lit corner. His arms wrapped around her and she leant against him.

'Did you miss me?' he asked. 'Hey, you're shaking. Whatever's the matter?'

'Do you see him?'

'Who?'

'That man from the nineteen thirties' Green Man who

tried to … well, I don't know what he tried to do.'

'Don't be ridiculous. He'd be about a hundred by now and besides, that chap's a lot taller.'

'But he had the same weird eyes and he was, well, creepy.'

'Come on, let's get you another drink.'

'Oh, I found these,' Paige said, pressing the banknote and coins into Wesley's hand before finding a seat in one of the alcoves.

Wesley returned with their drinks and sat down beside her.

'Did you find anything out about who might need us?' Paige said, and took a sip of Cherry B.

'No, he's still not here.'

'Oh. What time do you think he will be?'

'In about ten years.'

'What?'

'Okay, so I got the date wrong again, but you wanted to see this place in the eighties and here we are.' He pulled Paige in close and planted a kiss behind her ear. 'You see that lady with the dark hair, red lipstick and skirt up to her …'

'Yes. Who is she?'

'I've no idea, but she wanted to take me for a spin in her sports car and stop off at a cosy little hotel somewhere.'

Paige threw her head back and laughed. Wesley nuzzled her neck.

'You smell nice,' he murmured.

'Funny you should say that,' Paige said, and swung round to face him. 'Pete said the same thing earlier.'

'Did he now?'

'Yes, but don't you recognise him?'

'No, should I?'

'It's the chap who picked my hat up when we were in the marketplace where I bought my top – from Linda, who he's now sitting with.'

'But thirty-five years or so younger,' Wesley mused.

'Exactly. I asked him how he lost his fingers.'

'And?'

'Something happened in a place called George Yard. He can't remember exactly what but he's missing two fingers and has a scar like a chevron on the side of his face.'

'George Yard?'

'Yes. Apparently, it's at the back of here.' Paige looked at Wesley. 'You're not listening, are you?'

He didn't answer and she followed his gaze. Standing at the bar was a woman with wild red hair wearing bo-ho style clothes and carrying a large tapestry bag. Paige noticed Wesley shake his hand as if it was hurting. She looked back towards the woman but she was no longer there, although the man Paige had found creepy was now standing by the bar, not far away from where the woman had been.

'I think we should go now,' Paige said, as seductively as she could into Wesley's ear. He turned and their eyes locked. He tipped the last of his whisky down his throat and nodded.

'Come on, I'm starving,' Paige said. She stood up, took his hand and made her way towards the exit. 'And the smoke is choking me.'

They climbed the stairs and stepped out into the fresh air. 'I fancy Italian,' Paige decided.

'And I fancy you,' Wesley murmured and pulled her close. She kissed him and spun round, pulling him along behind her.

'Come on, which gate shall we use?'

'Baxter Gate. The same one that brought us here.'

'And don't forget to close it,' she teased as they made their way back.

Chapter 20

Caravelli's, Present Day

'This used to be the Old Manor House,' Wesley said, and pushed open a door with a large swirly 'C' engraved in the glass. It led into the Italian restaurant where Paige had said they should go to eat.

'I bet this place could tell a tale or two,' Paige said, taking in the atmosphere.

'Good evening, sir, madam.' A smartly dressed man greeted them. 'Do you have a reservation?'

'No. Should we have booked?' Paige asked.

'For two?'

Paige took in his name badge. 'Yes, please, Massimo.'

'I am sure we fit you in. Would you like to first drink at the bar, or go straight to table?'

'I think we'll have a drink at the table,' Wesley said, and Paige nodded.

'Then please follow me,' Massimo invited, and led them into the restaurant. A young waitress was placing wine glasses onto a table to the left, which was next to the wall on the near side of a pillar. Massimo indicated that this was to be their table.

'Good evening,' Paige said to a man drinking tea, who was sitting alone on the other side of the pillar, but he didn't seem to hear. Paige shrugged. Rude, she thought.

'Isabella, will be your waitress this evening,' Massimo told them. The young girl looked up.

'Er, oh, er, hello,' Isabella greeted – she looked nervous and knocked one of the glasses over.

'Go on,' Massimo hissed at Isabella, 'come back with your order pad when our guests have had time to consider the menu.'

The waitress nodded and walked away.

'I'm sorry, sir. She is new here.'

'That's quite all right,' Wesley said, and righted the glass.

'I think it must be his aftershave,' Paige said jokily, and winked at Wesley.

Massimo pulled out a heavy mahogany chair for Paige, who shrugged off her jacket and handed it to the Italian. She then sat down and shook out a thick, cream cotton napkin. Massimo presented them with the menus and wine list, and then returned to the bar.

Wesley was looking around and adjusting his white cuffs so that they protruded from the sleeve of his black suit just the right amount. It was Paige's turn to quiver; his cuff adjustment always had that effect on her. A voice from the table nearby caught her attention; the man on the other side of the pillar seemed to be talking to himself. Paige thought he looked familiar.

The door that led onto Sparrow Hill opened again and it caught Paige's attention. She put her hand on Wesley's arm. 'Look, it's that woman from the potions stall,' she whispered. Wesley turned and she noticed him stiffen when he saw Fenella, who tossed her wild hair as she too was shown to a table on the other side of the man drinking tea and talking to himself. Wesley was looking down at his right hand.

'Does it hurt?' Paige asked.

'No, it's fine,' Wesley said, and took her hand in his.

'You saw her in the Green Man, didn't you?'

'Yes, but she hasn't changed, not like your friend Pete.'

'Did you leave the gate open?'

'No. At least I don't think so.'

Massimo came over and placed a dish of olives on the table. 'What would you like to drink?' he asked.

'I'll have Cherry B, please,' Paige said. Massimo went to speak then paused before saying: 'I'm sorry, I'm afraid we don't-a 'ave that, madam. Is it new?'

'Not exactly,' Paige said, 'but never mind.'

'Red wine?' Wesley asked.

'Yes please,' Paige replied, disappointed that she couldn't have another Cherry B – she'd acquired a taste for that particular drink. Massimo left them and Paige chuckled. 'Do you know what Pete, who bought me the Cherry B in nineteen eighties Green Man, said I could have?'

'No, enlighten me,' Wesley said.

'A legover!' she said, and stifled a giggle.

'A what?' Wesley said in a stage whisper.

'A legover. It's Cherry B and cider. Very potent, apparently.'

'We must try it,' Wesley said, and squeezed her hand.

The man on the other side of the pillar was still talking to himself. Paige tipped her head to indicate the diner to Wesley, who craned his neck to see. He laughed and then turned his attention back to deciding what to eat.

The sound of cutlery clattering to the floor interrupted their deliberations. The man behind the pillar was frantically scrabbling around under his table, picking up knives and forks that had tumbled down. Paige began to giggle again when he mouthed 'sorry' to them, but Wesley wasn't laughing, he was watching the clumsy man toasting the red-haired woman with his teacup. Paige was also drawn in – Massimo approached her table with his order pad. Suddenly, the woman announced that she wasn't hungry after all and flounced out of the restaurant.

'How strange,' Paige said. 'She must only have been here

for a few minutes.'

'She presumably had time to go to the cloakroom though,' Wesley remarked. For the second time that evening their eyes locked. No words were spoken. Paige realised that something was amiss. She was sure that Wesley knew it too.

Isabella returned with her notepad and took their order, the wine waiter poured the wine, and Paige took a sip.

'What are you thinking?' Wesley asked.

'That woman, Fenella, went upstairs, we assumed to the cloakroom, came back and left without eating.'

'She did,' Wesley agreed, and took another sip of his wine.

Paige pushed her chair back. 'I'm just popping to the ladies – I won't be long.' She left their table and made her way out of the restaurant, through the bar and up the stairs. She paused at the top. The toilets were on her left and another narrow staircase was in front of her. She turned to the right and made her way along the landing. She paused in front of a large mirror that almost spanned the whole of the wall on her right, and admired her new blouse – it really did suit her. Further along the corridor were more bedrooms and the door to one named Hastings was slightly open. She peered in through the narrow gap and, with a shiver, she recognised the man standing by the fireplace – the one with the freaky eyes – he appeared to be looking for something. A door behind her opened and she jumped, hitting her toe on the open bedroom door. The man looked towards her and she turned away, frantically looking for somewhere to hide. To her right was a door marked 'staff only'. She grasped the handle, opened the door, slipped inside and closed it behind her. It was pitch-black but she daren't risk looking for a light switch.

A door close by slammed to. She didn't hear footsteps and assumed the man was still in the room. She'd wait another minute or two before leaving her bolt-hole.

'Good evening, sir.' She heard a woman's voice from further down the corridor, 'can I help you?'

'No, thank you,' Wesley replied and Paige opened the door a little – she could see Wesley approaching. As he reached her hiding place, she pushed the door wide open, grabbed his arm and pulled him inside.

'Ooh, how cosy,' Wesley said, and closed the door behind him. They were in complete darkness.

'Sshh,' Paige hissed. She felt his arms encircle her and he pulled her close. Before she could speak he covered her mouth with his and she pressed against him.

The loud bang of a nearby door shutting disturbed them and Paige pulled away.

'Why are you in here anyway?' Wesley asked.

'Why are we in here, you mean,' Paige whispered. 'That strange chap with the weird eyes we saw, or rather I saw earlier in the Green Man, was in the next room. He'd left the door ajar and although he's about thirty-five years older now, I definitely recognised him – he looked as though he was searching for something.'

'Shortly after Fenella of the philtres and potions was up here,' Wesley said as he kissed her neck; his lips tickled as he spoke.

'Exactly,' Paige answered, just as she was pressed back against the wall. She felt Wesley's hands on her hips and she closed her eyes, even though it was dark. He began kissing her again and she felt something soft behind her; it was cushioning their movements. Then it dawned on her.

'I think there's something soft, strong and very long next to me,' she said.

'Ooh, you say the nicest things,' Wesley said, his words punctuated by kisses.

Paige froze for a moment.

'What's wrong?' He stroked her back.

'I think we're being watched,' Paige whispered.

'Don't be ridiculous.'

'Seriously, we are being watched.'

Paige stretched her arm out and began to feel along the wall for a light switch. She found it next to Wesley's shoulder and flicked it on. They both blinked in the brightness. Behind her was a cushioning stack of toilet rolls and in the far corner was Henry, the vacuum cleaner, his eyes wide in shocked amusement. Wesley snapped the light off again.

Some while later Paige rearranged her clothes and made her way back downstairs, pausing in front of the mirror to straighten her hair. She returned to their table, took a sip of wine and smiled at the man on the other side of the pillar, who looked as though he was about to leave. Wesley joined her. Isabella, still seeming nervous, almost spilled his starter of Funghi Farciti as she placed it in front of him, and he winked at her.

Chapter 21

The Green Man, 1993

A crowd of people were laughing and jostling their way up the stairs. Several carried items; a stool, a metal knight, glasses. It seemed like they were ransacking the place. Rooted to the ground, Robert felt that he and Fox were like markers in a race that the revellers needed to swerve past. Some were less successful than others. First Robert stumbled to the left, and then to the right as he remained momentarily oblivious. He came to his senses as a young woman collided with Fox.

'Oi, watch it, Guy!' It was the young woman called Sharon with a group of young men.

'You alright, Shazza?' The youth who spoke put his arm round Sharon's shoulders. 'Mind my girl, thicko!' he directed at Fox. Just then another spotted Robert's recent acquisition.

'Hey, that's my jacket! He's wearing my jacket!' Robert's arm was grabbed again. Several young men moved so that both Robert and Fox were surrounded.

'Peace to you all! This is easily resolved, my friends,' said Fox, holding up his hands to placate their obvious anger. ''Twas an error of judgement, merely, on the part of my acquaintance, Mr Hooke, a man of science.'

'I'll give you an error of judgement,' said the young man

with a picture of several wild-haired faces in garish colours on the front of his shirt. He held his stool feet first towards them, and drove them back to the doorway of the hostelry. Sharon held his arm in an effort to restrain him.

'Mind my stool! That's my 'last night at the Green Man' trophy, that is. Don't you break it'

The young man shook her off aggressively and addressed Fox. 'Make your friend put it back where he found it, Guy!' Several of the group giggled as Fox and Robert teetered at the top of the stairway.

'Come on.' Robert grasped at Fox and they ran down the stairs. He shrugged off the jacket as he reached the bottom and held it out to the offended youth.

'I am most sorry,' he offered.

'Put. It. Back.' Each word was accompanied by a push from the stool, shoving Robert into the drinkers and dancers. Several shoved back. Drinks spilt but a path opened as the two were menaced across to where they had found the jacket. Robert laid it across the chair.

'Again, I make my sincere apology.'

'You need to learn a lesson, mate.' The stool was jabbed in their direction. Sharon tried again, grabbing at his elbow.

'That's enough, lover!'

He shook her off. One of the aggressors had picked up a bottle and another had his fists up.

'We all learn lessons from life. Let peace reign, now,' said Fox.

'I don't think that's going to work,' Robert asserted, pulling Fox away as he watched a tall broad fellow dressed all in black.

'Security! What is going on here?'

'He stole my jacket,' said the stool-wielder, holding out the coat in question.

A comely and dapper man, who had appeared from

behind them, spoke up placating the youth: 'And now you have it, so everything is back to normal. Settle down or move on out.'

Normal? Would that it was, Robert thought. The peacemaker seemed somewhat older than most of the crowd in the hostelry. He stepped forward, coming between Robert and Fox, and the gang of the aggrieved. Robert watched as he held up his hands to the rest of the crowd.

'Nothing to see here,' he announced. As he commanded their attention, a woman who had been sitting at the far end of the serving counter stood up and gestured to Robert, pointing to the door behind her. Clearly basic sign language remained the same in any century. Understanding that she was showing them the way out, he pulled Fox along with him. They passed through the door the woman had pushed open and into a small corridor. Robert opened the door to the right and revealed a room full of barrels. The sight made him start momentarily. 'Ale, not powder, you fool,' he muttered as they ducked inside, pulling the door to behind them and crouching down out of sight. He could feel the vibrations rippling through Fox. Robert's teeth were chattering and his legs felt weak as he spoke in a low voice.

'Hide. We'll hide here for a moment.'

'Never hide from a problem. Face your troubles, that's my belief.'

'You might think so, but we don't know this world, Mr. Fox. We need to know more before we take such a stance.'

They were both whispering, but still the door opened. They both kept low, in an effort to avoid discovery.

Chapter 22

The Green Man, 1993

'We're going to go through Pinfold Gate this time and that should be the correct one to take us to 1993,' Wesley said as they made their way along Albert Place and towards the town.

'Will it be third time lucky?' Paige asked.

'I believe it will,' Wesley answered.

'But it's the furthest gate from the Green Man.' Paige knew she sounded like a petulant child.

'I hope you're not complaining,' Wesley said, slipping his arm around her waist and pulling her close.

'Of course not. I'm just stating a fact,' Paige countered.

'And you want your Cherry B,' he teased, and they walked along Pinfold Gate and into 1993.

'Do we have the correct kind of money, because ...' Before Paige could finish speaking a group of people pushed past them, laughing and joking.

'Ain't it a shame,' one said.

'The town won't be the same wi' out it,' another commented.

'Come on, let's see if we can grab a souvenir,' a third voice shouted, and with that they hurried on into the town.

'I wonder what that's all about,' Paige mused.

'A closing-down sale by the sound of it,' Wesley said, then instead of carrying on into Swan Street he turned into the marketplace.

'The Green Man's down there.' Paige pointed back over her shoulder.

'I know, but I would just like to take a look at the place they call George Yard.'

'At this time of night?'

'It won't take long, I promise,' Wesley said, and they walked on past a couple of unlit shop windows, then stopped at the opening to a dark alleyway.

'Here we are, and if I'm not mistaken, this will lead us to the back entrance of the Green Man.'

'OK, let's check it out.' Paige relented, and they stepped into the gloomy passageway. 'I can't see a thing,' she said, 'it's too dark. Let's come back in the daylight.'

Wesley pulled a box of matches from his pocket and struck one. It gave little light to the passageway. Paige yelped and the match fell to the floor.

'What's that?' Paige whispered. A dark mound that the match-light had shown up had spooked her. Her heart was thumping and her mouth had dried. She stiffened when she heard a growling noise nearby.

'Sorry to disturb you.' Wesley was speaking to the dark bundle. He lit another match. 'May I ask you a few questions?' he enquired.

'No you can't. Piss off and leave me alone, unless you've got a spare blanket.' It was a man's voice, and he must have had a dog as the growling continued.

'Come on,' Paige hissed, 'let's go.' She sensed Wesley doing some weird movements – he was taking off his coat. He dropped it over whoever the rough-sleeper was, wished him goodnight and steered Paige further along George Yard.

'He'll probably sell your coat tomorrow for alcohol.'

'Maybe, but at least he'll be warm tonight.'

Paige felt someone brush past her, but couldn't see anything, she just caught a waft of a strong smell of apples. Then it was gone. The smell of the passageway returned and filled her nostrils. She wrinkled her nose.

'Let's get out of here,' she said. 'It's too creepy for me, and it stinks like a, well, like a public urinal.'

At the end of George Yard was a small car park illuminated by street lights, but there was no obvious entrance to the Green Man. Paige watched as Wesley walked over to a pair of doors without handles that were set into the wall. He ran his hands around them, shrugged and re-joined her.

'Come on,' he said, 'let's see what's going on down there, it sounds very lively.'

They made their way round to the front entrance, descended the staircase and entered the bar. It was packed, music was playing and it appeared to be standing-room only. They managed to weave their way to the bar and buy drinks with some irregular shaped coins that they still had and then move to the end of the counter where there was space to breathe. Paige noticed that most of the lovely paintings that were there in 1983 had gone and huge mirrors hung where they had been. She wondered if the knights-of-old were still there, underneath. A woman with a powerful voice was singing through the loudspeakers and Wesley took Paige in his arms and sang along, telling her that he would always love her. As the song finished there was shouting from near to where they had come into the bar. The people around them were moving away from what appeared to be a disagreement over a jacket.

'There!' Wesley sounded triumphant rather than concerned.

'Where?' Paige asked, standing on tiptoe to see better.

'Look,' he continued, 'they don't belong here. That's why we're here!'

Paige looked at the gentlemen who were being set upon by an angry young man and his friends.

'It looks as though they may be in trouble,' Paige said, knowing she was stating the obvious. She looked up at Wesley, who finished his drink, cocked his head towards the fire exit at the rear of the bar, and then walked over to where a bouncer was trying to calm the situation. She watched him stand between the angry young man and the two awkward-looking gentlemen, who he spoke to before turning back to keep the mob at bay. The two men looked like foxes fleeing from a hunt as they made their way towards her. She pushed open the door for them, putting her index finger to her lips as they passed. When they were through, she pulled the door to, leant on the bar and continued to sip her Cherry B.

Wesley returned and ordered another whisky.

'What was that all about?' Paige asked.

'That lad there,' Wesley pointed to a young man wearing a leather jacket, 'accused them of stealing his jacket and then, when they gave it back, got all hot under the collar, wanting to teach them a lesson. Are they in the cellar?'

'Yes, I've closed the door from this side.'

'Good. We'll get them out the back way, when I've finished my drink.'

The music continued and folks began to leave.

'How bizarre,' Paige said, as she took the last mouthful of her Cherry B. 'They're taking the stools, and that chap has one of the statues of a knight.'

'It must be a tradition here in Loughborough,' Wesley said. 'Come on, let's get those two out of the cellar.'

They went through the fire exit door. Wesley climbed a staircase to the back doors and Paige noticed him take a large key from a wall hook and undo the padlock that kept them chained to. She then pushed open the door to the cellar where the two men were crouching behind the barrels. She told them to follow her and they made their way up the staircase and out into the night air. Paige kept her eye out for any of the earlier aggressors and heard Wesley tell the men, who were definitely dressed for a different century, to go through George Yard and into the marketplace. He returned to her and for a second time, they made their way round to the front of the Green Man.

People were still pouring out of the underground bar and many made their way across the road to the building called Casablanca.

'We now have our quest,' Wesley said, as they walked along Swan Street and onto High Street.

'And what might that be?'

'They need to get back home. I told them to go to what they know as the Manor House tomorrow and we'd meet them there to see how we can resolve their predicament.'

Chapter 23

Outside the Green Man, 1993

They had emerged into a small thoroughfare. A faint stink of piss hung in the air. Robert looked from side to side in the evening gloom noting the stationary vehicles lined to the left of the small red-brick building on the opposite corner, and the fact that there were two ways out. One seemed to lead to the highway they had been on before. Robert began trotting in the opposite direction because their rescuer had said to go through the marketplace. He looked round to make sure Fox was behind him and saw that he was following with large, measured strides. But behind Fox he caught a movement. A whiff that reminded him of little green apples caught his nose.

'One moment. I think I saw ...' Robert held up his hand to stop his new friend and then pointed back to the red-brick lean-to.

'There! Someone is there. I think it maybe that woman.'

'Surely not, sir. She must be long gone.'

'I saw a flick of red hair. I'm sure of it. I am minded of the witch trials of a few years back.'

'No one could forget those times. The legacy of the Witchfinder General, as he called himself, lives on. People are still accusing each other of witchcraft, mostly to settle petty disputes or explain things they do not understand. That man had much to do with confirming my faith. I never did hear such poppycock. Treat any man as you would be treated yourself. That's how I live.'

'Oh, I agree. There is much we do not understand. One needs to look for small details. My micro-glass is good for that, but some might call it witchcraft. Would that I could capture an image in the way of that paper.' Robert spoke as he walked swiftly, but quietly, back to the small building, with Fox in tow. They paused at the doorway.

'One look cannot harm, surely?' The old green wooden door was slightly ajar. Robert pushed it open and stepped inside. There was a pause. A rustle. A flash of bright light erupted and for a split second they both saw the aura of the woman they had pursued before she disappeared, leaving a fruity tang behind.

'Did you see her?' Fox gasped.

'I did! I am sure I did. But where is she?' Robert felt around the walls of the building, one of which had two strange greyish white appliances attached. 'Help me, would you?'

'What are you doing?'

'Looking for an explanation. There has to be some kind of opening.' He ran his fingers over the brick. After a moment Fox joined him.

'Some things only God can explain, but yes, it is right to check. He pushed open the doors of two cubicles. 'This is some kind of garderobe, I do believe.'

'You are right, Robert whispered, in reply. The shape of the seats were unmistakable to him, even though the accompanying smell that he would have expected was absent. 'She is gone. But how? I cannot explain it though I saw it with mine own eyes.' Robert sank down the wall he had inspected and sat with his knees hunkered up and his arms wrapped around them. 'This world is very strange.' Robert bent his head into his arms to close off their surroundings. He felt Fox lowering himself to the floor next to him, and heard him speak.

''Tis true, young man. 'Tis true.'

Robert raised his head after a few moments. 'That man told us to get to the Manor House, and he seemed to know what he was talking about, but I'm not sure I can go on just yet.'

'If the Manor House is still in the same place three hundred years or so after our time, it isn't going to disappear in a matter of hours,' Fox told him. 'God has given us some shelter. We have it to ourselves, so let's stay here until it's light, at least. Perchance we might wake and find ourselves restored.'

Chapter 24

Caravelli's, Present Day

Florence put a hand out to steady herself as she climbed the staircase. That last large red had been a mistake and at forty-six she really should know better, but all that talk of witches and the look on Sandbach's face. Florence guffawed. Placing her hand over her mouth she glanced back, thankful that no one was behind her. Laughing quietly she took her room key from her back pocket as she got to the top of the stairs. 'Toilets on the left, another staircase in front and three bedrooms to the right,' she muttered, mimicking Massimo's directions earlier. 'And mine is the furthest away – hurr-bloody-ra!'

The key turned and she pushed her way gratefully into the room, as her phone began to vibrate in her jeans pocket.

'Well, hello my friend. How are you both?'

'Ah, so you've enjoyed the red again.' Caitlin laughed. 'We're fine. Tom is currently asleep, for a change, on my lap and we've been watching a Danish thriller. Not sure he likes the subtitles though. So how was dinner? Did you and the detective make amends and bond?'

'Well, the day has been eventful.' Florence sighed and sank onto the bed. 'As you know, I met up with a couple of old colleagues and Detective Inspector Sandbach. His ideas and thoughts regarding the cases are so far away from making any sense, and yet I always knew there was something very different about them.'

'Florence, you're rambling. What are you on about? You told me before that there were unexplained things going on. In fact, whenever we've talked about it you've said that there were things you couldn't explain. Surely, Sandbach is the man to unravel it all?'

'Well, yes and no. The thing is, Cat, it's a bit more complicated than I thought. We are not simply talking unexplained.'

'You're making no sense, Florence. What is it that's ...?'

'Witches!' Florence shouted, sitting up and instantly regretting doing so as her head began to pound. 'The man is talking witches,' she continued in a quieter voice and he's serious, Cat. Like shit, the man believes in witches!'

Florence stood up and started pacing the room. The magnitude of what Sandbach had said was suddenly very real. 'I thought he was joking. I even waited for the punchline, but no, he was deadly serious.' Florence walked to the mirror and stared at her reflection. Her eye-liner had smudged, she wiped at it, absentmindedly. 'The worst of it all was that it made sense. All those questions, all those unanswered queries and thoughts we'd had. Opened wide and explainable by bloody witches and magic and all the things I'd feared as a child.'

'Bloody hell!'

'Yes, bloody hell, indeed!' Florence's shoulders dipped and closing her eyes she rested her head on the mirror.

'Florence. Are you being serious? Are you really saying that something magical, maybe even something sinister, is to blame for the disappearances?'

'Well, Sandbach was being serious and in so many ways it makes sense, but the police officer in me, the rational woman, questions how can that be even remotely possible? I tell you what though, Cat, I started to take the piss, but the look on Sandbach's face made me stop, and the way he explained ...' Florence stopped talking as she remembered her meeting with Sergeant Boyle at the police station. Boyle had been animated, far more so than Florence could ever recall, and then there was that briefcase, the contents of which she never got to see. Boyle, despite being totally job-obsessed, had agreed, quietly, and only ever to Florence, that there had been something more to this case than they could ever hope to explain.

'Florence, are you still there?'

'Yes, I'm here – I just need to think and hopefully sleep. Look, I'll call you in the morning, okay?'

'Yes of course. I totally understand. Try to get some sleep and I really hope that it all seems clearer in the morning. Night, my friend.'

Florence threw her phone onto the bed, picked up the kettle and headed to the bathroom. A large cup of coffee was most definitely required for what was inevitably going to be a long night.

Part Two

Chapter 25

Disappearance, 1993

Sally North peered out from under her fringe. A large pair of shiny black shoes were on the pavement in front of where she sat, cross-legged, as was the custom for beggars and people sitting still for long periods of time. Her hat, within which she collected the takings from the day, was placed in front of her. The man's right shoe tapped and somewhere way above the shoes the owner cleared his throat. This was most unusual. The majority of people walked past with barely a glance. Stan, her best friend and fellow sleeper on the streets, said that it was because people didn't want to see the flip side of the coin, and didn't want to be reminded that other people struggled.

Leaning back against the wall of McDonald's, Sally's favourite pitch as she was often given a burger, she allowed her eyes to travel up from the large black shoes to expensive-looking grey suit trousers, covering masculine thighs. Tipping her head back, Sally absentmindedly flicked her fringe as her eyes met those of the startlingly good-looking man standing in front of her.

'How long have you been homeless, miss?'

'Who says I'm homeless?' Sally replied, tearing her eyes from the man's face and glancing to her left, wondering where the blithering hell Stan had got to.

'Okay, let's start again. My name is Matthew Hopkins and I work for a company that helps people get off the streets and into accommodation. How about I buy you a coffee and we can talk and see if I can help you?'

Yikes! Not a good idea to look back at him again, but dear God he was handsome, Sally thought to herself. Almost too handsome, and his eyes – wow, they were a colour Sally had never seen before; they shone like amber.

With a jolt, Sally realised that she was staring and started to scramble to her feet. Her right leg had other ideas though and she pitched forward into Matthew's arms.

'Christ! Sally, you idiot!' she exclaimed, balancing on her left foot as he steadied her. 'Sorry! Me leg's gone numb – must have been sitting down longer than I realised.' She bit her lip. Normally she wouldn't tell a stranger her name so suddenly, but he was attractive. Rubbing her leg Sally thought about what the man had said. Well it couldn't hurt to hear him out and a cup of coffee was always welcome.

'Who do you work for again?' The feeling in her leg was returning and Sally gingerly placed her foot back on the pavement. She was of average height, standing at five feet, five inches, but the man towered over her. He was still holding her arm, the pressure a little tight, and Sally stared at his hand until he released her.

'Sally, is it? Well, come on then, Sally,' Matthew said, 'we can walk and talk. I know a great little cafe around the corner.'

Sally watched as he stepped away from her. She looked down at her meagre collection of belongings. Her sleeping bag was rolled up and propped against the wall behind the rucksack that she sat on to keep her things safe. Everything she owned in the world was in that bag; three t-shirts, four pairs of pants, walking socks and her wash bag. She was wearing her one-and-only jumper under her one-and-only jacket. Her beloved navy velvet hat that had belonged to her grandma in what now seemed to be a distant life ago, was by her feet waiting in hope of any monetary offerings that may be donated throughout the day. Stan's stuff was next to hers and she wondered again how long he was going to be. He'd only gone to the toilet.

'I have to wait for my friend. He'll be back any minute,' Sally said, gesturing towards the market square. Stan was known among the stallholders and she'd no doubt he'd got talking to one of them.

'Why don't we go and look for him and then you can give him your stuff while we talk?'

'Don't you want to talk to him too?'

'Erm, yes.' Matthew glanced around and then checked his watch. 'I don't see why not. I just hope he's not too long.'

This re-homing business was obviously on the clock.

'How old is he and where does he come from?' Matthew asked.

'Bit older than me – been on the streets twice as long. He's from Scotland.'

'Where are you from?' Matthew asked, leaning back against the wall, his eyes fixed on Sally's.

Goodness, those eyes. Tiger-like, Sally mused as she looked right back at him. It was almost as if they were normal when he was looking around, but the moment he locked his gaze – wham! You were done for. And what kind of a name was Matthew? He certainly didn't look like a Matthew. Adonis, maybe or Troy. Sally chuckled.

'What's so funny?'

Sally jumped at the intrusion into her thoughts.

'Oh nothing.' She waved her hand dismissively.

Sally looked up at Matthew. His dark brooding gaze had returned and she felt a shiver run down her spine. 'Look, maybe I should stay and wait for Stan. Why don't you just tell me here? In fact, give me some money and I'll go into Mac's myself and get us drinks. You can sit with us and …' Sally looked around and laughed. 'Experience the true meaning of living on the streets.'

Matthew coughed. 'Well that sounds lovely, but I have a meeting at two and if we walk to the coffee shop I had in mind, I'm then almost where I need to be.' He took her arm again and started to back away. 'Come on, Sally, it's most definitely time to get you off these streets, into a warm home with food and money. Surely you'd like the chance of a better life?'

Chapter 26

Loughborough Market, 1993

Light filtered across the floor as Robert awoke. His face was resting on the cold surface of the gritty ground, and he watched the motes of dust dance in the shaft of light that crossed the room. For a moment he could not think where he was. Then he remembered. It was only a matter of hours since he had been in his time with his friend, Hall. That girl, the one with the contraption that emitted pink light. It was her fault, surely, the predicament we're in, he thought, his cheek grazing the floor. He knew what she meant though, with that last utterance, her fervent plea to 'go home.' He wished with all his might that he could go home.

Sounds. Noises were reaching through his ears, disturbing his thoughts. Metal on metal. People calling. Mechanics. He pushed himself up on one arm and looked at his companion sleeping on the floor beside him.

'Fox! Mr Fox!' Robert shook Fox's shoulder. 'We're still here!'

'Where?'

'In 1993. Or whenever. At least, I think we are.' He got up and pushed the door open, blinking in the light. 'I think the market is down there, though.'

'Our market?' Fox was getting up. Robert helped him to his feet. 'I am able to manage, thank you. I have slept in worse places, I can tell you.'

'I fancy, I have not.'

'A spell in Leicester gaol is all that you need to convince you that this is not so bad.' He was fiddling with the metal contraptions on the white wall-hung containers. Water suddenly spat out. 'Ha! A marvel. God provides!' He bent and drank. Robert copied, quenching his thirst.

'That's enough for me. Let us go. One must always move forward.'

At the end of the thoroughfare they paused. Robert noticed the street name plate, which read George Yard. 'You see, we are not mad. Our world was here. Proof that St George's Guild used to be here,' he said. But Fox was looking ahead and when he spoke it was with longing.

'Such a sight. 'Tis enough to lift the spirits of even the most ungodly. It is the market.'

'Yes, it is. But not the one we left, we can be sure. Look at the way they are putting up the stalls.'

Metal poles such as Robert had never seen had been covered with a thick striped material and lifted to cover the stalls below. Hucksters were setting out their wares, and Robert could recognise victuals and materials. The smell of food cooking pervaded his nostrils; onions mixed with something that made his stomach rumble. It was coming from a white shelter that was marked 'Hot Food' in large red letters. He watched as a man behind the counter filled what looked like a yeast cake with a patty of meat and those onions. The man handed it to his waiting customer, wrapped in some thin material. Paper? Not unlike the material of the publication from the night before.

'Thanks, mate. It's me breakfast.'

'Happy to oblige. Sauce is over there,' the trader responded, depositing the proffered coins in his apron pocket.

They watched as the buyer parted the two halves of bread and squeezed a bottle, one of those on the bench indicated. It couldn't be glass, as it didn't break. The man's fingers pressed in, making both sides indent with ease, and a worm of red curled onto the patty.

'I have to have one of those,' Fox said.

Hooke forced his thoughts from the bottle of strange pliable material. He was certainly hungry. 'My aspiration, too, but we have no monies.'

'I have coins,' Fox replied, reaching out his leather purse.

'I have some also, but I fear our coins are unlikely to pass here. We need to observe carefully.'

'Says the scientist. The realist in me says "we need food."'

'The scientist in me says "I know that, sir, but we must play this world as we find it." Let us look about and take stock.' Robert watched Fox arch an eyebrow in his direction, his piercing blue eyes conveying scepticism, but he didn't reply. Fox turned and began to walk past the delicious smelling hot food into the market. Robert followed, and they both walked slowly up one side of the thoroughfare looking at the stalls. It was early morning, but other people were doing the same. They seemed to have a range of appliances, Robert thought – a young woman pushed a small carriage with an infant inside it. An old woman pulled a rectangular receptacle, where she had clearly stowed her shopping.

'That man, Fox! Look how old he is. I know not how he is still walking.'

They watched as a stooped and aged man held onto silver handles and pushed a wheeled trolley in front of him.

A girl pushed past them carrying a large pillow in a shiny see-through covering over her shoulder. Fox stepped back to let her pass and collided with a passer-by. He staggered, almost losing his footing in his efforts to hold onto his hat.

'Pardon me," he said as Robert reached out to steady him. The grey-suited man pushed by without a word. He looked back briefly.

Good looking man, but strange eyes, Robert thought. A man in a bright orange doublet pushed a handcart full of cartons towards them. They steered cautiously past him, past stalls with almost familiar products like wool, clothes and books with vivid pictures. There were stalls with tools, the purpose of which was beyond them. Some had loud music playing. It was mesmerising. His brain was being assaulted by new things, new ideas.

'It's all wonderful!'

''Tis as baneful as the charavais,' remarked Fox.

At a fruit and vegetable stall Robert stood transfixed. He could recognise the deep-red beets with green tops and bunches of carrots. Potatoes were familiar, though in abundance here. Apples, yes, but those curved yellow things, nestled together. A notice named them 'bananas, £1 a bowl.' A collection of green and yellow globes patterned on the outside and topped with spiky leaves. Pineapple, apparently. He bent to smell the display.

'Take stock, you said. I don't think you meant literally,' said Fox at his shoulder, guiding him backwards.

'Or right, me darlings? Been to a fancy-dress party, have we? What can I get ya?' A big woman in blue pantaloons and wearing an apron with a large pocket in the front was speaking to them.

'Ah, nothing at the moment, kind lady.' Fox bowed.

'Oooh, you're a pair of cards. Please yourself then.' She laughed and it seemed a friendly enough exchange, though this time they both raised eyebrows at each other. Her meaning was lost on them. They watched her serve another customer. This one was juggling bags from hand to hand with a red and white cup. She took sips between ordering her vegetables. She stood the cup on the side of the stall, pulled off the lid, and discarded it. She drained the last drops and then crumpled the cup, throwing it to the ground before walking away with her purchases.

'Dirty mare! She should put it in the bin,' the suddenly less-jovial market woman said, indicating a receptacle just a short distance away.

'Allow me, madam.' Robert scooped up the crumpled cup with its deformed M design. He sniffed and looked up.

'Come this way. I smell coffee.' Robert indicated a way through the stalls to more permanent trading places beyond. Robert's nose led them to a building adorned with the same M – McDonald's. The windows were covered with what appeared to be pictures of comestible dishes and beverages.

'Yes, fine. But we still have no coin.'

To one side of the door to the hostelry was a young girl, sitting crossed legged on the floor. Her undressed hair was long and cut roughly across her eyes. She had on a jacket, and a simple round-necked top, with the now familiar blue pantaloons. A bag of heavy material with straps was by her side.

'Fifty-p for a cup of tea,' she said, as two men in coats stepped around her to push open the door. They watched the men pull a small number of silver coins from their pockets and throw them into an upturned navy hat.

'Get yourself a job, darling,' one of them told her as he turned away.

Another man approached her. Robert caught Fox's arm.

'Look! 'Tis the man who knocked into you.'

'Nay. He's long gone.'

'Verily, it is. His habit has the same sharp appearance, and if I see his eyes I will know.'

'His eyes?'

'You did not see them? The oddest, most striking colour. More striking indeed, than yours.'

Fox fixed him with his famous stare. 'People have remarked that my eyes do pierce.'

'They do, but not like this. What is he doing?'

The man and the girl had exchanged some words. The man took the girl's arm. She wrenched herself free and made to pick up the hat, but the man pulled her away.

'Her hat. We must get it for her. We must return it.' Fox began to run over to the abandoned hat. Robert watched the man lead the girl around the corner out of sight.

'Quickly! I like this not. We must follow,' he said, running after his companion. There was a pause as they both took in the small pile of silver-, gold- and copper-coloured coins. Then Fox folded the soft, velvet edges of the hat in as he picked it up. He rolled it inside his own, wedging them both inside his jerkin, and the two of them ran down the road.

Chapter 27

Caravelli's, Present Day

The dining room was empty and Florence made her way to a table in front of the window. Checking her watch, she pulled a chair out and sat down. She was on time, an unusual feat, especially considering the amount of wine she'd drunk the night before.

She'd made herself a coffee in an attempt to get her thoughts in order after the magnitude of what Sandbach had been suggesting had really begun to sink in – and the effects of the wine had receded. She had drunk far more than usual, the collection of drum-playing frogs in her brain a constant reminder.

A door opened and one of the waitresses walked towards Florence, a smile on her face and a menu in her hand.

'Good morning, Miss Carter. Would you like tea or coffee while you consider the menu?'

'Good morning, Ellen. I'm meeting Mr Sandbach, but he hasn't come down yet so I'll have coffee while I wait, please.'

'Oh, Mr Sandbach has been down for a while; he's been on the phone in the courtyard. I'll bring his tea over with your coffee. In the meantime, please help yourself to cereals, fruit or pastries.'

Florence smiled in response before casting her eyes over the menu. Unsure as to whether she could face a full breakfast, she stood and wandered over to the sideboard. *Maybe a croissant, oh and definitely one of those apricot pastries, a handful of prunes to help my stomach, but then maybe have some of that very healthy granola and yoghurt, but what to put on it? Dried fruit or that yummy looking compote?* Florence chuckled. *Or, how's about both?*

'Ahem.'

Florence turned to see Sandbach, his expression firmly fixed on the towering plate of food she had in one hand, and the large bowl of granola clutched in the other.

'Hungry?' he asked with a raised eyebrow.

Florence laughed and walked back to the table. 'Well, I wasn't, but then once you get there it all looks so good. I only normally have porridge or a piece of toast at home, which I usually end up sharing with Tom.' Florence placed both plate and bowl on the table and sat down, draping her napkin over her thighs before picking up a knife and cutting the croissant in half. Pausing with the knife midway to the butter she looked up.

Sandbach was gazing out of the window, his expression unreadable.

'Ellen said she'd be out in a mo' with tea and coffee, but we were to help ourselves to anything else we'd like first,' Florence said, pointing with the knife to the array of food. 'I'm not sure I can face a full English this morning.'

'Hardly surprising, considering the amount of food you have there. Shouldn't you eat the granola first? Isn't there some sort of breakfast etiquette in these places?'

'And that from a man who believes in witches.' Florence looked again at Sandbach, who was yet to sit down. 'Are you going to join me, or are you simply going to stand there and ridicule my choices?'

'I'm sorry it took so long.' Ellen had bustled back into the room carrying a large tray. 'The canteen has broken so I had to wait for the kettle to boil. Here we go – coffee for you, Miss Carter and a pot of tea for you, Mr Sandwich.'

Florence snorted and dropped the knife onto the butter dish. She sneaked a glance at Sandbach who had made no reaction at all and was still standing by the chair. Maybe he was used to people getting his name wrong, she mused.

'May I take your breakfast orders?' Ellen continued, seemingly unaware of the gaff she had made, 'what can I get you both?'

Florence glanced at the menu and then at the pile of food on the table in front of her. 'Erm, I think I'm okay. Maybe some toast, and can that be brown please?'

Ellen nodded and turned to Sandbach. 'And you, sir?'

'Full English, please, with beans, mushrooms, no tomatoes and white toast for me.'

'Lovely, now to remind you, chef does cook from scratch so it'll take a little while. Do help yourself from the sideboard.'

Florence watched as Ellen left the room before pouring herself a large mug of coffee. 'God, that smells amazing,' she said, taking a sip. 'And unusually it lives up to that promise. Thank the gods for the Italians. They do know how to make good coffee.'

'Not a coffee drinker myself,' Sandbach said, as he walked towards the sideboard, 'however, the granola and Danish look nice. What's the filling?'

Florence picked the one she had selected and took a bite. 'Apricot, and there's the smallest amount of custard and it is absolutely delicious.' She sighed dramatically and then laughed. 'Caitlin's always astounded by the amount of food I eat. She says, by rights, I should be at least two-stone heavier. I say, exercise, not getting married and living with a cat is the epitome of happiness.'

'Who's Caitlin?' Sandbach asked, as he returned to the table and finally sat down.

'My friend and the only person I trust with Tom, my cat,' she explained in response to his quizzical gaze.

'Not a cat person, and to be honest, I'm not that keen on dogs either,' Sandbach said, taking a bite of his pastry. 'Yes, you heard me,' he muttered, looking at the floor. 'You were right about this Danish, it is delicious.'

Florence looked down at the floor, but could see nothing of note. She watched as Sandbach closed his eyes in obvious appreciation, sighed and then took a swig from his teacup. 'Anyway,' he said, 'let's get on with today's plan. What we have and what we know so far.'

Unprepared for the sudden change of direction, Florence realised that she was staring at Sandbach and that the rather large amount of blackcurrant jam she had been spreading on her croissant had jumped off and was making its way back to the table.

'So,' she said, ignoring his amused expression and scooping the jam off the tablecloth and back onto the croissant, 'where did you want to start?'

'I think that we should continue to pursue independent lines of enquiry in order to cover more ground. Despite the powers that be deeming my attendance necessary, they don't always have the patience required that a case like this often takes to resolve.' Sandbach pointedly looked across the room and Florence waited while Ellen approached with a plate in each hand. 'Plus,' he continued in a hushed voice, 'we are working across, at over a twenty-five-year span, with multiple missing people and an incredibly small number of witnesses.'

Florence took a huge bite of jam-filled croissant and waited while Ellen placed Sandbach's breakfast and their toast on the table.

'Is there anything else I can get you?' Ellen asked, looking at Florence. Caught mid-chew, and with a sizeable amount of croissant still in her mouth, Florence could only shake her head.

'Thank you,' Sandbach said, as he picked up his knife and fork.

Still chewing, Florence watched Ellen walk away.

'Okay, well, ahem.' Florence coughed as she swallowed the slightly larger-than-she'd-have-liked mouthful of croissant. 'How's about I retread some of the locations that were so relevant back when the case was live? Places like the marketplace and George Yard? I still have a couple of contacts as well as Boyle at the nick, so I will have a chat with them too.'

'Yes, that all sounds good, but I want to visit George Yard myself.' Sandbach paused and sipped his tea. 'I need to be able to picture the location and get a feel for the area. So, you head to the police station and I'll go to George Yard. I know from yesterday that the market is in the same area so I can ask a few questions while I'm there.'

'Great. Let me know what time you finish and I can either meet you in town or back here,' Florence said, sitting back in her chair. 'Good grief, I'm so full.'

'Hardly surprising.'

'Are you always this charming, or is it a dimension of your personality you've only discovered since meeting me?' Florence asked with a grin.

Sandbach stood up. 'I'll see you later, but in the meantime, feel free to contact me if you come across anything noteworthy.' Sandbach strode across the room towards Ellen, who had just appeared from the kitchen.

'Goodbye, sir. Will you require dinner later?'

Sandbach nodded at Ellen and looked at the floor. 'Yes, please. Is seven okay?'

'So, reserved solely for me then!' Florence chuckled to herself and rubbed her very full tummy.

Chapter 28

Loughborough Market, 1993

'Get off me! I've changed my mind,' the girl said, while trying to pull her arm out of the grip of her companion. Robert could see that he was holding her far more tightly than a friendly gesture would warrant. They slowed as they came nearer to the pair. Except they weren't on their own. The red-headed woman from last night was approaching from the other direction.

'Coffee. I just offered you a cup of coffee, Sally,' the man was saying to her.

'What's wrong with McDonald's coffee then? We don't need to go all the way up Church Gate.'

'This little place I know has the best coffee, hot chocolate if you like. Delicious toasted sandwiches. Cakes. Come with me. You'll be fine.'

'I've got to go back first. My hat. You made me leave my hat. It's got my money in.'

Fox pulled at the hat in his jerkin with his free hand, but Robert stopped him. This wasn't the time, he thought.

'Hey, you! Yes, You! Let her go this instant!' As the red-haired woman spoke the man they'd followed whipped his head round.

'Get out of here, witch, this is none of your business,' he

hissed in reply, spittle flying in her direction as his seemingly benevolent expression turned to one of rage. He turned back to the girl, and then spotted Robert and Fox.

'It's none of your business, either, travellers. Be gone!' Robert froze on the spot. He heard Fox beginning to speak.

'Unhand her, sir,' he said, but none of the three were listening.

'I'm making it my business. You will not have this girl. You know they have to go with you willingly, and she is not willing.' The woman was reaching into her large tapestry bag as she spoke. She took out a tubular object, perhaps as long as Robert's arm, and whirled it around her head, once. He watched its circuit, realising that they had seen it before, and then that all around them activity had stopped. Movement, noise, everything was still. Except them. Well, Sally was. The man called Matthew dropped his hand from Sally's statue of a body.

'What have you done?' he uttered, but that was all because the tube was swinging round again. Robert watched as she uttered incomprehensible words and hit Matthew on the side of his head. He disappeared. Robert could not believe what he'd seen. He started forward.

'Gadzooks! I cannot believe it. I will not believe it,' Fox was muttering, while rubbing his eyes.

The woman had turned to the girl. She lifted the tube again and touched Sally's head with it.

'This is no place for you. I send you to a better life. You will be happy and well,' she said. Sally disappeared.

'Madam, that was one step too far! The young woman had done no harm. Who are you to act as God?' Fox had lifted his finger and was pointing at the woman, fixing her with that stare from his commanding eyes.

Robert found his voice: 'I know not what that was. Science or magic. Where is she? Who are you?'

'I am known as Fenella, and in your time I was indeed called a witch, it is true, but that is not what is important for the moment. Do not be too hasty to judge; all this is not what it seems. You have your own problems. Problems that you need to solve yourselves. You are out of time, here, and beyond my powers.' She touched herself on the head and the light they had seen the night before flashed, obscuring their view, the aroma of apples reaching their noses. As it cleared they could see she was gone and all the life had returned to the strange world they were in. Vehicles were moving on the thoroughfare more quickly and more noisily than Robert thought possible now that they were away from the market. People were opening shops for the day's trade. They stood and watched for a number of minutes before either of them spoke.

'Well, we have solved our first problem,' Robert said suddenly, breaking into the moment.

'To what are you referring? Nothing is resolved as far as I see,' Fox answered.

'We now have coins. Surely enough to buy some sustenance.'

'Oh, no! What I have here belongs to that young woman. We cannot use it. We must find a way to return it.'

'That is preposterous! She is gone. Think of it as benevolence from God. He provides, does he not?'

'He does,' Fox admitted. 'And I am hungry.'

'I was on my way to take a cup of chocolate with my friend when we were wrenched from our world. That man mentioned chocolate and you are the only friend I have here. They were making in that direction,' Robert said, pointing. Then he turned and looked at the buildings behind him. 'And there,' he said, pointing again, 'is our clue to getting our bearings. The thoroughfares have names as they did in our day. This is Swan Street.'

'So it is,' agreed Fox.

'So where they were going is towards Church Gate. And that solves another problem. That man told us to go to the Manor House, which is also in that direction. If we think logically we can find our way.'

'Perhaps you can use your logic to help us negotiate through these mechanical carriages then,' observed Fox, as he surveyed Swan Street with what Robert knew was considerable trepidation, because he was feeling the same way. Last night and today, however, there did seem to be a system.

'Cars! They are called cars. That paper last night said so. On this side of the road they all move from right to left, and on the other side they move from left to right,' Robert offered.

'Even I can work out that logic, my friend,' Fox said, caustically.

'You would think there would be some logic to crossing over, though,' Robert added, as they both watched a young man dodge his way through the cars from the opposite side of the thoroughfare to their side, using trotting steps, and disappearing into the market. Choosing his moment, Fox stepped out between the cars and ran to the middle of the road. Robert did the same, his heart in his mouth. Then they both dashed over the second part together. Reaching the other side, Fox had his hands folded across his chest and his eyes closed. Robert put his hands on his thighs and bent forward to catch his breath for a moment or two. Straightening up, he could now see ahead of them the name plate reading Church Gate.

'Another problem solved,' he said, after reading the plate out aloud. 'We know where to go, and on the way we will have an adventure and spend some of our ill-gotten gains.' His attempt at humour got another 'look,' but Fox strode out around the corner into Church Gate with alacrity, so Robert followed on as quickly as he could.

Chapter 29

Carillon Court, Present Day

'OK, so this is where the infamous Green Man pub used to be,' Sandbach said, surveying the flower shop in front of the Carillon Court shopping centre.

Terrence stayed close to his side – he didn't like crowds.

'Can I get you anything, darlin'?' A woman asked from behind the buckets of roses. She appeared to be in her late forties, short hair with jeans and a fleece under a green tabard. 'Special occasion?'

A green badge told him her name. 'No, sorry, Sharon, I'm just looking,' Sandbach replied.

'Certainly. Just let me know if you need any help deciding.'

'No, I mean I'm just looking at the building. Can you tell me – is this where the Green Man pub used to be?'

Sandbach held out his ID badge and smiled.

'It is, but you're a couple of decades too late I'm afraid,' she said with a wry smile. 'There's the Bell Foundry right behind you if you're thirsty.'

'Ha ha,' Sandbach replied, humouring her. 'No, I'm trying to find out a bit more about this place. Where it was, what it was like. That kind of thing. Is it possible to get inside, do you know?'

Sharon pursed her lips and peered into space – the look of someone concentrating hard.

'The Echo did a thing about it a while ago. Went down and took some photos. It looked so sad and run down. I remember when it was open years ago, it was a great place. Not the most glamorous establishment, and it had its share of fights and what have you. But the atmosphere was … I dunno, fun.'

'The Echo?' Sandbach repeated, hoping for some clarification. The irony of repeating the word 'echo' wasn't lost on him, but he felt it would just confuse the situation to mention it.

'The local newspaper,' she replied. 'It was amazing; the first chance we had to see photos of the place since it closed.'

'So how did the newspaper get in if there's no front door? Is there a back door accessible from the alleyway behind?' Sandbach pointed to the little road just to the left of the shopping centre.

'George Yard? No, there's nothing down there. At least not as far as I'm aware. No, they got in through a hatch in the floor, inside the shopping centre itself. Crazy, we'd all seen the outline in the floor but hadn't really figured that was a way in. Of course, you'd need someone from the council to let you down there, you can't just wander down by yourself.'

'Thank you. That's really helpful,' Sandbach said with a smile.

'You're welcome. You want to buy some flowers to say thank you?'

'No, sorry,' he said, turning away.

'Tight git,' he heard her mutter, then she turned to speak to a customer.

'You are a tight git,' Terrence added.

'Oh shut up.'

'What did you say?' Sharon had turned back towards him, a hardened expression on her face. 'Look, I've got a business to run here you know. I don't have to give my valuable time to people asking stupid questions about places that have been closed for years. So you needn't be rude with me!'

'No I'm sorry, I was talking to .... Look, why don't I buy some flowers after all?'

The seller shrugged, and her face relaxed.

'What sort would you like? A nice bunch of roses? Some carnations?'

Sandbach mentally played spin the bottle with the flowers on offer, then shrugged and pointed at the nearest bucket.

'Lilies eh? Someone's funeral?'

'Whatever. They'll do. How much?'

'To you, fifteen pounds,' she said, with a raised eyebrow.

Sandbach handed over the money, feeling slightly fleeced. He realised he had no idea how much these things would usually cost.

'Thank you,' he said, taking the flowers with a forced smile.

'You've still got it,' Terrence said and chuckled.

Sandbach felt drawn to the little alleyway running down the side of the shopping centre. He knew it wasn't supposed to have any connection with the pub, but he wanted to see for himself anyway. There were plenty of people bustling along trying to get where they were going down the main road, but no one seemed to want to go this way. It wasn't very long; about enough space for a couple of cars end to end, including the loading bay area at the far end, where a white Transit van had parked. About halfway down was a turning to the left. He examined all the doors and openings along the right-hand wall as he walked down, in case one of them could be a secret entrance into the pub, but they all looked fairly normal for the shopping centre itself.

He reached the corner and turned left. At first it looked

like any other alleyway you might find in a town. And then he recognised it as being the same alleyway Fenella had disappeared into the day before. Probably just coincidence but it piqued his curiosity. He walked the length of it, again checking doors and entrances. This time for anywhere a person could escape quickly. In theory, there were a couple she perhaps could have made use of, but it seemed unlikely. Any doors there look very secure, not the kind to leave unlocked. He even tried the ones to the disused toilet block, just in case. Nothing. Just enough of a rattle to suggest that they were not going anywhere without the appropriate key to gain entry.

Sandbach felt an odd tingling sensation up his back and Terrence began to growl.

'You!' A voice spoke, indignantly.

Sandbach turned just in time to see the familiar floaty figure of Fenella. She held something in the air and was bringing it down over his head. Not fast like a weapon, but gently as if she was going to tap him on the head with a rolled-up newspaper. But it wasn't a newspaper, it was smaller, like a tube or something leather-bound, which looked familiar.

It touched his head gently. He expected to feel a sensation to match the size of the object; it hadn't been swung hard, but it felt completely different – as if his head was made of jelly and she'd rested a baseball bat on it. His head seemed to give way, bending and squashing very oddly. He felt the object getting warm, then hotter and hotter until it began to burn. He was vaguely aware of someone muttering words but he couldn't make them out. As the object was lifted from his head, he thought he saw orange and yellow sparks fly in slow motion; the alleyway began to spin and blur. Everything went black.

Chapter 30

The Green Man, Present Day

Everything was dark, completely dark. Sandbach couldn't see a thing. He had to blink a few times and he waved his hand in front of his face to be sure, but still nothing.

'Hello. Is there anybody there?' he called out. He realised that sounded like he was participating in a corny seance, trying to reach someone from beyond the grave. The vague possibility then crossed his mind that perhaps he was dead, and that he was now reaching out to the living. Would someone be picking this up on a Ouija board in a back room somewhere? Not likely, there was probably a much simpler explanation.

There was a slightly damp and fusty smell, plus he realised he was lying on a solid and fairly uncomfortable floor. He felt around with his hands. The ground felt gritty and dusty. His face stung from where sharp bits were digging into his skin.

'If there's anyone there, can you tell me where I am?'

'That has to be the stupidest thing anyone's ever said,' Terrence whispered.

'There you are. Where are we then?' Sandbach replied.

'I have no idea. Were you expecting me to do a recce while you were having a nap?'

'Would've been nice,' Sandbach said, making the effort to

sit up.

A thought occurred to him and he reached into his jacket pocket for his mobile phone, which thankfully was still there. He fumbled for the button on top and finally there was light. Not enough to see any further than the screen in front of him, but enough to realise he probably wasn't dead. He clicked around the settings to find the torch function that he knew had to be here somewhere. If only there was a five-year-old here to show him how to use this new technology! After adjusting the speaker volume and accidentally taking a selfie, he finally managed to switch on the light and illuminate his surroundings.

'Looks like we've missed last orders,' Terrence said.

They appeared to be inside a pub or bar, but one that must have been closed for a long time. There was no carpet or floor covering of any kind, only concrete, with what looked like a blackened area off to one side. Presumably there had been a fire here at some time in the past. On one side of the pub was a dark wooden bar, on the opposite an alcove with seating, no table, but it did have a very detailed painting on the wall, a castle by the looks of it and soldiers in uniform rows in front. The ceiling was painted red and the walls mostly white or cream, but most unusual was the fact that there were no windows.

'OK. I think I know where we are,' Sandbach said, feeling a slight shiver run down his spine. 'And if I'm right, we've missed last orders by more than twenty-five years.'

Sandbach got to his feet and looked around. There were more seating alcoves and archways into other areas, but no doors or way out that he could see.

'I think we're going to need some help from outside on this one,' Sandbach said.

He managed to get the phone into making-a-call mode, which he often felt seemed surprisingly difficult given the original nature of the device, then fumbled in his jacket pocket for the business card Carter had given him earlier. She would undoubtedly be overjoyed to receive a call from someone who had been less than polite to her previously, especially given the predicament he found himself in now, but he couldn't think of anyone better to call.

'Hi, Carter, how are you?' Sandbach said, doing his best to sound polite.

'What's wrong?' she replied, flatly.

'All I said was "how are you?" I resent the accusation that I would be nice to you because I need something.'

'She's got a point,' Terrence said.

'Be quiet will you?' Sandbach hissed.

'Be quiet?' Carter replied angrily. 'You rang me!'

The line went dead. Carter must have hung up on him.

'Very smooth,' Terrence said with a chuckle.

'If we can't find a way out then we're both going to be stuck here in the pub that time forgot.'

Sandbach, realising the light on his phone was still on, made his way to the seating next to them. There was no cushioning on any of the seats, which he'd noticed already but for some reason was still surprised when he actually sat down with a thud.

'So, why are we here?' Terrence asked.

'Good question. I don't know.' Sandbach replied. 'That woman, Fenella? She hit me with something. I thought she was going to try and knock me out with that bar or whatever it was.' Sandbach pondered for a moment. 'But she didn't, she ... I don't know what she did, but now we're in here.'

'Perhaps she did knock you out and you don't remember anything because, well I don't know, because she knocked you out?' Terrence said, with lashings of sarcasm.

'I don't have a headache and I don't feel like I've just been knocked out. I feel, well, like I've just had a good night's sleep. I'm not saying that waking up on a dirty floor in a pitch-black, abandoned pub is my dream getaway, but it could have been worse.'

'Right, but how did she get you in here? You said it was a really difficult place to get into, literally. She also didn't seem to be built like a Russian weightlifter.'

'High-fibre diet?' Sandbach said with a shrug. 'Perhaps there was a doorway off George Yard and she pushed me inside.'

Sandbach was mulling over the location of the doorways he'd passed along George Yard, wondering whether any of them might lead here. He didn't remember seeing anything obvious. Presumably that was the idea to keep it hidden or secret, so that people didn't try to break in and use it as a drug den or something. His phone rang; it made him jump – Carter's name was on the screen.

'Hello?' Sandbach answered, cautiously.

'What do you want?' Carter asked. 'Presumably you called me for a reason?'

'I did. Sorry about before, I wasn't telling you to be quiet by the way, it was ... someone else.'

'It sounded like you!'

'No, I mean I was talking to someone else. Anyway, you're right, I do need something. I need help opening-up the Green Man pub.'

'Ha, that's not going to happen in a hurry. Do you know you need permission from the shopping centre manager, and to have the Fire Service on site? There's no normal door or stairway inside you know.'

'Really?' Sandbach said, trying to sound genuinely puzzled by what Carter had just told him. 'So how do you get in then?'

'Through a hatch in the floor near the lift shaft,' Carter continued. 'So, like I said, you won't be getting in there for a few days at least. We'll have to get the office to make contact formally. But it's not like some idiot has got trapped inside.'

'Yes, about that ...'

Chapter 31

The Green Man, Present Day

Words failed her, but Florence knew that Sandbach wasn't the sort to mess about.

'Hello ... did you hear what I said?' Sandbach's voice echoed through the car's hands-free set-up.

'Yes. I just heard you admit to being a complete idiot,' Florence muttered, before continuing in a louder voice, 'I heard you say you were trapped in the Green Man. I need to ask you two things: One, how did you get in there – bearing in mind that there's no bloody door? And two, how the buggering hell am I going to get you out?'

'It's complicated, and you might not believe me ...'

'Oh for the love of God. Are we back to witches again?' Florence exclaimed, slapping the steering wheel in frustration.

Silence.

'Hello ... Sandbach ... Can you hear me?'

Florence could hear muttering – it sounded like Sandbach was talking to himself.

'Yes, I'm here. The short version is that I saw Fenella and she tapped me on the head with a tube and then it all went dark.'

'Oh my God. Was it a wand?' Florence gasped, before adding, 'Jesus Christ, Sandbach, listen to me – you are making me sound like a bloody idiot!'

'Look, I just need you to get that help you were talking about and come get me. It's not the most welcoming public house I've been in.'

'No? Well you may want to start making yourself comfy, this could take a while, plus I'll have to call Boyle and rearrange our meeting at the nick. Just keep your mobile on and maybe put it onto power-saver mode. Oh, and Sandbach?'

'Yes?'

'Get me a large glass of red, it's most definitely your round.'

Florence ended the call, indicated left and pulled into a lay-by. Reaching into the footwell she grabbed her handbag, pulled her phone from the side pocket and entered the four-digit pin.

'Jules, Jules, Jules – where are you?' she muttered, scrolling down her contacts list, before pressing the call button.

'Florence Carter! As I live and breathe. How the hell are you and please tell me you are back safe in our fair town?' Jules's familiar, deep voice rang out.

'I'm good, thanks and yes, I'm here – for a short while anyway. Listen – I have a problem. You still working Blue Watch?'

'Of course. Once an arsonist, now a fireman. Why? What you done?' Jules's laughter echoed down the line.

'For once it's not me in trouble, although I do want your help and it needs to be on the q.t. Can you meet me at the Green Man asap?'

'Where? The Green Man in the town! The underground Green Man with no direct access. You do know the Green Man's been closed since 1993, don't ya girl?'

'Yeah, I know. Just meet me – please.'

'Okay. As it's my day off I can be there in fifteen.'

'Brilliant. Oh, and Jules?'

'Yes?'

'Bring some rope with you. Some thick, long rope.'

'Oh my God. What on earth …'

'Bye.' Florence hit the end-call button and sat back in her seat. Flicking through the recent calls she selected Sandbach's number.

'The cavalry's on its way,' she said when he answered the call. 'Now, sit tight – I can't wait to hear more about how you've ended up in there.'

'It isn't like there's a door, Carter. I didn't walk in!'

'Yeah, okay. Whatever. I'm on my way.'

'Did you just say "whatever" like some highly strung teenage …'

'And that's enough from you,' she said, stabbing her call display with her finger, before she pulled back into the traffic and headed towards the town centre.

Chapter 32

The Old Manor House, 1993

The eatery was just inside the small thoroughfare that led off Church Gate, just as the man they now knew as Matthew had predicted. Fox got there first, and Robert watched as he paused to look at the wares on display. Saliva gathered in his mouth as the unmistakable smell of bacon cooking reached his nostrils. A list of commodities had been posted in the window.

'All day breakfast. Bacon, sausage, eggs, beans, hash brown, fried bread and a mug of tea, £2.50.' Robert read slowly. 'I don't know what hash brown is, but the rest sound wonderful.'

Fox had also been reading, it seemed.

'They do hot chocolate drink, too,' he said, pointing to the items listed under beverages.

Robert pushed open the door, and as they entered they were greeted with: 'Good morning, gents. How can I help you?' from behind the counter. The middle-aged woman, with strange purple hair and one large earring, wore a red apron and a friendly smile.

'Two breakfasts, if you please, madam, but might we have hot chocolate instead of tea?' Robert asked.

'Course, me ducks, if that's what you want. Anything for a pair of gents like yourselves. Sit yourselves down over there and I'll bring it over when it's ready.'

Fox's eyebrow had raised, but he nodded his head at the woman and they both sat as she indicated, at a table with four chairs near the window. Fox retrieved his hat from inside his jerkin. Unrolling it to reveal Sally's hat once more, he placed his own on one of the two extra chairs. There was just one other customer, who was drinking from a mug and reading a periodical at a nearby table. The lady behind the counter was cooking with her back to them. Fox leant forward.

'Do we have enough coinage, Hooke?' he asked, placing Sally's hat open on the table and picking up one of the gold coins. He read: 'One pound – 'tis a fortune!'

'I doubt that,' said Robert, taking up another and biting it. ''Tis not a gold pound as we know it. There are no marks. Currency is most likely devalued from our day.'

'So says the scientist,' said Fox sardonically, piling up the copper pennies into twelves. 'Several shillings, here.'

Robert was drawn to the silver coin with seven sides. 'Fifty-pence,' he read. 'I think we will manage. The breakfasts are two pounds and fifty pennies each. There are five of the gold coins, three of these and several of these silver twenty-pence and ten-pence coins. Hide the hat though. Put the coins in your pocket, for now.'

Fox pushed the hat back inside his jerkin and slipped the coins into its front pocket. A few moments later the woman bustled over with two mugs of steaming brown liquid.

'Here we are, duckies. Sugar's on the table,' she said, indicating a bowl of small packets. 'I'll bring your breakfasts in two ticks.'

As she retreated Robert's eyes met Fox's blue ones. They lifted their mugs together, without words, and sipped. Robert gave a little gasp. The hot liquid had burnt his lip, but the taste was … the taste was like nothing he had ever tasted before. Fox smacked his lips.

'This is good, very good. Better still than I had expected, Hooke.'

They savoured the drink in silence for a few moments before their food was put before them. Hooke stared at his plate that contained a half of what was clearly a baked tomato, two eggs, two slices of bacon, two long burnt brown meaty objects, a shaped browned item that looked vegetable based and some round orange beans in sauce. It smelled like heaven. Balancing on the side of each plate there were triangles of fried bread.

'Knives and forks, and your bill,' the woman announced, putting metal implements wrapped in some kind of thin paper to the side of each plate, and a slip of paper on a shallow dish in the middle of the table.

'Wonderful. My thanks to you, dear lady,' Hooke managed. He unwrapped the implements while Fox watched and then copied. After a moment of inspection they both set to, cutting and forking the food to their mouths.

'Onions,' Fox commented, as he tasted the unfamiliar shaped object. That was all either said until the plates were cleared. They used the bread like a trencher, wiping round the plate to soak up the egg yolks and orange sauce. Then they both drained their mugs.

'Oh, my,' Hooke said, replacing his mug on the table. 'That was the most marvellous meal I can remember. And I will remember it forever.'

'Indeed, my friend,' Fox responded. 'But now that we are replete we must return to our mission. The Manor House is not far from here, I believe. I met with Friends there not so long ago.'

'Hall was telling me about Bromskill and his meetings. He is not too pleased about them making themselves known so close to the church.'

'It matters not where people worship. God is all around us. One does not need a steeple house and all the rituals therein to find Him. The church is the people.'

'I am sure you are right. And perhaps it has worked out that way in this new time. Let us proceed as you suggest. But first we must pay our way.' Hooke opened the slip that the woman had left. The scrawling writing read:

2 all days	£5.00
2 hot chocs (surcharge)	£1.50
Total	£6.50

'Indeed,' Fox agreed, selecting the five gold and three silver, seven-sided coins. 'Hopefully, I have counted right.'

They both stood up and Hooke watched Fox approach the woman behind the counter and proffer the coins. She gave them a quick look, pressed some buttons on the machine behind her and a drawer popped out. Hooke tried to see how that had happened, but the woman let the coins slide into the drawer, and pushed it shut.

'Mind how you go, me ducks,' she said. Hooke took that strange advice as a dismissal.

'Thank you kindly, madam.' Both of them nodded their heads to her as they left, Fox adding a wave of his hat.

'Well, that was a success, my friend,' Fox declared, once outside. 'Lead on.'

Hooke stepped out, and within a matter of a few minutes they came to another large thoroughfare busy with a variety of vehicles as before.

'Ready, Fox?' Robert asked, as they teetered on the edge of the walkway. He wasn't surprised when a matter of seconds later, without answering, Fox launched himself between the vehicles and negotiated his way across, dodging this way and that. Several honks sounded making them both jump as Robert followed in his wake. On the other side he had to step back into the path of the cars to avoid colliding with a strange two-wheeled contraption. 'There must be an easier way,' he gasped, watching as the rider, who was wearing a bright pink helmet, kept going at speed, apparently unperturbed by their near miss. Once he had caught up with Fox he asked: 'Did you see that? How does he balance? I must know.'

'This world is full of the most wonderful and curious mysteries,' Fox replied. 'But they will have to wait. We need to keep going. We have tarried enough.'

At the top of Church Gate the way opened out. Robert pointed.

''Tis the church. All Saints. Our church. Right there in front of us, Fox.' His voice had gone up so that he was almost squeaking.

'Yes, I see the steeple house, as you say. Come, the Manor House is opposite, is it not?'

And there it was. Essentially the same, Robert thought, gazing at the décor.

'The Old Manor House.' Fox read the large writing across the building. 'It is another place for eating. Look, there is a list of wares to be had.' Robert looked over his shoulder and read from the list that appeared below a notice on the door, which read: 'Closed.'

'Prawn tails in salsa rossa on a bed of spinach. Bruschetta. I do not know these things.'

'Loin of lamb in anchovy sauce with wild mushroom gravy. Now that would suit me. There is certainly some familiar fare.'

They peered through the left-hand window and saw tables set with pink flowers and an array of shiny cutlery. The right-hand window revealed sofas, and pink walls hung with large paintings.

The door opened. A man stepped out and looked them up and down with a rather unfriendly expression. 'Can I help you?' he asked.

'Ah! Good day to you, sir. We are interested in the

building. It has been here a long time, I trust?'

'Some five hundred years, so yes, indeed. It is one of the oldest buildings in Loughborough. You'll need to come back later if you want to look around. We're closed just now.'

'How kind,' Fox added to Robert's greeting. 'But we're hoping to meet someone. Two people in fact.'

'I'm sorry. I can't help you. As I said, come back later; we're open at seven o'clock.' With that, their new acquaintance stepped back inside.

'What do we do now?' Robert asked, staring at the firmly closed door, which signalled that the exchange was over.

Chapter 33

The Old Rectory, 1993

The obvious thing to do was to cross to the church. After all, it too looked much as it had done in their day. Certainly, Robert thought, there had been some embellishment, but it was essentially the same. All Saints' Church it was called now, he saw, looking at the wording on the board that was fixed to the stone wall.

'There was a school on these grounds,' Fox broke into Robert's musings having caught him up.

'Yes, Thomas Burton ran one for the boys of the parish.'

'It is a good thing to educate the young, though not just boys. Girls should also benefit from improving their minds.'

'I have met some uncommonly clever women, but I'm not sure about school, Fox, my fellow. Now, before we were snatched from the marketplace I was staying at the rectory, which is behind the church. Or it was. Let us hasten there and see if it remains.'

Both men set off, following the perimeter of the stone wall. They could see tree-tops of what was, perhaps, an orchard. Some way along their route the wall ended, rounding to a gateway. A notice proclaimed it the Old Rectory Museum, restored by Loughborough Council and the Archaeological and

History Society. It advertised tours and displays about the building, which had been used as a home of the rector of All Saints Church for 800 years. They stared up the long gravelled pathway to what was left of the house.

'Oh, my stars! There is only a small part of the house remaining. What has happened?'

'Hundreds of years. That's what.'

Robert was getting used to Fox's dry wit, if that's what it was, but the shock of seeing his friend Hall's house like this was staggering.

'Those pillars stand like sentinels; they were the main part of that beautiful residence. Only one wing has survived.' Robert was drawn forward by the awful discovery, though there was a kind of beauty in what remained; the remnants of the house and the gardens with their fruit trees and brambled walls, had some charm in the sunlight that filtered through the branches. They walked through the archway, which joined the pillars to the abiding wing, and pressed their noses to the glass of the window near the arched doorway to the museum. It was closed, but they could see the flagstone floor and display cabinets full of curiosities.

'I can't help feeling that Hall will suddenly appear and open the door to us, though this place is nothing like he would have known,' Robert murmured.

'I told you they'd come, didn't I?' said a female voice.

Both Robert and Fox jumped with shock, straightening up and turning as the answer came.

'Indeed you did,' said the man with her. They were their rescuers from the night before.

They all shook hands in greeting.

'I am Robert Hooke, and this is George Fox.'

'Robert Hooke from the Royal Society and George Fox of the Quakers?' the young woman said. 'I thought you both looked familiar.'

'Our sincere thanks for helping us last night,' Robert began. 'I can't begin to tell you our story.'

'We know some of it,' the man, who had introduced himself simply as Wesley and his companion as Paige said, and guided them to a wooden bench nearby. 'We know you are out of your time, through an accidental occurrence, and you need to return. We can help you.'

'You know? How can you know?'

'If we told you we travel through time ourselves you would probably not believe us,' said Wesley.

'What is this? Some kind of sorcery?' Fox exclaimed.

'You could say that,' said Wesley. 'That's what it looks like, and certainly what you would've called it in your day. In fact, it might be the right word on any day.'

Robert laid his hand on Fox's arm.

'Let them speak. There is much we do not understand in this world we find ourselves. We have already seen marvellous inventions and tasted the most wonderful fare.'

'That much is true. 'Tis a place full of unworldly creations and people with strange, ungodly powers. They have tools to communicate and tools to transport. Take that flame-haired woman, for example.'

'You've seen her?' the young woman interjected, but Fox spoke without pause.

'First, we saw her conceal strange tubes within a wall covering. And then she made a young woman disappear.'

'And on both occasions she stopped time with one of those tubes,' Robert added, unable to stop himself now that Fox had started the story.

'She did what?' Wesley and Paige's expressions showed mixed feelings.

'She stopped time? Are you sure?' Paige asked.

'She did! She did indeed! And it was just as well, because that fellow, with extraordinary eyes, was about to abduct a young woman, for what purpose I can't guess, but she made that young woman disappear. She said it was for the young woman's own good, and she made herself disappear – twice.' Robert ran on, without taking a breath. He paused for a moment, and then asked, 'Is that normal, in this time? I am a scientist, and I would know how it's done.'

'No. It's not normal in any time,' Paige said. 'Wesley, what do you suggest we do?'

'We can't get involved, you know that. We just maintain the status-quo.'

'But this is about keeping the status-quo. We can't have people stopping time and taking the law into their own hands.'

'So you are suggesting that we do just that?'

Robert and Fox both looked from one to the other, following the debate.

'You know that we've done it before, when we've had to. And we already know that Fenella woman's up to something in the present day. I think we have to at least share this information with the police. It seems that the missing people might be linked.'

'Why would they believe us? We'll need something to convince them. You know anything that doesn't make logical sense will be dismissed.'

'We'll have to take them with us.' Paige was pointing at Robert and Fox.

'Take us where, exactly?' Fox asked. Robert was thinking the same thing.

'No!' Wesley said, a fraction of a second later.

'If we agree to help, then how?' persisted Robert.

'Will you come? Please? I think it will help.' Paige looked earnest and sincere to Robert, who could not help but like the pair, though even his scientific brain was not sure what she was asking.

Wesley stood up, suddenly: 'Okay, okay, you win.'

Paige kissed him on the cheek. 'I knew you'd see it my

way,' she said, and kissed him again. She then turned back to Fox and Hooke. 'If you would follow us, we'll see what we can do. And then we promise to return you to the moment that your lives changed.'

Robert glanced at Fox, who shrugged his shoulders and raised his hands in a questioning motion. Exactly what Robert felt. What choice did they have?

'We both need to go home, so if you can make that happen, we will help,' he told them.

'We might be out of sight for a little while, but it shouldn't be for too long,' Paige said. She linked her arms through Robert's and Fox's so that the three of them walked together, behind Wesley, through the gardens to the graveyard of All Saints. They followed him down the path to the lychgate in the churchyard wall.

Robert watched Wesley unlatch the gate and hold it open. As they passed through, Paige said, with a bubbly note to her voice, 'and don't forget to close it properly.'

'No worries! The latch is firmly shut,' they heard Wesley reply behind them.

Robert's first impression was that evening had come quickly. In the beams of light passing over them he caught the look from Fox's eyes, which were round with surprise. Following his gaze, Robert was transfixed by what he saw – cars of the future. The future-future!

Chapter 34

Caravelli's, Present Day

Sitting cross-legged on the floor, Florence tried to stem her racing brain. Her yoga teacher had introduced the idea of attaching an imaginary red balloon to individual thoughts and then allowing them to float blissfully away.

It wasn't working today.

Witches and magic consumed her mind, coupled with the overwhelming fact that this was not something explainable. She couldn't just rock up at work and start talking to colleagues about this – they'd have her sectioned in a heartbeat, and more startling was the fact that there was no one who would believe her.

Caitlin would, and her mild acceptance on the phone was testament to their years of friendship. They trusted each other; trust that had formed instantly on the assault course they had met on all those years ago. Florence smiled at the memory. She'd been halfway up an enormous wall on the Army assault course near Lichfield when a female voice from the top had drifted down – along with clear instructions as to how to climb. The friendship had been made and they'd crossed the line of the course together, much to the disgust of their sergeants, who'd initiated the wager.

A loud knock on the bedroom door interrupted her thoughts. Uncrossing her legs, Florence stood up.

'Evening, Boyle,' she said, opening the door to the smiling face of her friend. 'Come on in. What would you like to drink? I can make something hot or maybe you'd like something from the bar downstairs?'

'No, don't bother with rushing around. Just pop the kettle on and let's have a cuppa. Nice room,' Boyle replied, as she walked over to a chair and placed a black briefcase on the table in front of her. 'I've never stayed at Caravelli's – eaten here a ton of times, but never got to actually venture upstairs.'

Florence eyed the briefcase as she switched the kettle on. 'Is that the bloody case you had when I met you at the nick yesterday?'

Boyle laughed. 'Yes, after you called to say you couldn't make it earlier I thought I'd better come to you. We went through far too much for me not to share what I've found.'

Florence sat on the bed, crossed her legs and eyed her friend. 'Come on, Mrs, spill – what did you find?'

'Documents – well to be exact, reports and photographs.'

'Oooooh, tell me you have some old pictures of witches and wizards.' Florence leant forward on the bed. 'Seriously, Harriet, start talking – I need to know.'

'Witches and wizards?' Boyle laughed. 'I know it's all gone a bit weird, and I will never forget that burning page, but really, Sandbach is a believer?' Boyle turned to the table, pulled the case to face her and then flipped the locks open.

'Like you would not believe! And I kinda do get it but imagine actually filing that report! Anyway, carry on, please.'

'Okay, but we are definitely coming back to this,' Boyle said, opening the case. 'So, after we got scattered to the far corners of the county I thought that I'd passed that feeling – you know, that we'd missed something – and I'd just get on with my job, but I didn't and I guess those missing people just wriggled under my skin. They just couldn't have disappeared – so I decided to go searching.'

'But where?' Florence asked, as she got up to make the drinks. 'Tea or coffee, or even a swanky hot chocolate?'

'Ooooh, hot chocolate – is there enough for two? Go on, then,' Boyle replied in answer to Florence's nod. 'I left it a while and then started looking– you remember Ann in records?'

'Yes. Tall, short dark hair, smiley,' Florence said as she passed a mug of steaming hot chocolate to Boyle.

'That's her. Anyway, after you left, she and I met on a course – turns out she loves art too, so we started going to galleries together. Nice break away from the job and she didn't have a family either, so it made sense for us to meet up occasionally. One of the days she mentioned the misper case, and we got talking. She told me that the case-file notes, truck loads of them, were only sitting in the records office waiting to be shipped to HQ for storage.' Boyle shrugged. 'Well, I wasn't going to miss that opportunity.'

'What did you do? And did Ann get you access to those records?' Florence sipped her drink.

'Oh yes. And before you splutter about access and confidentiality, I know, but it was so easy! I seriously could not believe that I just waltzed in, picked up a box, opened the first file and started reading.'

'How long did you search for?'

'Just over six weeks. I took a cushion and plonked myself on the floor. I had to fit it around work, obviously, but I often popped in on refs any chance I got – I reckon the lads thought Ann and I were at it.'

'Harriet!'

'What? You know they all thought I was gay – they were unable to comprehend that I just wasn't interested in any of them – I had to be gay or there had to be something wrong with me.'

Florence laughed. 'Yup, if you didn't fancy Muzy then you

had to be a lesbian, so what did you find?'

'A few things that the super obviously didn't want us to know at the time,' Boyle said, passing some paperwork over to Florence, 'namely witness statements about people disappearing through doors; without opening them first,' she answered in response to Florence's raised eyebrow.

'Okay, well there has been quite a bit of that reported too,' Florence agreed, flicking through the pile of statements, 'by Sandbach, it has to be said, but still. He may be weird, but he's believable weird – if you know what I mean?' Boyle nodded. 'Bloody hell, Harriet, these two mention sightings of a woman with red hair.'

'You don't think ... you can't possibly mean ...'

'I absolutely do – it's got to be Fenella! Let's get looking through those photographs. I'll put next month's salary on the fact that she'll be on one or more of them.'

'Okay.' Boyle removed three folders from the briefcase. 'You look through that one and I'll start here.' Boyle passed a folder across and then turned her chair to face the bed. 'Let the witch-hunt commence,' she said as she flipped the file open.

Florence chuckled. 'Jesus, by the end of this Sandbach'll have us both believing and we'll all end up in the same home for the deluded and mentally unstable.'

'Come on, let me in on this whole magical convention of witches and wizards dropping into this little town every so many decades.'

'Apparently, and this is according to Sandbach, the red-haired woman is connected to this whole mystery around the missing people and he believes that she was responsible for putting him inside the Green Man.'

'What do you mean inside the Green Man?'

'Ah, I didn't tell you that bit did I? Well, Sandbach had witnessed her disappear in George Yard yesterday and this morning he took off after breakfast to go solo – not one for working with someone, and to be fair, we'd hardly be the next Lewis and Hathaway – anyway ...'

'Carter, did you just really say disappear?'

'Yes, I know it's a lot to take in. Anyway, he went on his way and I was coming to see you. During the drive he called and told me he was inside the Green Man and could I come get him out. I don't think he realised that the only way in and out was through the trap door, which is at the foot of the stairs up to the carpark and next to the lifts.'

'What did you do?'

'Well, come on Harriet, there's only one person you could call, with access to long thick rope, for something like that on the q.t.'

'Jules.' Boyle guessed with a laugh.

'Exactly. Anyway, we managed to get to the access panel with some bullshit about checking for a gas leak, and we got him out.'

'Did you go down there?' Boyle put the photographs she had been looking through on the bed and picked up the next pile. 'Nothing of interest in that lot.'

'Give them here and I'll add them to this pile. Did I bugger – not a chance of me ever going into a bar that's been closed for over twenty-five years. I did peer down the hole though and it did look very creepy. I certainly wouldn't have wanted to get trapped—' Florence had resumed her cross-legged position on the bed with the photographs balanced on her calves, placing each scrutinised photo to one side before lifting the next. Glancing at the ceiling, she closed her eyes. 'Harriet, I think I've found her.'

'What? Have you really? Pass it here and let me have a look.'

Florence looked again at the picture in her hands. 'I'm sure it is, there, standing right outside Grudgings,' she muttered, handing it to Boyle. 'What do you think?'

Florence watched as Boyle studied the photo. 'I'd also bet a month's wages that this was her – and she looks exactly the same.'

'Probably uses an expensive face cream,' Florence muttered, uncrossing her legs and quickly flicking through the remaining photographs in front of her. 'There might be more of her so let's have a quick look and see.'

'It makes you understand why the top brass shut this case down so quickly.'

'If the top brass actually knew …' Florence let the words hang there. 'What if only our old super knew and he closed it down?'

'But why would he do that? And more importantly, could he do that?'

'Harriet, we're looking at evidence that a woman, looking exactly the same over twenty-five years ago as she does now, was in and around the marketplace at the time we were searching for those people. Florence sighed. 'I never sought promotion – I always knew that traffic cars and firearms was the right path for me, but you and I have both worked with some complete arseholes higher up the ranks. I'm not saying it wouldn't have been difficult, but probably far easier than attempting to explain that to other bobbies, and then the public. Jesus, can you imagine the panic?'

'Not forgetting the weirdos it would tempt out. There would be magical types all over the bleeding place. So, what are we going to do about this?'

'Here she is again.' Florence turned the photo she was holding so that Boyle could see. 'Christ, Harriet. I really do not know. Part of me is desperate to find out what the hell is going on and part of me can totally understand why whoever buried this, bloody buried it. First and foremost, I need to get these to Sandbach.'

'Well it's time I was off anyway, but you must promise to

keep me in the loop regardless of whether this gets buried again.'

'Yes, of course. Whatever happens, I'll let you know.'

'Okay then. I'll leave all the photos with you shall I?'

'No, just these two – they definitely give enough detail so that the area and the people are recognisable. Just take the paperwork and the other photos but leave the two statements that mention the sighting of the woman with red hair.'

'Well it was great to spend some time with you again, Florence. Make sure we get together soon – without the threat of being turned into a frog.'

'Oh, I doubt she'd turn you into a frog, Harriet. Far more likely a cat or a dog. Only young handsome men get turned into frogs. Please tell me you've read the stories?'

'You daft sod. Glad to see some things haven't changed.' Boyle collected all the folders, put them in the briefcase and closed the lid. 'Keep safe, and keep in touch.'

'I'll walk you down and then go see where Sandbach is,' Florence said as she grabbed the key, opened the door and followed Boyle from the room. 'Are you back in work tomorrow?'

'No. I have three days off now and was intending on nipping down to London with Ann, and before you ask, no, we are not seeing each other. We are just good friends.'

'Harriet—' At the foot of the stairs, Florence stepped into the foyer. 'The thought hadn't crossed my mind, honestly. My closest friend, with the exception of Tom, my cat, is Caitlin. I've known her for years. We travel and hang out. So much bloody easier than spending time with a bloke.' They'd reached the main doors and Florence turned to look at her friend. 'You surely don't give a rats what people think, do you?'

'No, and you're right. I shouldn't, but sometimes it's just difficult to ignore the incessant judgement folk place on each other. Right, I'm going. Remember, keep safe and let me know.'

Florence smiled at Harriet's retreating figure as she watched her stride across the road towards the church. Releasing the door, she turned and was surprised to find Massimo behind the bar. Maybe he's just materialised through the floor, she thought as she approached the bar.

'Would madam care for a glass of red?' he asked, politely.

Sandbach could wait for a bit – give her time to untangle her thinking. Smiling, she pulled a stool back and sat down. 'Make it large, please.'

Chapter 35

Caravelli's, Present Day

'I don't think I could eat another thing,' Paige said and slumped back into her chair. 'The dessert menu is tempting, but after antipasti and a main course, I'm absolutely full, thank you.'

Ellen looked downhearted.

'Just two coffees, please,' Wesley said.

'Of course. With pleasure.' Ellen nodded and went back to the bar area.

'It's a lovely evening.' Paige turned to Wesley. 'The moon's lighting up the church's tower.' She noticed a lone drinker, who she was convinced was either police or military, sitting in the bar with a large glass of red wine, but her attention shifted when Massimo approached their table carrying a tray with their coffee and two small shot glasses containing a yellow liquid.

'I hope you have enjoyed your meal.'

'Superb, as always,' Wesley answered.

Massimo placed the drinks down in front of them. 'Please accept a little Limoncello – on the house.'

'I don't mind if I do, thank you. Can we have the bill too please?' Wesley asked. Massimo nodded and left them.

Paige sipped the lemony liqueur. It was sharp but sweet,

and her taste buds tingled as it slid over her tongue.

'Ooh, that's really nice.' Paige smacked her lips. 'I could get used to those.'

The waitress they knew as Isabella walked towards their table. 'Your bill, sir,' Isabella said, 'and this note has just been handed in for you too.'

'Thank you.' Wesley took the paper and opened it out. Paige detected a frown fleet over his face as he read the letter. He took out his wallet, sighed and threw the paper down onto the table along with some bank notes.

'Problem?'

'No, just an inconvenience. You go home and get to bed.' He stood up and kissed Paige on the cheek. 'I won't be long,' he whispered in her ear, and then walked towards the exit.

Paige picked up the note and read the cursive handwriting that scrawled across the page: 'Sir, your assistance is needed outside in the churchyard as a matter of urgency.'

'Those two again.' Paige shook her head. She looked around the restaurant. Earlier diners had left and the room was less busy, although she could see from where she was sitting that one or two remained in the bar area. Suddenly something, or rather someone, caught her eye. A woman with flaming red hair crossed her line of vision and turned towards the staircase, as if she was heading for the cloakrooms.

'Fenella,' Paige said under her breath. She placed her napkin on the table, stood up, pushed her chair back, and made her way into the bar and past the young woman holding a glass of red wine, who hadn't moved.

Paige climbed the stairs. When she reached the landing she stopped and peered around the corner to her right. Fenella was standing outside the Lovell room with her back to the staircase and appeared to be fumbling with something. Presumably her room key, Paige thought and slipped inside the cloakroom, which was to her left, to wait until she heard the

Lovell room's door opening and closing. A lady was drying her hands; she said hello to Paige and then left. Paige was alone. After a while, and although she hadn't heard a door open or close, she decided to take a look. She crept out and headed along the landing. No one else was there so she tiptoed in closer. Once outside she could hear low voices coming from the Lovell. They sounded urgent – not an argument but a heated exchange. She pressed her ear onto the door's woodwork, but it was thick and muffled the conversation. Paige's concentration slipped as she felt someone behind her – Wesley must be back and had decided to follow her upstairs. A smug grin spread across her face; this could wait, and she spun round to embrace him. The smile slid from her face and she stepped backwards, her heel thudding against the door.

'Heard anything interesting?'

Paige looked up into the eyes of the tall man who was blocking her way; they were a mysterious amber and seemed to look deep into her soul.

'Who are you?' Paige asked, 'and why are you here?'

'I'm here for you,' the man replied and took her elbow in a painful grip; she could feel his thumb pressing into the flesh of her upper arm.

'I know what you are,' he snarled and drew her towards him.

'What I am? What are you talking about? Get lost, I don't know you – let go!' She tried to pull free but the grip grew tighter, and it hurt like hell. She opened her mouth wide to call out to whoever was inside the room but a sweaty palm slammed across her face.

'Keep your mouth shut and do as you're told.' He spun her round so that he was behind her, still with his hand firmly over her mouth. In one swift movement he let go of her arm and thrust open the bedroom door propelling her inside with such force that she fell to the floor.

'You again, Hopkins!' It was the man she had seen talking to himself yesterday. 'What the hell are you doing?'

'This is the offender that we've been searching for, the woman I told you about, DI Sandbach.' The man, who had just been called Hopkins, said and prodded Paige with his toe. 'She's the key to all of this.'

'What?' she said. 'Don't be ridiculous.'

She tried to get up but Hopkins pushed her back down. Her head slammed into the wooden bedstead and she passed out.

Chapter 36

Caravelli's, Present Day

'Well that wasn't embarrassing in the slightest,' Sandbach said, changing into a fresh drab grey suit, but one that didn't smell of damp, mould and decades old cigarette smoke. 'I suppose she's going to hold it over me for the rest of this case now.'

'If it wasn't for Carter and her friend with the fire engine, you'd still be stuck down there,' Terrence replied with glee.

'You would be too.'

Terrence shrugged and turned to lick himself.

'But I suppose you're right. Perhaps I could buy her a coffee.'

'You are getting flash with the cash,' Terrence scoffed.

'Oh shut it,' Sandbach replied as he headed to the en suite bathroom.

He'd just closed the door when there was a soft metallic rattling from just outside. It sounded like the door to his room. He was about to call out and announce that he would be with whoever it was shortly, but something didn't seem right. Anyone working here would either know that room was occupied and leave him alone, knock on the door, or would just have a key to let themselves in. No one should be trying the door or fiddling with the lock. There was a click and gentle swooshing noise of the door being opened. No heavy footsteps he noticed – hopefully this meant no violent confrontation with someone twice his size, but he could definitely sense movement outside the bathroom. The outer door clicked shut.

'Could be ninjas,' Terrence whispered.

Sandbach raised an eyebrow and glared at him, before whipping open the bathroom door and jumping out.

'OK, who's there? This is Detective Inspector Sandbach, please identify...'

He paused when the bedroom appeared to be empty.

'Well that was strange, I could have sworn ...'

Sandbach frowned, convinced something was still amiss.

'Fine. I'm going down to reception.'

He stomped towards the door to his room, opened it, took a few more noisy steps on the spot, and then shut it again. He waited silently, looking over at the double bed with an almost disappointed expectation. Sure enough, a red-haired woman emerged from behind it. Her eyes initially darted around the room but froze once they met Sandbach's. Fenella stood up slowly and scowled at him.

'That has to be the most pathetic trick in the book,' she said.

'Worked though, didn't it?' Sandbach replied casually. 'What do you want?'

'Nothing from you,' she spat. 'Why are you even here?'

'Interesting question – you broke into my room.'

'You should still be stuck in ... never mind.'

Fenella bent down and picked up the large bag she had been carrying with her earlier. She reached inside and pulled out a familiar-looking leather tube.

'You'll just have to go away again,' she said, stepping closer to Sandbach.

Sandbach raised his hands and stepped to the side; he didn't want to get trapped in the doorway, but inside the room he didn't really have anywhere to go either. He didn't fancy magically appearing back inside that old pub again, so he had to stop her. He could try and wrestle the tube from her, but he was never much good at the physical stuff. Perhaps she could be reasoned with.

'Let's not be too hasty with that,' Sandbach said, keeping an eye on the leather tube.

Fenella smiled. 'You don't even know what this is all about do you? Working with Matthew Hopkins, that, that ... murderer.'

'He is working with us as a consultant, nothing more.'

'He pours lies into people's ears, that's what he does. That's what he's always done. You think he's your saviour when really he's the one you should be afraid of. He's the one you need to lock up.'

'Wait, stop! Look, you might be right,' Sandbach pleaded, 'he approached the police, apparently. We've not brought him in. But there's so much he's told us that doesn't make sense. I don't trust him. And he certainly is not in control of this operation.'

Fenella paused for a moment, then shook her head. 'It doesn't matter. Either you are working with him, or you're so stupid you're helping him whether you understand it or not.'

'I understand that inside that leather tube in your hand is a missing page from a thirteenth century bible. And that this page, along with others like it, has some more unusual properties.'

Fenella lowered the tube slightly.

'So, are you hanging on to any of the pages for safekeeping?' Sandbach realised she was clearly still looking for the missing pages herself. This was a delicate moment and he didn't want her to leave, or send him somewhere else, before he could get more information. 'Because Hopkins is,' he told her.

Fenella's eyes lit up.

'I knew it! How many pages? Does he keep them with

him? Are they kept in his room here?'

She seemed to lose interest in Sandbach and began to walk towards the door. Sandbach moved to the side to get out of the way. Fenella glared at him momentarily, then walked past him.

'I can't let you confront Hopkins,' Sandbach said boldly.

'Ooh, that's a good idea.' Terrence winced and said, from the bed, 'yes, why not antagonise the lady with the magic tube?'

Fenella turned back to Sandbach and held out the tube in a threatening manner.

'Let the police handle this,' Sandbach continued, 'we can get to the bottom of it, but we need more information. Who is in possession of these pages? Which pages are unaccounted for, and perhaps, most importantly, what do they all do?'

Fenella shook her head and backed away towards the room door.

'You can't help, you people never do, you just get in the way.' Fenella opened the door.

Sandbach caught sight of Matthew Hopkins on the landing behind her. 'Wait!' he shouted.

Fenella spun round but Hopkins, clearly seeing what she was holding, snatched the leather tube from her hand and quickly tapped her on the head with it. There was a strange ripple in the air around Fenella, like a heat haze but much stronger. She vanished. Orange sparks fluttered toward the ground, marking the only sign that anyone had been there.

'So that's what it looks like from the outside,' Terrence said.

Sandbach nodded, abstractly fascinated by this bizarre sight, before he turned his attention back to Hopkins who stood in the doorway with a self-satisfied expression on his face.

'There you are, Sandbach,' Hopkins declared, 'that's the witch taken care of.'

'Why did you do that?' Sandbach asked, desperately

trying to hide his frustration. 'I want to know what's going on here, what's really going on.'

'I've told you already, and she wasn't going to tell you anything.' Hopkins turned away and slammed the door behind him. Sandbach sat back on his bed, trying to come to terms with what had just happened.

'You handled that well,' observed Terrence, from the floor.

'Shut up!' Sandbach sank down onto the pillow and closed his eyes. Moments later he could hear voices. Hopkins, and a woman. Not again. There was a thud against the door. He got up and opened it to find out what was going on, just as a young woman was propelled towards him. She fell through the doorway, onto her knees. 'What the hell are you doing now? Who is she?' Sandbach shook his head in amazement.

'This is the offender that we've been searching for, the woman I told you about, DI Sandbach. She's the key to all of this.'

'You're a consultant. You don't have the right to arrest anyone.'

Citizen's arrest – section 24A of the Police and Criminal Evidence Act. Am I wrong?' Hopkins said, looking smug.

Terrence practically choked with laughter, almost falling off the bed. Sandbach felt his normally calm and collected demeanour being sorely tested. But he couldn't afford to upset Hopkins at the moment. They needed more information.

'Right, well there's an officer here now so you can hand her over to me. And just to be clear, what exactly are the grounds for arrest?'

'She's been practising witchcraft with Fenella; she's a known criminal.'

'What? Don't be ridiculous!' said the woman, as she tried to get up

Hopkins pushed the young woman roughly and she fell back knocking her head on the bedstead and lay still.

'You didn't need to do that,' Sandbach admonished.

'Police brutality!' Terrence said, nosing at the young woman's still form.

'He's not the police,' Sandbach said, bending over and checking that the prostrate female was breathing, which she was.

'You are, though,' the dog pointed out.

'Just shut the fuck up.' Sandbach's teeth were grinding as he looked at his canine sidekick, but Hopkins had clearly thought Sandbach was speaking to him.

'Of course. I'll leave you to it, shall I? You'll take her to the station? She has an accomplice. I need to get to the Rectory museum, where I believe he is waiting for her. I shall arrest him too!' Hopkins said frostily.

'No! Just stop arresting people will you,' Sandbach said as he edged over to the window, keeping an eye on Hopkins all the while. The window looked out onto the carpark at the back and the road behind. Sandbach stole a glance outside. There was no one in the carpark. Then he noticed someone on the road. Could be something, could just be a dog walker. He turned back to Hopkins, who was still there.

'You stay here and get help with her. If there's any arresting to be done, I'll do it. What does this person look like?'

'Medium height, medium build, dark hair.'

'Well that narrows it down.' Sandbach walked towards the door. 'Give me that,' he demanded, holding his hand out towards the leather tube.

Sandbach went to take it but Hopkins pulled it away at the last minute and wrapped Sandbach on the head with it. The room around him went dark and melted away, leaving Sandbach in darkness. There were footsteps and muffled voices hurrying away into the distance. Sandbach moved towards the sounds then tripped over something in front of his feet. He fell forward and hit his head on something hard and smooth. The noise sounded hollow and looking down he saw a thin even strip of light below it. He realised it must be a door and so felt around for a handle but there wasn't one. He got up from the awkward position he'd fallen into and reached for the phone in his jacket pocket. He never knew how to get the torch function working but the screen gave him enough light to see something of his surroundings. It was a very small room filled with boxes and containers, and the thing he'd tripped over was a Henry vacuum cleaner. Its smiling face mocking his predicament.

Using the light from the screen Sandbach found the door handle – it was locked.

'Of course it's locked,' he muttered.

'What did you expect?' a little voice replied. Sandbach almost wished it was the hoover talking so he could kick its smug face. 'Now we're going to need rescuing again aren't we?'

Sandbach began hammering on the door and shouting for help. It was embarrassing. He didn't know which storeroom he was in but had a feeling he was still in Caravelli's. With that realisation he stopped banging and decided to ring Carter and get her to fetch someone with a key.

A few minutes later the door opened, momentarily blinding him and revealing a puzzled looking member of staff – Isabella, the moody one who had served his meal earlier. Sandbach stepped out into the corridor to get his bearings. He had been in the storeroom right next to his own bedroom.

'Do I even want to know why you were in there?' Carter asked him.

'No, probably not, it's a long story. Look, there is a remote chance that Hopkins has arrested a suspect and taken her to the station, but I doubt it. In which case this is going to be a long night.'

'Ooooooookay,' Carter replied, with a puzzled expression.

'I need you to call the station, just in case Hopkins does actually take her in. They won't be there yet, obviously, but get them to notify us immediately if they do.'

'And what are you going to do?'

'I'm going to the church's old rectory.'

'Why?'

'Hopkins mentioned an accomplice and I think he may be heading that way. Get some back-up sent over there while you're at it, he could be dangerous. Then grab a coat and meet me down there. Oh, and Carter, go check his room and see if there's anything there that could help us.'

'On it,' Carter said, and disappeared back into her room.

'So, what's going on at the old rectory?' Terrence asked.

'Good question. I have no idea, so let's go and find out.

Chapter 37

Caravelli's, Present Day

Paige opened her eyes. She was lying on her side and the bed beneath her felt comfy. She closed them again but snapped them open when realisation began to flood her brain. She sat up and took in her surroundings. She was in an untidy room, a different bedroom. She tried to get up but couldn't. She flopped back and tried to remember how she'd ended up here. Her head hurt – of course, she'd fallen and hit it on the corner of the bed in the room that she'd thought Fenella had entered, but there had just been that strange police officer. She tried to remember his name – Sandwich was it? Or Sandbank? But that didn't matter, she must have knocked herself out and now that she'd come round she was in a different place. She heard a noise from what she assumed was the bathroom, the door opened and the man she now knew was called Hopkins stood in front of her. Behind him there were pictures stuck to the painted wall above the tiles, and they were connected by red lines. It reminded her of the working walls you see on television crime shows.

'What's all that? Where am I?' She had brain fog and felt slightly sick.

'Never mind what that is, or where you are,' Hopkins said, closing the bathroom door. 'It's where you're going that you should be worried about.'

'I don't understand,' Paige said, rubbing her head. 'What is all this? Why have you brought me here? I'm nothing to you.'

Hopkins pushed her back onto the bed and leant over her. She sat up, pulled her legs towards her and backed away.

'Get away from me.'

The blow that struck across her mouth knocked her back down and Hopkins climbed onto the bed and straddled her. She pushed her body into the unforgiving mattress and kicked against it as she tried to get away. He grabbed and held each wrist above her head and she twisted her shoulders, desperately trying to break free. He leant in towards her.

'What's your name?' His face was inches above hers.

'Why?'

'Just tell me.'

'Get lost.'

'Tell me.' His voice was threatening. She felt his grip tighten and he pressed down onto her.

'No, I won't, until you get off me.' She squirmed under his weight and he laughed – a maniacal, humourless sound.

'You will, witch!' A shower of spittle sprayed onto her face and she closed her eyes. 'Tell me!'

'Go to hell.'

Hopkins snorted and pulled her hands down so that they were level with her waist. He knelt on each one so that she was pinned down by his weight. Pain shot through her wrists and she feared they might snap. She tried to raise her legs but he pushed his feet over them so that she was held down completely. He was heavy and she struggled to breathe.

'Say. Your. Name.'

She pursed her lips and shook her head.

He took each cheek in his large, sweaty hands and began to press his thumbs onto her eyes. The pressure sent everything black and she gasped.

'Say it!,' he shouted, and pressed even harder.

A kaleidoscopic light pattern swam in front of her and the pain became too much.

'Paige.'

'Louder.'

'Paige.' She trembled at the thought of what he might do to her.

'Paige what?'

'Just Paige.'

'I knew it! You conniving she-devil!'

He released his grip as suddenly as he had taken hold of her and climbed down. Paige kept her eyes closed for a moment until the grotesque patterns cleared. What the hell did he mean? She sat up and slid across the bed to its edge, but Hopkins was too quick and the blow that struck across her cheek sent her crashing to the floor. He grabbed her arm and roughly pulled her up. Moving behind, he put his arm across her throat and held her in a vice-like grip, pulling her backwards and into the bathroom. She struggled and tried to kick out, but he was too strong. She fought to breathe as he squeezed pressure onto her windpipe. Lack of oxygen was making her light-headed. She heard a chinking sound and sensed that her captor was doing something with his right hand while holding her with his left, but she couldn't see what it was. Then something cold and damp was clamped over her mouth and nose and held there. The smell was like ether and a droplet fell onto her throbbing lip where it mingled with the blood that was oozing into her mouth. The cocktail was sweet yet metallic. He changed his grip to under her arm and lifted her back into the bedroom. She tried to wrestle herself free, but her head began to swim and her legs felt heavy. Her whole world was closing in as he threw her onto the bed.

Chapter 38

Caravelli's, Present Day

Heart pounding, Florence pushed herself back against the door until it quietly clicked shut. The Hastings room appeared to be empty, and after looking behind the curtains and under the huge old bed, she turned her attention to the en suite bathroom. The door was closed. Florence moved across the carpet, her right hand instinctively going to her hip, but there was no gun holster and more significantly, no gun. God, she hated being on secondment. Her left hand fumbled in her jacket pocket for the extendable baton she kept with her. Very few people offered resistance when faced with a gun, but today the baton would just have to do.

Taking a deep breath Florence placed her hand on the door plate and pushed, flicking the baton out at the same time.

'Bloody hell!' she exclaimed. The bathroom was empty, but the walls were covered in photographs and pages full of lists; a make-do incident board full of faces and writing. Red pen lines traversed between the photographs in a myriad of patterns. Notes had been made beside and below them, the handwriting spider-like, scrawling along the wall.

Putting the baton under her arm, Florence stepped closer, her attention caught by one face.

'Well, this explains the do not disturb sign on your door, Mr Hopkins,' she muttered, looking at the huge blown-up picture of Fenella, which was placed centre stage above the bath. The word 'Witch' was written in green above the picture in large letters, and as Florence scanned the room this word appeared above another face. Stepping into the bath, Florence peered at a photograph of a young woman. Her face was familiar. There were four more pictures of this woman, one of which featured a man.

'Ah, now I know.' Florence laughed. 'That's the fit bloke you were sitting with earlier, but why the sodding and buggering hell are you up there on this wall?'

Turning abruptly and stepping back out of the bath, Florence looked around the room, her baton extended, and pointed at the pictures with the word 'Witch' above them.

'I suppose what I should be asking is why the word 'Witch' is branded above your head?'

To the right of the bath was a walk-in shower; the walls inside this were empty. The sink and toilet were on the left. Luckily for Hopkins the room was only half tiled, so more photographs could be stuck to the painted wall above.

'Well, my mum did always say you could never go wrong with a packet of Blu Tack in the drawer.'

There were lots of pictures of people in what looked to be the marketplace. It was difficult to tell, as the majority were extreme close-ups and the background out of focus. Huge photocopies of photographs dominated the space above the toilet with one single, small picture in the middle. It was of a young girl standing outside McDonald's and she appeared to be looking directly at the camera. The spidery-scrawl was in blue this time and identified the girl in the picture as Sally (homeless). The numbers 1993 were written next to her name and a big red X was underneath.

'Not the most flattering photos of us,' Florence muttered, catching sight of her own face in a different picture with

Sandbach, 'but at least my eyes are open.'

There was a brown-coloured bottle on the sink along with a pink cloth. Florence leant forward and sniffed the cloth. There was no smell but it was damp. Carefully, so as not to destroy any evidence, Florence touched the cloth and then licked her finger. A slightly sweet taste, not necessarily unpleasant, but not something you'd want pressed against your face.

Pulling her phone from her back pocket, Florence tapped recent, and then pressed call on Sandbach's number. Stepping through the door she scanned the room. A large leather-bound book was on the bedside table, and with the phone to her ear she read the title: The Discovery of Witches.

After six rings the phone switched to voicemail.

'For God's sake, man, answer your bloody phone – you really need to see this. I'm in Hopkins's room. There's no sight of any woman, but there's a book about witches, a bottle of chloroform and a damp cloth. Oh, and I'm looking at some weird shit that will totally backup your theory about witches, wizards and Hogwarts actually being a real school.'

Chapter 39

The Old Rectory, Present Day

'Where are we?'

Robert was distracted from the vision in front of him by his companion's question. 'The future,' he replied.

'We were already in the future before!' Robert felt Fox's urgent grip on his arm, demanding his attention. 'But that is not what I meant. I meant what location is this?'

'Why, the same location, just another time, isn't that right?' Robert turned away from the carriageway in front of them to seek corroboration from their new companions, but he and Fox were alone. The lychgate, which opened onto the church grounds, was behind them and the church itself was lit up so that it looked magnificent.

'How have they done that?' Robert asked, almost to himself.

'More to the point, where are those people, Wesley and Paige? They seem to have brought us here and abandoned us.'

Fox's words communicated outrage, but his tone wavered so that Robert could feel the panic underneath; a feeling that was also creeping up on him. Clearly the couple were not in front of them, or he would have seen them, Robert thought, so they must be in the church grounds. Robert started for the gate.

194

'Wait! Stay a moment!'

'What is it? They said they might be out of sight for a while, I think, but we need to find those two!'

'What if we go back through the gate and move again in time?'

That was indeed a good question.

'I do not believe that would happen. After all, people pass through here to worship regularly, presumably without mishap. It was something about those two that made it work.'

However, Fox's words had created a doubt, and Robert didn't feel he could risk moving to heaven knows where.

'Let us return to the rectory entrance, and gain access that way.'

They walked briskly along the paved walkway that bordered the high stone walls, as they had before. This time, Robert took in the housing on the left, which had clearly replaced the Shambles, the slums of his time. Even in the dusk of the evening the shapes of the trees on the other side of the wall could be made out, gently illuminated by the church lighting.

'There is an unnatural feeling about this place,' Fox commented as they reached the entrance to the rectory and peered into the gardens. 'If I did not believe that everything in our world could be explained, this sight might persuade me that supernatural powers do, indeed, exist.'

'This is not our world,' Robert remarked under his breath, but he didn't want to investigate those thoughts any further. They were able to gain access into the garden without too much trouble, but walking on the gravelled path had made quite a crunching sound. For some reason Robert felt they needed to be quiet.

'Let us move onto the grass,' he suggested.

Fox gave a shrug, and then followed as Robert stepped carefully towards the lawn. They made their way over the wet grass towards the old house. As they drew closer they could see a wavering beam of light, different from the glow of the church lights.

'What is that?' Fox asked. 'That beam is seeking us.'

'Shhh! More like who is that?' Robert replied in a whisper. 'Someone is searching for something.'

They crept towards the light. It was moving around the front of the building. They could see a man holding something from which the light emitted. He shone it over the doors and windows.

'He is trying to gain access,' whispered Fox.

That much was obvious. They held their breath as they watched the beam and the shadowy body moving for what seemed like several minutes. It seemed to Robert that Fox was as unsure of their next move as he was. Then there was a sudden rushing movement from the right. The light dropped to the ground. A figure picked it up and Robert heard Fox's gasp. In the glow from the beam both of them had seen a red-haired woman. The light went out.

'It cannot be her,' Fox whispered.

'It looked like her, did it not?' Robert responded. He was thinking rapidly. 'And she … she stopped time while we were watching didn't she? Twice, now! Is it so much of a jump, therefore, to think she could travel in time. But why is she here, and why now? Is she following us?'

'Maybe this is to do with why Wesley and Paige wanted us to come here.' Fox didn't wait for a response. He began striding to the location of the altercation. Robert followed. There was no one there.

'We did see them, did we not? That man with the light and the flame-haired woman?' Fox asked, looking around in the gloom.

'We did. But we cannot be surprised that they have disappeared. We have seen that before … though I wouldst like to know how they did it. And I, for one, want to know what is going on. It is as if you and I are on the fringe of a mystery. We see things but nothing becomes any clearer.'

'We have no choice but to go on, Robert, my boy.'

Robert felt Fox's hand on his back in a reassuring gesture. He was slightly startled by the use of his Christian name. Thus far Fox had been conventionally formal.

'We were making our way to the church grounds. Let us continue.' Robert led the way. Soon they had to climb over a stone wall like the one around the perimeter of the grounds, but lower. Then they were in the church yard, surrounded by gravestones and shrubs. It was brighter here, and they could see that the church was illuminated by boxes of light at ground level; the boxes were placed in among the bushes and the lights angled up the walls. They could see the lychgate ahead as they came around the side of the church. Both of them were avoiding the gravestones and walking on the grass at the side of the gravelled path when Robert heard a noise. A sort of groan.

'Did you hear that?' he whispered to Fox.

'It came from over there,' Fox said, indicating off to the right, towards the stones. 'It sounds like an unworldly being, and I have had enough of things I do not understand. Leave it be. Let us go forward.'

'Someone is hurt,' Robert said, the groans coming again. He darted sideways and spotted a body lying prone behind a large stone. As he watched, the person struggled to a sitting position.

'Wesley!' he gasped and ran forward.

Wesley put his hand to his head and Robert saw that it was covered in blood.

Chapter 40

The Old Rectory, Present Day

Sandbach returned to his bedroom, kicking himself for being so stupid.

'I don't know who that woman was, but Hopkins thinks she's important in all this. The thing is, I think he might have a different agenda to the one he is presenting to us,' Sandbach said aloud, staring out of his bedroom window at the dimly lit, empty street below.

'Well, duh,' Terrence replied. 'Smart move by the way – leaving her with the strange man.'

'Thank you, that really helps.'

Movement caught his eye and he could see a figure crossing the road away from him. Although Sandbach could only see the back of the figure below, he recognised Hopkins at once. He was alone.

Sandbach rushed back out of the room and down the stairs. He got to the back door and opened it as quietly as possible. He stepped out into the night and shut the door behind him. Hopkins had been heading in the direction of the road on the other side of the church. Sandbach jogged quickly but tried to keep the sound of his footsteps quiet. Reaching the corner, he slowed and made his way round carefully, keeping as close to the wall as possible. Hopkins was up ahead; he was walking at a reasonable pace but looking straight in front. Perfect. Sandbach began following at a similar speed. Until that is, the sound of a burglar alarm from a nearby building cut through the silence and echoed around the streets. Sandbach flinched and ducked down behind the wall and peered over. Hopkins turned around immediately. Sandbach couldn't see his face, but the body language suggested he didn't want to be found. Hopkins ran. Now that he no longer had the element of surprise, Sandbach chased after him as fast as possible. Hopkins sped past the church, past a metal gate to a new-looking building and then just as he got close to the end of the road, he turned right and darted through a gap in the stone wall.

Moments later, although it felt like longer, Sandbach arrived at the gap too. He stopped and tucked himself in tight against the wall. He waited and tried to listen for any sounds, something that might give away Hopkins's position. He could be just the other side, or he could be long gone over a fence on the far side or whatever this place was. There was no sound. Sandbach slowly peered around the corner of the building. There was a path leading through an open grass lawn to an old building at the other end. There were a few small bushes next to it, but no sign of Hopkins within the grounds. He'd probably disappeared through a gap in the fence up ahead. But maybe Hopkins was still here, in the building. Sandbach crept along the path, feeling vulnerable, exposed because he was out in the open. He reached what had looked like a door from a distance but turned out to be an archway into an open area with the ruined building. The place next to it looked solid enough and he heard something, possibly a door bumping on the far side of it. He crept closer. As much as he detested using guns or tasers, some kind of protection would have seemed like a good idea. Hopkins was clearly dangerous.

There was a faint noise just around the corner, the sound of movement on the gravel pathway. Sandbach took a deep breath and feeling ridiculous as he had no skill in hand-to-hand combat either, not even basic martial arts, he made his move. He jumped around the corner, arms raised ready to grab Hopkins, but there was no one there. The scent of apples hung in the air. He heard movement behind him, then felt the familiar melting sensation as the world fell away from him.

*

Sandbach woke with a jump; he opened his eyes and sat up but found himself blinking in complete darkness. He knew he was indoors as there was no breeze or cool night air. There was instead a familiar fusty smell. He pulled his mobile phone from his jacket and pressed a button, just enough to get it to switch on and let the screen light up his surroundings.

'Oh, you've got to be kidding me,' he said, standing up and immediately searching through the list of contacts on his phone. 'Not again.'

Terrence gave a chuckle. 'She's going to love you.'

Chapter 41

Caravelli's, Present Day

Paige knew she was conscious again, but although her eyes were open, she couldn't see a thing. The blackness was so complete that she thought she might have been blinded. Her mouth was filled with some kind of fabric and the tapes that sealed it were burning her painful cheeks. She felt nauseous and knew she was going to retch, but fought it back thinking that she might choke on her own vomit if she was sick. Her senses gradually returned and she realised that behind her was a cold wall. She could hardly move; her wrists were tied to her ankles so that she was forced to sit in an upright foetal position. Stretching out her middle finger she felt along the restraints – plastic, no wonder they hurt. Where the hell was she? And what the fuck was all that about her name? She listened. Nothing. The floor beneath her was hard and her bum hurt. She knew she had to do something so she leant sideways – her shoulder nudged a solid wall. She tried the other way – same thing. Rocking from one buttock to the other, she moved forward until her feet touched something solid. The bastard had gone and left her, probably to die, in this godforsaken crypt. Now what? She didn't even know where she was. She might still be in the hotel, but then again, Hopkins could have taken her somewhere else. Even if she was in the hotel he'd put the do not disturb sign on the door, so no one was likely to enter his room, if it was his room.

Well I can't just sit here and wait for you to come back, you gobshite, she thought, and moved a little further forward. Lifting her bound feet and hands together she dropped them against the solid barrier. It wasn't a wall – it sounded wooden, a door maybe? She raised her feet again and repeatedly hit whatever it was. Having her wrists strapped to her ankles helped her to lift them, but it was also excruciatingly painful as the plastic dug in. She stopped and tried to shout, but a muffled moan was all she could produce. She began repeatedly kicking out at the barrier again until the strength drained from her legs and she fought against the incredible sleepiness that was trying to envelope her once more.

Paige's energy slowly returned. Her shoulder was on fire, her face burnt and her wrists screamed with pain. She was shivering with both cold and fear and she began to cry. Gradually, anger and frustration welled up inside her. She screwed her eyes tight and shook her head to send the last remaining tears away. Once again she thought about her jailer.

Aaargh. Scumbag! You weasel-faced shit. Her opinions of Hopkins were interrupted as a clock struck in the distance. She listened more intently. Nine o'clock then – morning or afternoon? It sounded like a church clock so she was, most probably, still in the hotel. And then another sound came from the other side of the panelling that she had been kicking. Oh God, was it Hopkins? She sat still, trying not to shake with cold, and waited. After a minute or two she heard a woman's voice. Paige began to thump on the panelling with her bound feet again. That bloody lump of cloth in her mouth still prevented her from calling out, but she tried anyway.

Chapter 42

Caravelli's, Present Day

Ellen was in the back, waiting for an order when she heard the click she knew meant someone was using the door to the yard. No one used this way in, especially when the restaurant was open. She peered into the hallway and caught sight of some shadowy figures outside. Strange that they should use the back way, but then some people did like to slip out for a smoke.

'How long for table twelve's desserts?' she directed at the kitchen staff.

'Uno minuto, solamente.'

'Ok, pronto,' Ellen replied. She did a bit of the lingo. Italians were always saying pronto, they even answered the phone with it when calling fellow Italians. 'Pronto! Pronto!' Obviously not to customers though. Ellen picked up the plates from the pass – one in each hand. She pushed open the door with her bottom. Two men stood in the hallway, supporting a third between them. He had his hands on his head, and their arms were around him, helping him to walk. 'What's happened?' Ellen asked, her attention on the injured man. Wasn't he one of their customers? Table fourteen?

'He is somewhat confounded, Miss, having sustained a blow to the head.'

Ellen turned her eyes to the speaker as his choice of words diverted her concentration. She froze. The plates she was holding started shaking. Her heart was pounding and a rushing sound assaulted her ears. She swallowed hard. She had seen these men before – and they were looking surprised too. Both of them were staring at her and they were dressed in a fashion Ellen knew of old.

'It is you. The girl who caused us to be here,' said the one with the wide-brimmed hat clutched to his chest.

'You're ... you're, George Fox,' Ellen heard herself say. 'You were in the market speaking in 1663. Oh my God, I did it again!'

'Well, this is a situation,' commented his companion. 'We come looking for one person from the past and find another.'

The injured man looked up. His gaze moved from one to the other and Ellen could see the surprise on his face.

'You know each other?'

None of them answered him. 'I am Robert Hooke,' said the second supporter, making a little bow to Ellen.

'Robert Hooke, the scientist? Bloody hell. I don't believe it.'

'The very same. I assure you.'

The injured customer interrupted, muttering: 'You met in the past? Why didn't I know that?' Ellen ignored him. She was clutching at the plates, as if her life depended on it. She pushed open the door to the kitchen, and rested them back on the counter. As it swung back, closing them into the hall once more, she demanded: 'When did you get here? How did you get here?' Her mind was trying to come to terms with what she was seeing. Surely they would have arrived in the market? That's how it had worked for her; the time changed but the location stayed the same. They hadn't been touching her, so if they'd moved it could have been to any time. That had happened before when she was younger. But the place one moved to had always been the same.

Fox interrupted. 'Young lady, this gentleman needs our assistance.'

'I'm working,' Ellen said, stupidly. But she was involved. 'What can I do?'

'Would you fetch Miss Paige please? I think we have a situation that needs to be dealt with, and we'll need her.' The injured man stared at each of them. 'There is some explaining to be done here.'

'You're Mr Wesley, aren't you?' Ellen's query was answered with a nod. 'Won't be a mo.'

Ellen recovered the plates she had abandoned and carried them through to table twelve, placing them in front of the customers as she usually did, but without the friendly banter. Ignoring a request for attention from a nearby table, she glanced over to where Mr Wesley and his girlfriend had been sitting earlier, and confirmed what she'd thought – it was empty.

Back in the hall, Ellen's hands wrapped themselves inside her pinny, as she did her best to keep calm.

'I'm sorry, sir, but there's no one there.'

'What time is it?'

'Half-past nine, sir.'

'Where is she?'

'I don't know, sir, but you need to sit down and rest. Can I show you to our staff room and get you a drink of water or something?' Usually she would have called Massimo in straight away, but how could she? This whole situation was bizarre, and needed careful, discrete handling.

Fox and Hooke kept silent. Mr Wesley had a quizzical look on his face.

There was a moment of indecision, and then, although nothing specific happened, it felt to Ellen that they had all agreed. Before they could move they were disturbed by Izzy coming through for an order.

'What's going on, Ellen?' Izzy asked. Ellen could hear her

tone was overlaid with anxiety.

'Something's come up. You'll have to cover for me. I need to take these people upstairs to the staff room.'

'What can be that important? Can't you wait? We've almost finished our shift.'

'Please, Iz. It's to do with my past. I can't tell you anymore for the mo, except that I last saw these two in 1663.'

'You what? Don't talk daft.'

'I'm serious. Cover for me, please? There's two more desserts for table twelve to go out. I'll do those, and then disappear. OK?'

Ellen watched as Izzy sighed. 'OK. But I want the full story. All the details.' With that, she went back into the restaurant.

'She won't believe you,' Wesley said. 'Better to keep your own council.' Fox and Hooke were both nodding.

'I'm working, in case you hadn't noticed,' Ellen repeated. 'But if you go on upstairs and wait, in a few moments I'll take you to the staff room, where we can talk.'

Ellen pushed open the door to the kitchen and picked up the two remaining desserts for table twelve. Massimo was serving at the bar. She let the three men out of the corridor and watched them go up the stairs before taking the plates she was holding to the waiting customers, with an apology for the delay. She stopped at the table she'd ignored previously and with another apology, took their drinks order.

'Another two glasses of Amaretto to table thirteen, please,' she said, handing over the paper docket. Massimo took it with a nod. He didn't look at her; he was saying goodnight to some customers, who were just leaving. Ellen walked quickly towards the kitchen but turned up the stairs before she got to the door.

Chapter 43

Caravelli's, Present Day

Sliding her mobile back into her jeans pocket, Florence grabbed the doorknob and pulled. As it began to open the door creaked slightly, but not loud enough to muffle a thumping sound. Poking her head out of the door Florence listened. The corridor was lit by a night light and all the other doors were closed.

The thumping sounded again; this time accompanied by a low moan and was most definitely behind her. Florence held her breath and turned slowly, allowing her body to lean back against the door, pushing it closed with her bottom. Retrieving her baton from her jacket pocket, Florence looked around the room again. It was dominated by a huge fireplace in the middle of the far wall, two sideboards stood either side of this each of which had a large glass vase in the centre. Wood panelling covered the remaining walls halfway up, the otherwise intimidating dark brown softened by the pale walls above. Paintings framed in gold hung from the picture rail, depicting countryside life complete with streams, fields of green and blue skies.

The thumping sounded again. Florence moved along the wall, past the bathroom door and towards the fireplace. She stopped and listened. The sound seemed to be coming from the corner of the room, but Florence couldn't see any sign of anything disturbed.

Putting the baton onto the nearest sideboard, Florence stepped back and started to tap the wood panels from the side of the bathroom door, working her way towards the fireplace.

A long low moan accompanied one loud thump and Florence took two paces forward. The noise was definitely coming from behind the panelling to the right of the fireplace. Pressing and pushing she worked her way around the single panel. Suddenly, with a gentle creak, the panel moved and Florence could see that there was a hinge attached to the wall behind. With a gentle shove, she eased the panel to the left. A young woman was sitting in the very tight space between the panels and the wall, her hands and feet tied. Her mouth was gagged and her face was wet with tears, but it was the fear in her eyes that motivated Florence into action.

'It's okay, I'm going to get you out,' Florence said, dropping to her knees and taking hold of the corner of the tape covering the woman's mouth. With a quick yank she pulled.

'Maaawwww,' A stream of profanities filled the air. 'Bloody hell, you could have warned me.'

Florence reached into her jeans pocket and pulled out her penknife. 'I'm sorry, but in the end it's just a better way to do it. Now hold still and I'll cut these off you. Are you hurt? Is anything broken?' The battered girl shook her head. 'Come on then; let's get you out of there. I'm Florence Carter, by the way. And you are?'

"Paige.' Her voice was weak and croaky.

'Okay? Can you stand?'

Gently, Florence placed her hands under Paige's arms and started to lean backwards, allowing her body weight to pull her forward.

'I'm sorry, but my legs are numb. I need to sit down, but not here. What if he comes back?'

Florence wrapped her arm around Paige's back.

'Come on,' she said, ignoring the anxiety in Paige's voice and pointing at the door, 'let me help you. My room's just along the corridor.'

Allowing the other woman to lean heavily on her, Florence guided Paige towards the door, but as she did so Paige tripped and both women fell against the bedside table, knocking the lamp and books flying onto the floor. A thick cream folded piece of paper had been dislodged and was poking from between the leaves of The Discovery of Witches. Supporting Paige with her left hand, she reached down, pulled the folded sheet out and pushed it into her back pocket.

'Those big things will have to wait.' Florence winked at Paige, before opening the bedroom door.

Pulling her room key from her back pocket, Florence unlocked the door to her room and then helped Paige to the armchair. She watched as the other woman leant forward and rubbed both her ankles.

Crossing the room, Florence returned to the door and turned the key in the lock.

'Ah, don't worry,' she said in response to the frightened expression on Paige's face, 'It's only to keep us safe. We don't want him being able to just walk in if he finds you've escaped. Now, I'm taking it that Matthew Hopkins popped you behind the panelling and this isn't something else I've walked into?' She paused as Paige nodded. 'Good.' Walking over to the cupboard by the window, Florence bent and opened the door. 'I'm a police officer and have been working recently with DI Sandbach on a missing person's enquiry that started more than twenty-five years ago. Thank God – they've restocked the bar,' she exclaimed, retrieving two small bottles from the minibar with a flourish. 'Now, I'm a gin drinker myself, but I've always found in situations like this that brandy is the best option.'

'Yes, brandy would be fine, thank you.'

As Florence poured the drinks, sighing with relief to find a bottle of Fever Tree tonic water nestling in the door of the fridge, she could sense that Paige was watching her. As she passed the other woman her drink she met her inquisitive gaze.

'Have you found anything that would answer why he wanted me?' Paige asked, her hands clasped around the glass of brandy.

'The short answer is no,' Florence said as she took the other seat and sat down, 'and we may well be dealing with a case of mistaken identity, but I can tell you that this is a complex case. I'm going to phone Sandbach as I think he's gone off on some misguided mission, but first, are you okay?' Florence leant forward in the chair, 'I mean, he didn't hurt you,' and gestured towards Paige's face, 'other than what I can see, obviously?'

Florence watched as Paige looked around the room, before settling her gaze on the floor. 'I really thought he was going to, you know ... but he just wanted my name.'

'Your name?' Florence asked with a frown. 'What the bloody hell would he want with your name? How can a name be of any benefit to anyone?' Standing up, she pulled her phone from her pocket, 'I'll make that phone call and get Sandbach to come back here. There'll be statements to make and a load of questions for you, but in the meantime, sip that drink. You're safe now.'

*

The brandy was decidedly welcome and Paige wondered if there might be another one in the minibar. She looked down at the red, raw marks on her wrists; they burnt like hell. Florence had been gently questioning her about how she'd ended up in the priest's hole and, although some of the details remained fuzzy, most had been disclosed from when she'd followed Fenella upstairs, briefly seeing the other policeman, and the brutal way in which she was forced to tell Hopkins her name.

'I need the bathroom,' Paige said, 'and another brandy if there is one, please.' She pushed herself up and made her way across the room, entered the en suite and closed the door behind her. Her head was still muzzy from either chloroform or brandy. She turned on the taps and splashed her face with warm water. The face that looked back at her from the mirror above the sink made her gasp. Darkening patches framed her eyes and cheeks. She wiped a trickle of blood from her chin and winced when she caught her swollen lip.

'Are you okay in there?' Florence called.

Paige dried her face and went back to the bedroom.

'I'm fine, but I look as though I've done ten rounds with a cage fighter!'

'Perhaps you have.' Florence, Paige thought, was trying to make the situation less chilling. She gratefully accepted a second brandy and watched as Florence pulled the paper that she'd picked up in Matthew Hopkins's room from her pocket.

Paige took a sip of her drink, then closed her eyes and tipped the rest down her throat. She shook her head and opened her eyes again. The sight that met her made her nervous.

'Florence, are you all right?' she asked. The police officer's face was drained of colour. Her rescuer looked straight at her and then she, too, drained her second drink in one. Paige walked steadily over and stood slightly behind Florence so that she could read whatever it was that was unnerving her self-assured ally.

'It's a letter.' Paige's voice was low. 'Oh my —'

The two women stared at each other. 'So that's why he needed to know my name.' Paige felt sick. 'I've seen his father,' she said, 'back in 1933, he tried to take me then.'

'Take you?'

'Long story,' Paige said. The look on Florence's face was quite comical. 'I think Fenella might be in danger too – she's obviously the she-devil with flaming hair.'

'Oh, don't tell me, she was there in 1933 too.'

'Yes, and I think she helped to save me that night.'

'I need another drink,' Florence said, and moved towards the minibar.

'What was that noise?' Paige hissed.

'What noise?'

'Someone's outside.' She froze momentarily when she thought Hopkins might be returning, and then she recognised one of the voices. 'It's Wesley!' Paige rushed to the bedroom door, and before Florence could stop her had opened it and flung herself at Wesley.

'Ah, there you are,' he said.

'Yes, here I am,' she said, her head buried in his chest, 'and where the hell were you when I needed you?' She pulled away slightly.

'I was a little indisposed,' Wesley said, pointing to his bleeding brow.

'Indisposed? Indisposed? What the F—. ' Paige couldn't align her emotions; she was relieved to see him but incensed at his levity.

'Language, my love, we are in the presence of a man of God.' Paige stepped back; the two men behind Wesley looked a little embarrassed.

'Oh, what a surprise – you're involved too!'

Paige was suddenly aware of the floor coming up to meet her; her head spun and everything seemed surreal. She felt herself being scooped up and taken back into the bedroom.

'I'm sorry, you must have been through hell,' Wesley whispered in her ear, and she felt his gentle kiss on her cheek as he put her down on Florence's bed.

She closed her eyes and waited for the nausea to pass.

'Florence Carter,' Paige heard the police officer introduce herself, 'and you really need to see this.'

When the room finally stopped spinning, Paige pushed herself upright. Wesley was reading the letter that she and Florence had read earlier. His hand began to shake and he crumpled it.

'Did he do this?' Wesley asked, taking Paige's chin gently in his other hand. She nodded. Wesley stood up and flung the letter down on the bed next to Paige. 'I'm going to grab the bastard by the neck and see what happens when I squeeze hard,' he growled.

'We don't know where he's gone,' Paige said, 'but he'll be looking for me when he finds out I'm no longer his prisoner.'

'Then I'll find him and give him a good throttling,' Wesley promised, and flung open the bedroom door.

Chapter 44

Caravelli's, Present Day

Ellen saw, as she reached the top of the stairs, that the Despenser room's door was open. Wesley was standing in the doorway.

'That's not the staff room,' she said, trying to keep her voice level, 'it's a guest room booked to Florence Carter.' What were these people up to now?

'We have another situation,' Wesley told her – he looked angry.

'Another one?' Ellen asked, her voice betraying disbelief and irritation.

'I'm afraid so.' Wesley stood aside to let Ellen pass. She stepped around Fox, who was holding the door of the en suite open. She could see Hooke exploring the appliances.

'An indoors garderobe? Fascinating. What does this do?' Hooke pressed the button flush. Ellen suppressed a laugh as he jumped back with surprise at the water rushing down the pan.

'Ellen?'

Wesley's voice made her turn and she took in the other occupants of the room. Paige was sitting on the side of the bed with her head bent low, as if she was going to be sick. Florence Carter was kneeling beside her. Paige looked up.

'What's happened to your face?' Ellen gasped.

'It's a long story,' said Paige. 'I'll mend.'

'You'll be OK. We'll sort this.' Turning to the others in the room Florence said: 'Paige was shut up in some cubby hole by that bastard staying in the Hastings room. I found her and brought her here.'

'Shut up? Shut up where?' Ellen said, a sick feeling starting low down in her stomach.

'You really should go to the hospital for a check-up you know. We have to report this.'

'Who to?' Paige asked. 'You said Hopkins was police.'

'He is. Well sort of. He's working as a consultant with the police. But I can assure you there is more to Matthew Hopkins than meets the eye. He seems to be mixed up with something very strange,' Florence replied.

Ellen couldn't help herself – the words poured out: 'Matthew Hopkins! I think he's dangerous. He's got these pictures and books and things related to witches, and if he's anything like the original Matthew Hopkins you're lucky you got away. Where? Where did he shut you up? Was it in Hastings room? It wasn't in the priest's hole was it?' Ellen's heart was pounding and she realised she was gabbling. Everyone had stopped to stare at her.

'Yes, it was.' Florence spoke. 'And how do you know all this? What are you doing here anyway, and while we're at it ...' she stood up, 'who the buggering hell are those two you've brought in here, Wesley?

Fox pushed past Ellen. 'Matthew Hopkins is a very cruel man who preys on the fears of ordinary folk for his own ends. He says he is waging a war against witchery, but he acts contrary to the word of God,' he said, wiping his jacket, which was covered with droplets of water. Hooke came out of the bathroom shaking his hands dry.

'What a marvellous invention,' Hooke declared, before adding, 'but that was in our time.' He came to stand near Fox. 'Don't forget we are centuries ahead now.'

'They look like each other though,' Ellen mused out loud. She was glad they hadn't delved more into the priest's hole. She didn't want to explain how she knew about it.

'Hold on!' Florence was looking from face to face. 'Our time? What's this our time business?'

'Oh dear,' Paige murmured. 'Wesley?'

'Florence, you're a police officer,' Wesley began.

'Yes and my patience, and beliefs for that matter, have been sorely tested over the last two days with revelations about witches and that Harry Potter was based on a true story. So unless you are going to add some validity to any of that or give me some pieces of this bloody complicated jigsaw puzzle I've been tasked with ...'

Wesley coughed and continued. 'I rather think that we all might have some of the pieces you're looking for. If we could just calm down and talk we might sort something out.'

'I am calm,' Florence exclaimed. She spread her arms out before taking a deep breath. 'There, all calm, so please continue.'

'I can't stay long. In fact I should have gone already. I'm still supposed to be working,' Ellen reminded the roomful.

'OK, Ellen. How about you start by telling us how you know these gentlemen?' Wesley suggested.

Ellen stood in front of the window, and reached into her pocket. She took out her phone and turned it over and over in her hands. 'I don't know them personally. But I do know quite a bit about them both through my studies. I'm doing a history degree, specialising in the seventeenth century. It's all because of my phone, you see. I never understood how it worked, but every now and again it transported me to 1663, or back to the present day – and if someone was too near me when it happened they moved too. It's happened before. But I didn't know about these guys. I didn't know him, Mr Hooke, then,' she said. He nodded as she mentioned his name. 'But I was watching Mr Fox speak in the market the first time I came back. I took my phone out of my pocket without thinking, and that's when it happened.'

'Can I have a look at your phone, please?' asked Paige. 'This can't be allowed to happen again. You've no idea of the problems it causes when people start popping off to different times.'

'Oh, it wasn't this one. I haven't got it any more. At least I have, but it's packed away in a drawer at home. I upgraded a year or two ago, and I haven't touched it since.'

'Well, that's a relief. It'll need permanent decommissioning then.

Paige turned to Hooke and Fox. 'And what about you, gentlemen? What do you think of Ellen's story?'

Fox spoke: 'It was an act of God, a supernatural event.'

'There was certainly something unexplained about it, but it was probably no more supernatural than that garderobe,' Hooke chipped in. 'It was her, though. She was dressed like a maid and she was in the market as we were. Just before we found ourselves in 1993. She held a silver object up in front of her, and a pink light wrapped around us.'

Ellen felt relieved. She sat down on the dressing table stool, as Wesley took over.

'These things happen sometimes, and we have to step in to restore the balance. As Paige has pointed out, one ripple in time can cause others. Imagine throwing a stone into a pond; the ripples fan out – it's like that. One small seemingly innocuous act in one place can cause serious problems elsewhere. And we have some extremely significant problems to solve. I think you can go now, Ellen, but please keep this to yourself.'

Ellen stood up again. 'I will,' she said, but her eyes were on Florence. She'd been quiet while they were speaking but now Florence addressed them all, speaking slowly at first.

'So, now I'm supposed to believe I'm in a room full of sodding time travellers?' Florence stood up, her hands on her hips. 'I don't know about stones in ponds, but it seems there's some bloody huge ripples that need sorting. Please don't go far, Ellen, I will want to speak to you again.'

'Oh yes, I'll be here until eleven, I'm not on breakfasts.' Ellen turned to Paige and Wesley. 'I don't know who you really are, but I hope you can put things right.' Then she addressed Hooke and Fox. 'I'm sorry if I've caused you any trouble.'

Hooke stepped forward and bowed. 'Young lady,' he said, 'we have had an adventure. And I for one will not mind if it lasts a little longer, as long as we can go home eventually.'

Fox lifted his eyes to the ceiling. Ellen couldn't help herself – it seemed like the situation was under control and she was relieved to be out of there.

'I know what you mean – there's no place like home,' she said, and clicked her heels. With Florence's burst of laughter ringing in her ears, she smiled and ran back downstairs.

Chapter 45

Caravelli's, Present Day

Robert's eyes followed the young woman he now knew as Ellen as she left the room. At least now the cause of their moving across time was established, even if he still wasn't sure exactly how it had happened. He rather thought that no one was sure, but the communication device seemed responsible, and evidently this wasn't a usual purpose for it as they had all seemed surprised. So, time travel wasn't normal for people in the ... er ... what must be the twenty-first century, he assumed.

'Mr Hooke.' His name brought Robert to the present once more.

'Yes?' It was Wesley speaking to him.

'Mr Hooke, Mr Fox, come and sit down, we have some questions for you.'

'Er ... yes we do,' the woman called Florence added, with some authority.

Robert caught Fox's eyebrows raising as they crossed the room to sit on the couch where Wesley had indicated they should rest. Paige had been sitting on the bed, propped up by the pillows. She swung her legs down and sat upright as she spoke.

'Florence is a police officer. The police uphold the law in these times,' Wesley said.

'Is that work suitable for a woman?' The question left his lips before Robert could stop it.

'Fie, Mr Hooke! Both men and women should be able to do any job they feel they can turn their hand and mind to, in my view.'

'How very modern, Mr Fox,' remarked Florence. 'So, let's move on from the time-travel thing. You clearly both recognise the name Matthew Hopkins. I think we all know, now, that he appears to be something more than he pretends. What else can you tell us?'

Robert thought.

'We have seen his like before. I don't mean back in 1663. Obviously everybody knows about him then. Witch-hunting is a big thing and he is a powerful man.'

Fox nodded. 'A dangerous man. One little whisper can cast a doubt that has caused whole families to be tried as witches and put to death.'

Robert continued: 'We saw him in 1993. He was trying to abduct a young woman, but he was unsuccessful.'

Fox interrupted the story. 'It was the flame-haired woman who stopped time and made her disappear.'

'Hold on a moment—' Florence spoke. 'Stopped time? Flame-haired woman?'

Robert watched her catch the glances that flashed between Paige and Wesley.

'You knew about this?' she directed at them.

'Sort of, but I knew they had to come and tell you themselves,' said Wesley. 'It sounds implausible, but we all admit there is something extraordinary going on, and you need to hear what they have to say.'

Okay, I'll go with it, especially if the red-haired woman is involved, but no more time-travel stuff. Stick to the facts.'

'I am a scientist and facts are my business, mistress,' Robert told Florence, who sprayed some of her drink back into her glass.

'Mistress? Florence is fine. Facts are fine. Let's have them.'

'Pardon me, but I have to mention time. It is a fact that we have seen the red-haired woman stop time twice. Once, as we said, when Hopkins was trying to abduct a young woman named Sally. She whirled her tube thing above her head and everything around us froze. All the people and all the vehicles stopped. Then she tapped Sally on the head, and she disappeared.'

'Fenella made Sally disappear?' Florence asked.

'She did, madam. She told us she had sent her to a safe place,' Fox told her.

'It's Florence, please!' Florence turned to Paige and Wesley. 'That might explain how Sandbach ended up in the Green Man.'

'I think it's because they're out of time that Mr Fox and Mr Hooke were not affected.' Paige looked at Wesley.

'Quite possibly,' Wesley agreed. 'Fenella does seem to be trying to keep people from danger, doesn't she? What's her motive, I wonder?'

Robert watched Wesley, who was clearly pondering the question he'd just voiced, and then it dawned on him that he'd heard a familiar name.

'The Green Man – that's where we were the first time she did it!' The words burst from his mouth.

Florence challenged him: 'The Green Man? You were there? You couldn't have been. It's closed.'

'In 1993. It was in 1993 that we saw her,' Fox said.

Robert watched Florence open her mouth as if to speak again before closing it and slumping onto a chair. She took another deep draught from her glass.

Robert felt his neck tense and his heart beat hard as he took up the story. 'Yes, we were sitting at a table when she came through the throngs, and she whirled the tube thing around her head. Everything and everyone around us stopped still. Even the smoke in the atmosphere held its place. Fenella took some tubes from her bag and held them to the wall. She tapped them with one tube that she kept and they disappeared. They seemed to melt into the surface. It only took a moment or two and then she moved quickly towards the back entrance, and as she left everything came back to life.'

Fox took over. 'It was so quick. We couldn't believe it had happened like that until we saw her do it again.'

'Oh come on! For fuck's sake.' Florence got to her feet, placing her empty glass on the desk next to her. 'There isn't enough alcohol on the planet for me to deal with this shit.'

'That's very useful,' Wesley confirmed to Robert. He turned to Florence and Paige. 'It's vital that Matthew Hopkins doesn't learn this information. Nothing of this must be told to anyone outside these four walls.'

'I'll have to tell Sandbach,' Florence said, pulling her phone from her pocket again.

That was the second time this Sandbach had been mentioned. Who was he? Robert had to ask.

'Who is this Sandbach person?'

'My colleague. Another police officer. He was keeping an eye on Matthew Hopkins. He's been gone a while —'

Fox interrupted. 'We haven't said what we saw at the steeple house.'

'The steeple house? Do you mean the church?' Paige said.

'Well, we didn't understand what we were seeing at first, but it seems someone was using a light to search the grounds of the church and the rectory,' Robert told them. 'It was only a moment, but we both saw red hair as the light fell. When we got to that point no one was there.'

'She can't have got him again, can she?' asked Florence.

'Again?' Wesley questioned.

'Yes, again. Sandbach believed that Fenella sent him into

the Green Man and I thought he was nuts, but how else could he have got in there? The silly sod was trapped and I had to call the fire brigade to get him out.'

At that moment there was a ringing sound from Florence's communication device and Robert watched as she placed it to her ear.

'Sandbach —' Florence paused and Robert saw her frown deepen before her mouth opened in shock. 'Okay, I'm on my way.'

'Right,' Florence addressed the room, 'Sandbach is indeed back in The Green Man and I've got to go.'

Chapter 46

Caravelli's, Present Day

'The Green Man?' Paige said, 'the basement bar that's all closed up?'

'That's the one,' Florence replied, shrugging on her coat.

'How the hell did he get down there?'

'I think,' Wesley said, as he moved around the room, 'it's something to do with Fenella again, the potions woman, and the papers that those two were talking about.' He pointed to Fox and Hooke. Paige saw Hooke open his mouth to speak, but close it again when Wesley continued. 'Let me get this straight. You,' he pointed to Florence, 'are investigating cold cases, and it seems that the missing persons might have been moved by Fenella, probably for their own safety. You two,' he pointed to Fox and Hooke, 'saw Fenella push something into a wall in the same Green Man, but in 1993. We can assume that the items she hid were pages, which Hopkins is looking for. This Hopkins character already has at least one page.' He looked at Florence for confirmation. She nodded. Wesley continued: 'He then took you, Paige, as he thinks you are crucial to him. And now, your DI Sandbach,' he turned to Florence, 'is underground, again, in the Green Man.'

'Well, that about sums it up,' said Paige. 'Now what? And

why are you rubbing your arm?'

Wesley pulled his hand away and turned to Fox and Hooke. He looked pensive.

'It's your tattoo, isn't it?' Paige persisted, 'is it changing?'

Wesley nodded and turned to Fox and Hooke.

'We came here in order to return you to 1663, so I shall need to work out how to do that as soon as possible. If this fades ...'

Paige looked at the two gentlemen who were out of their time. They looked fearful. Wesley continued: 'In the meantime, wait here, and stay out of trouble.'

'You can do it,' Paige said to Wesley, and she stuffed the letter that Wesley had flung onto the bed into her pocket and pulled a pink-and-maroon, checked throw-over from the bed. The painkillers Florence had given to her earlier had kicked in and she was feeling much better, even though her wrists were still sore. She caught Wesley's quizzical look.

'Going on a picnic, are we?'

'No,' Paige said, emphatically. 'It's cold out there and I haven't got a coat.' She wrapped the throw cape-like around her shoulders, and headed to the door. 'Come on then,' she said, and ushered Florence and Wesley out of the room. She turned to Fox and Hooke, who had moved to follow.

'He said stay put,' she told them. 'Wait here for Wesley and he'll take you home – and don't answer the door.' She pulled the bedroom door behind her shut and hung the do not disturb sign on the outer handle.

Chapter 47

The Old Rectory, Present Day

Ellen zipped her coat and lifted the straps of her neat leather backpack over her shoulders. She grasped both the black bags, which were twisted at the neck, and manoeuvred open the back door with her foot; she usually got rid of the rubbish bags on her way home. It was gloomy out here. The only light came from the small lamp over the back door and the distant street light. As she lifted the dustbin lid and launched the first bag she heard the door open again. She recognised the emerging shadowy figures instantly. It was that police officer, Florence, with the slightly strange couple, Paige and Wesley.

'Are you sure those two will be OK in your room?' she heard Paige ask Florence.

'As safe as they will be anywhere, I suppose. We don't have much choice. You have to find Fenella and Hopkins and I can't leave Sandbach stranded in that old dump, but God knows who I'm going to be able to find to help at this time of night,' Florence answered.

'He must have been looking for something important over in the old rectory for her to have got him again.' It was Wesley speaking. 'Something has given her power, though.'

'I don't want to believe it but it has to be these papers or pages, or whatever they are. Sandbach told me that Hopkins performed some kind of trick in the police station where he set a page of some kind of mysterious medieval writing alight and then it reformed, but I just dismissed it as fanciful rubbish.'

Ellen watched Paige catch Florence's arm as she stopped speaking.

'Yes, it has to do with pages. That's why he wanted me. Paige. Don't you see? I don't know why I am linked with antique writings, but the idiot seems to believe I am.'

Ellen threw in the second bag and replaced the bin lid with a clatter, turning as the three came closer.

'Ellen, is that you?' Florence called over to her.

'Yes. I was just putting the rubbish out before I went home. I couldn't help overhearing you. Sergeant Sandbach is in trouble?'

'It's Detective Inspector Sandbach actually, but yes, he is. We're going to find him now.'

'But you were saying something about the rectory and some medieval writing?'

Wesley answered: 'Why would that interest you?'

'Well, I lived at the rectory in 1663 for a while, and since I've been back I've kept close to here, and there, just in case ...'

'In case?' Florence asked.

'In case she got to go back,' Paige told her. Turning to Ellen she continued: 'That's obvious. But there's something else, isn't there?'

Ellen shuffled her feet on the path. She hated to admit that she'd taken more than a passing interest in guests' possessions. She looked up and Paige was looking straight at her. Something about the look in her eyes gave Ellen confidence. 'When I was cleaning Mr Hopkins's room he had all kinds of books and things lying about. One of the books was open and I knew I'd seen something like the writing in it before.'

'You had? Where?' Wesley asked.

'There's a page just like it hanging in a frame on the wall of the upstairs room in the old rectory, the one that was my bedroom while I was there, and now it has all kinds of artefacts and information in it.'

She watched the glances that flitted between the three of them.

'Another page? What are the chances that this is one they've both missed so far?' Florence asked, her lip curling slightly.

'Well, your friend Sandbach seemed to think there was something worth searching for fairly urgently only a matter of hours ago,' Wesley countered.

'He's not my friend ... well, I suppose he might be now.' For a moment everyone paused.

'It's worth checking out, surely?' Paige's voice broke the silence and her face showed her concern. 'What if we do that, Wesley, while Florence raises the alarm, or whatever you do to get someone over to the Green Man? It shouldn't take long. Ellen can show us, can't you, Ellen?'

'I suppose so,' Ellen said hesitantly. It was late. Did she really want to get involved with these people?

'There is the slight problem of getting in,' Wesley said, 'I have many talents but breaking and entering isn't one of them.'

Ellen looked at the three of them. They were serious that there was something wrong. Florence was the police, and that Matthew Hopkins ... he was dangerous and seemed to have links with the past. That was important to her.

'Actually, that isn't a problem,' Ellen said, swinging her backpack around and digging into it, her mind made up. She held up a large brass key.

'You're a dark horse,' Florence said with a snort of laughter.

'I'm a member of Loughborough's Archaeological and Historical Society and I take turns to open up and staff the museum.'

'But what about the alarm?'

'I have the code.'

'Well, that's it then – we have a plan. You get off and I'll get my end sorted.' Florence took her phone from her pocket and started pressing numbers.

Wesley kissed Paige on the cheek and offered both her and Ellen an arm each. The three of them left Florence and turned the corner out of the yard, walking briskly across the road towards the old rectory.

*

They stood in the gloom of the museum just by a table opposite the door that Ellen had closed behind them. She took out her phone and fiddled with it so that it emitted a small bright beam.

'I don't want to switch on the lights and alert anyone to the fact that we're here.'

'Absolutely, so where is it, this page?' Wesley asked.

'Upstairs.' Ellen indicated the wooden staircase in the corner over to the left. She led the way. There were all kinds of framed pictures and documents on the walls of the room, which was stuffed with tables and desks around the walls as well as in the middle. These were also covered with books and other artefacts. At the top of the stairs they separated and went either side of the tables to opposite sides of the room. Wesley ran his fingers over a number of the items on display. He picked up the receiver of a mid-sixties telephone.

'Would you look at this, Paige?' he whispered.

'Put that down —'

'The picture's over here,' Ellen interrupted. She was used to the eclectic mixture on display.

Wesley caught up. 'Oh yes. Yes, that looks about right.'

'I reckon that's spot on,' Paige added.

They looked intently at the framed page's curly writing, its first letter large and illuminated.

Ellen spoke: 'It's definitely medieval. It doesn't fit here, but then quite a few things don't seem to, so I've never questioned it before.'

Wesley reached up and took the frame off the wall. A strange expression appeared on his face. He tipped it towards him to get a look at the illustration. Then he let go and looked at his fingers.

'What's the matter?' Ellen asked him.

'Well, it's not so much the illustration itself, but how it made me feel. A buzzing sensation started in my fingers and moved out across my body. I felt powerful. It's still there, not as intense, but I can feel it.'

Ellen reached out and touched the picture, something she hadn't done before. She'd only photographed it on her original visit, five years ago.

'My fingers are tingling,' she said, looking down at them.

'We'd better wrap the thing up,' Paige said and pulled the makeshift shawl from her shoulders. She held it out to Wesley and he took it, although it seemed to her that he didn't really want to, and wrapped the frame.

'For goodness' sake, give it to me,' Paige said, taking the package and tucking it under her arm. 'This thing certainly has some power. Come on, let's get out of here.' They all headed back down the stairs.

Ellen pulled the heavy door to and locked it. She dropped the key into her coat pocket and turned as Wesley spoke.

'Right, I need to get Fox and Hooke back or they'll be stuck here forever. I'll see you back at home, my love.' He kissed Paige, turned and strode away.

'I'd better get over to the Green Man then as quickly as possible,' Paige said as they watched him head towards the gate.

At her words, Paige was enveloped in a low pink light. Ellen registered the surprise on her face and she stepped back in shock. She watched the frame slip from its covering and fall from Paige's grip. It landed on one corner with a sharp crack. The glass broke and shards fell over the path as the frame fell backwards and lay face down. It had been several years since she'd seen that pink light, the light that had moved her into the past, and now her companion was no longer with her. Paige was gone.

Chapter 48

The Green Man, Present Day

Inside the Green Man, the interior looked much the same as it had before; dirty and abandoned. As soon as Sandbach had realised where he was, he'd made the call to Carter to come and rescue him – again. Since then he'd been sitting at the bar going over the notes in his pocketbook.

'Handy that someone left a light on for you, isn't it?' Terrence piped up.

'Yes, isn't it just,' Sandbach replied, absent-mindedly.

Instead of being plunged into total darkness again, when he arrived this time, he'd found a candle burning in a wine glass, illuminating the abandoned pub. This was a bit of a mystery, but after a quick check of the premises he decided that whoever had lit the candle had departed. And to be fair, much stranger things had been happening over the last couple of days, so he wasn't going to worry too much about one candle. He'd keep an eye out for someone if they returned, but for the time being he felt fairly safe, albeit trapped.

'So, who do you think left the candle burning?' Terrence asked, continuing the subject.

'I don't know for sure, but I'd guess it was Hopkins, could be the crazy hippy woman I suppose, but my money would be on

Hopkins,' Sandbach replied.

'You think that's his style, do you?'

'Does it have to be anyone's style? If you want light in an abandoned pub with no windows, surely you look for whatever you can that will provide light?'

'But if Hopkins chose to come here, he would surely have been prepared and brought something like a torch or a lantern, at the very least something that doesn't burn up what remaining oxygen there is in this sealed up drinking establishment.'

'What's your point?' Sandbach asked, knowing full well that it was a very good point.

'You'd only do something like this if you were stuck and couldn't get out. And had to use what was to hand.'

But the point had been made. Sandbach tucked his notebook back into his jacket pocket.

'OK, who else is in here?'

There were soft footsteps from the far end of the pub. Sandbach spun round to see the familiar flame-haired troublemaker, last seen in his room at Caravelli's.

'Who are you talking to?' Fenella asked. 'I assumed you were on the phone to someone. Are you using a hands-free thingamajig?'

Sandbach looked at her puzzled for a moment, but with a glance at Terrence – now sitting on the bar wagging his tail – he understood.

'Yes, that's right. But they've gone now,' he said with a glare at the little dog. Terrence shrugged and began to lick himself. 'Thanks for that image.'

'What?' Fenella said.

'So, how did you get here?' Sandbach asked, quickly changing the subject.

'Presumably the same way you did,' she replied indignantly, 'which I assume means you no longer have the page.'

'The page?' This was starting to make some sense, but

Sandbach thought he would play ignorant. After all, it wasn't far from the truth.

'The thing inside the leather tube,' she said, rolling her eyes at him. 'I assumed you had figured out what it was by now. Presumably my expectations were too high. You are a policeman after all, a representative of the law, so naturally thick as pig shit.'

'Happy to disappoint,' Sandbach replied. 'So tell me more about this page. I assume we're talking about one of the missing pages from the Codex Gigas, or Devil's Bible?'

'I ... yes,' Fenella said, looking lost for words.

'Not all of us eat doughnuts and drink coffee all day, some of us are quite partial to a bacon sandwich too.' Fenella looked at him as if he had just messed himself. 'Anyway, Matthew Hopkins had shown me, and my colleagues back at the station, a page that had ... unusual properties, shall we say. I believe he showed us only what he wanted to share, leaving out some important details about the pages, and more importantly, his purpose with them.'

'So what are you going to do now?' Fenella asked.

'Good question,' said Terrence with a chuckle. 'What are you going to do now? It's not like you've got Hopkins cornered is it? You don't even know where he is.'

'Good point, but I don't think that matters right at the moment,' Sandbach replied.

'What point? I asked you —'

'It's true I don't know where he is now,' Sandbach said, cutting her off. 'I assumed he would have sent me somewhere that I couldn't get in the way of his plans. But you're here.'

'So?' Fenella replied.

'So whatever's going on here, you're a key part of it all. Hopkins doesn't seem to like you very much.'

'No shit, Sherlock,' Terrence butted in.

'But he needs you,' Sandbach continued.

'Ha!' Fenella laughed coldly.

'I could tell from the way he described you back at the station. His insistence that your interference was damaging, and that you'd stolen pages from this bible. He was keen to paint you as the criminal mastermind.'

'And what makes you think I'm not?' she replied.

'Because you carry all your important belongings with you in that big hold-all bag, because you don't have anywhere safer to keep them. And because you don't seem to be working with anyone else. I think you are all alone and you don't trust anyone.'

'Well, I guess that shows you're not much of a detective then, doesn't it?' she replied, acidly. But she had paused awkwardly before speaking and avoided eye contact with him. Sandbach smiled and nodded sympathetically.

'Oh, piss off!' she yelled and stormed off, back to the other end of the pub. Obviously she couldn't go too far away.

'Nicely handled,' Terrence said with a grin.

'Actually, that went better than I expected,' Sandbach replied under his breath. 'I don't suppose we can get a cup of tea down here. I'm guessing the water will be off, and the electrics. So even if we could find a kettle, it wouldn't be much use.' He leant over the bar to see what refreshments were available. Not a lot it seemed. 'I should have asked Carter to bring a flask or something when she comes to rescue us.'

'Perhaps some doughnuts too,' Terrence added.

'Now you're just being silly. Where is Carter anyway? She said she was on her way.'

There was a noise coming from the ceiling near the lift shafts, followed by light shining down onto him.

'I'm looking for a detective,' Carter's voice called down from the hatch in the ceiling. 'One who's daft enough to get locked in an abandoned pub, twice.'

'That'll be me,' Sandbach replied cheerily. 'Don't suppose

you've brought anything to drink, have you?'

'What?'

'Never mind.'

'Not you, hang on.'

There was some muffled talking as the hatch was partially closed, followed by light again. Carter began climbing down the steps leading from the hatch.

'Thank you, no I'll be all right. Just stay there please,' she called backup before reaching the bottom and jumping off the last step.

'You needn't have come down,' Sandbach said. 'Now that the hatch is open, we can just climb up.'

'We?' Carter looked at him with a puzzled expression.

'I wasn't on my own this time, she who is to be known as Fenella was already here.'

'Fantastic. We think there's important evidence down here and she's just the person to help us find it.'

'What evidence?' Sandbach asked.

'The pages of course,' Terrence added.

'Oh, the pages,' Sandbach repeated.

'Yes. There's reason to believe the missing pages are down here somewhere, or at least some of them. Fenella was seen hiding them here.'

'Ha!' Fenella cackled from the back of the pub, she walked out into the open. 'Acting on new evidence, are you?' she asked in a mocking voice.

'Yes, actually,' Carter replied.

Sandbach looked at her, questioningly.

'Long story,' she muttered, shaking her head.

Carter walked over to join Sandbach and Fenella.

'So, do we know where these pages are?' Sandbach asked, glancing back and forth between Carter and Fenella.

'I was hoping she could help us,' Carter said, looking at Fenella.

'Help?' Fenella exclaimed. 'Help? That's exactly what I've been doing all these years. The pages have been hidden for a long time and with good reason.'

'I think this is a matter for the police to decide now,' Carter said, calmly. 'Don't you think?'

'You don't get it do you?' Fenella shouted, 'who do you have working with you? Hopkins! The devil himself. The very man I've been trying to avoid for so long. He's the last person you want to take possession of these pages, believe me.'

'Well he's not here now,' Carter said.

'But he soon will be. He's the one who sent me here, isn't that right, Detective?' she said to Sandbach.

'She's got you there,' Terrence said, pacing up and down the bar. 'You know it's just a matter of time before he turns up. We should leave.'

'Fenella's right,' Sandbach said, feeling suddenly impatient. 'Hopkins must know the pages are here, but presumably he can't get them without help. Which is why I'm guessing he sent you here,' he said, looking at Fenella. 'You're the key to this aren't you? For the time being, we need to get you out of here. Carter, can you escort Fenella back to the police station, I'll wait for Hopkins to arrive and then we can talk.'

'Do you really think you can take him on?' Carter asked. 'No offence, but you're hardly a bodybuilder.'

'I can talk my way out of most situations,' Sandbach replied, not feeling entirely convinced. 'But probably best to call for backup, if you don't mind.'

Carter nodded then turned to Fenella. 'Come on then, let's get you out of here.'

Fenella followed Carter back to the steps and Carter gestured up to the hatch in the ceiling, signalling for Fenella to go first. Fenella shrugged and did just that.

'Do you want me to stay?' Carter asked, looking worriedly at Sandbach.

Sandbach shook his head.

'My hero,' Terrence muttered.

Carter nodded and began to climb.

Chapter 49

The Green Man, Present Day

Paige landed with a bump.

'Ouch.' She stood up and rubbed her knees. 'Where the hell am I now?' she said, but there was no one to hear. Wherever she was it was cold and she flung the makeshift shawl around her shoulders once more. The space she was in, although dark, looked vaguely familiar. She sniffed; it smelled musty and damp. Light was seeping under a door a few steps away and she walked towards it.

The door creaked as Paige pushed it open, and a swish of movement revealed Detective Inspector Sandbach; he spun round to face her.

'You're not Hopkins.' Sandbach was frowning.

'No, thank goodness,' replied Paige. 'So this is what the Green Man looks like now.'

'Paige!' It was Florence – she was halfway up a ladder. 'What are you doing here? More to the point, how are you here?'

'Ah. I can't explain right now.' Paige eyed Fenella, who had also climbed the ladder and was hanging on just below the hatch opening.

'Oh yes, she's very clever. Can we go now?' Fenella sounded impatient and was leaning down.

'Hang on a minute,' Florence said, jumping from the bottom rungs. She ran over to Paige. 'Are you all right? Look we all need to get out of here. Sandbach is going to wait for Hopkins.'

'That's right,' Sandbach confirmed.

'He'll kill you.' Paige turned to Sandbach who nodded to the floor.

'That's a good point.' Then he looked up and announced to the room: 'You know what? Perhaps we should all head back to the station. Let's get some backup and deal with this properly.'

'What a good idea,' Florence said, sarcastically.

'Brilliant,' Fenella piped up, just as a small orange flash lit the room. 'Let's go.'

'Let's not,' a familiar male voice said. Paige felt her stomach lurch and her mouth felt as if she was biting on cotton wool balls. 'How about we all stay and get to know each other better.' Paige turned to see the sneering face of Matthew Hopkins. Now they were in trouble.

'Come and join the party, Fenella. I insist.' Hopkins was gloating. He pulled a mobile phone from his pocket and held it to his ear, never taking his eyes off those around him. His head jerked upwards a shade. 'Sterne. Is everything taken care of? Good. Close up.' He put the phone back in his pocket and the hatch above the ladder slammed into place, directly over Fenella's head. She visibly jumped and nearly fell off the ladder. Paige shivered as the room became gloomy, lit only by the flickering candlelight. It was as if the temperature had dropped twenty degrees.

'I never thanked you properly for this, by the way.' Paige saw Hopkins waving a leather tube in Fenella's direction. 'It's made life a lot easier since I acquired it. And you, Detective Inspector,' he said as he turned to look at Sandbach, 'your incompetence has been most appreciated.'

Paige could see that Sandbach was uncomfortable. She watched him shuffle his feet and what she imagined was an embarrassed smile flitted across his face.

'I want the rest of the pages, Fenella,' Hopkins demanded.

'Well you can't have them.' Paige heard the retort and watched as Fenella worked her way down the ladder and stepped onto the pub floor, crossing her arms and challenging him with her glare.

'I could burn you where you stand, witch', Hopkins said through gritted teeth. It would be no more than you deserve.'

Paige gasped as Fenella taunted back: 'Do it then. And you'll never see the pages.' They were as bad as each other. This was getting dangerous; more dangerous than being incarcerated in that bloody priest's hole.

Hopkins took a step toward Fenella. Sandbach had moved; he was clearly trying to intervene, his arms raised in an effort to calm both of them down. At least someone was trying to defuse the situation, although Paige wasn't confident that he had what it would take.

'How about we try and work this out between us, then no one needs to get burnt,' she heard Sandbach say.

'What?' Hopkins said, stepping closer.

'If you set fire to anyone then we all die from smoke inhalation and suffocation. Not the nicest way to go,' Sandbach told him.

Hopkins simply waved one of the leather tubes in the air.

'Good point. You can go wherever you want with that, I suppose,' Sandbach conceded.

'I repeat, give me the pages, Fenella.' Hopkins's voice sounded loud and strident.

Fenella straightened herself, flicked back a tress of copper hair and lifted her chin. She stepped forward. Paige felt a frisson of concern; Fenella looked a little too confident given the situation. She held her breath as Fenella moved determinedly and stopped right in front of Hopkins, looking him up and down.

A smile appeared on her face and Paige caught a swift movement. Fenella brought her knee up sharply between Hopkins's legs and he crumpled into a heap on the floor, clutching himself and moaning.

'And what exactly are you going to do about it? Send me here again?' Fenella sounded triumphant.

Hopkins, still lying awkwardly, reached across to his bag, which was on the floor next to him, and brought out a different leather tube. To Paige it looked identical to the one he held in his other hand, except for the symbol near the end, which clearly meant something. Hopkins darted forward and quickly jabbed at Fenella with the tube, striking her on the ankle.

Paige reeled back in horror as Fenella burst into flames and fell to the floor, screaming.

Florence was looking frantically around the pub and shouting.

'Fire extinguisher! Now!'

Sandbach immediately started searching. Paige pulled off the makeshift cape from around her shoulders and threw it over Fenella, rolling her on the ground.

Hopkins laughed at their frenzied efforts as he pulled himself up to a sitting position against the bar. 'It won't do any good,' he sneered.

Paige patted the lying form all over. She could hear Fenella whimpering, and felt her writhing in pain underneath the cloth. She pulled back the edge but flames burst out and Fenella started her terrible screaming again.

'Stop it!' Paige shouted at Hopkins. 'You need her. You said so yourself!'

Hopkins shrugged, got to his feet slowly and walked over to the writhing mass on the ground. He tapped the bundle of fabric with the tube. The screaming stopped. Paige pulled the cover away to reveal Fenella, a shaken and terrified look on her face, but otherwise completely unharmed. No sign of burns or blackened skin.

'That's the page you showed me at the station, isn't it? Inside that tube.' Sandbach spoke, breaking the momentary silence.

'It is, indeed.' Hopkins held the tube defensively in front of him like a weapon.

Florence made a move; Paige thought she was going to confront him, but Sandbach held up a hand to stop her.

'But you showed me this page burning up then reforming, not setting fire to things by itself,' Sandbach said.

'The pages have many properties, I showed you just one of them.'

'So what do the other pages do?' Paige said.

'Good question.' Sandbach was looking at the ground, then he looked up at Hopkins. 'What do the other pages do? And why?'

Paige looked around the room at the faces of the people there. It was clear that they were all somehow connected, but how? Florence obviously wasn't going to keep quiet any longer.

'Sandbach and I have been led on this bizarre trail, looking for missing pages and missing people, and you seem to have done quite well out of it, Hopkins.' She looked from Fenella to Hopkins and then at Paige. 'And now Paige and her other half have been thrown into the mix. It's about time you told us what the hell is going on?'

'I thought I had made myself quite clear. I simply want the missing pages. This witch has the pages and I want her to give them to me,' Hopkins stated quite firmly.

'Or what? You'll kill her?' Florence challenged.

'No, she'll die anyway, but I can make it quick and painless or she can burn the slow torturous death of a witch.'

'You're mental,' Florence said, shaking her head.

The room suddenly felt a little hotter and less comfortable. Paige was unnerved, but also unsurprised by

Hopkins' lack of deceit or attempt to hide his violent intentions. She found her voice.

'Can't we find a reasonable solution? If you get what you want then surely no one needs to come to harm?' she asked Hopkins.

'She will die,' he replied flatly. 'But you can all go first, if I need to encourage her to give me what I want.'

'Burn them,' Fenella said. 'I don't care. I'll never give you the pages.'

'No,' slipped from Paige's mouth at the same time as Florence spoke.

'You're fucking joking me!'

'I'm afraid I am deadly serious,' Hopkins said, with that leering smile Paige had seen before. 'I can do away with the detective here,' Hopkins waved the tube towards Sandbach. As he was speaking Paige could see Fenella struggling to get to her feet. She stood and folded her arms in defiance.

'Or her.' He pointed the tube in his right hand at Fenella, and then suddenly swung it to point at Paige. He lunged.

'No!' Florence shouted, as Paige felt the most excruciating pain as her leg burst into flame. She threw herself to the floor and rolled. Shrieks filled the room and she knew that this time they were her own. Through the haze of agony she saw Florence grab the pile of material from the ground and run towards her.

'Stay back or you'll burn too,' Hopkins yelled.

Florence ignored him and charged as if intending to go through Hopkins to get to Paige, but Hopkins took a deft sidestep. Paige flinched as she watched Hopkins strike Florence, who fell to the ground. The smell and sound of Paige's own body burning filled her nose making her cough and retch. One minute she was in interminable agony and the next the pain had vanished and with it the flames. She shook her head and looked up. Hopkins stood beside her with a tube in his hand.

'I can be reasonable, if you give me what I want,' she heard him say.

'Okay, okay. You win, I'll give you the pages. You don't need to burn anyone again,' Fenella told him, and Paige momentarily closed her eyes in relief as Florence crawled over and sat down next to her.

Hopkins smiled and nodded. 'Where are they?' he demanded.

'They're already here.'

'No, they're not. I've checked every inch of this building, using traditional methods and some not so traditional ones.'

'They are here, they're just ... out of time with us.'

'And what does that mean exactly?' Hopkins looked as if he was running out of what little patience he had. Paige shivered and Florence squeezed her arm.

Fenella moved her glance from one to another, without speaking. Paige knew what she was eventually going to say. Of course! Fox and Hooke had told them they'd seen Fenella hiding papers in the Green Man in 1993. They must only be available then.

Fenella continued: 'The pages are here in the Green Man, but removed from the usual flow of time.'

Florence looked at Paige, and a mirthless laugh escaped her lips. She, too, had clearly realised the implications.

Sandbach looked nonplussed. He opened his mouth as if to ask a question, but Fenella got in first.

'They no longer exist in the present time,' she confirmed.

'Unless you can go back to 1993, when the pub closed, you're out of luck,' Florence taunted. Paige wished she hadn't said that.

'Oh yes, this miserable establishment closed on the seventh of March that year, I believe,' Hopkins mused. 'Good.' He leered and nodded. Opening the leather tube, he took out the page that had been inside it and then carefully placed the tube back into his bag. He then took the other tube and did the same. Holding the two pages together, one hand on top and one underneath, he began to mutter something quietly under his breath.

'No,' Paige whispered.

'Stop!' Fenella screamed at Hopkins.

'What is he doing?' Sandbach shouted to everyone in the room.

'He's combining powers,' Fenella warned.

'To do what?' Florence asked, but Paige knew. She braced herself. Nothing was going to stop the muttering and she was sure that some of the letters and illustrations on the pages were moving. She gulped as a small green circle lit up on the front of the top page, quickly followed by the corresponding green circle illuminating the underside of the second page.

'This can't end well,' Paige directed at Hopkins.

'It certainly won't end well for the witch!' Hopkins spat towards Fenella, before returning to his quiet chanting. He twisted the two pages in a circular fashion, turning one in the opposite direction to the other. For a moment the two circles flashed red. Paige felt a deep thud reverberate around the underground pub and it shook the ground, causing dizziness and ringing in her ears. She felt sick with the knowledge of what he was doing. Where the hell was Wesley when she needed him? Then they were all plunged into darkness.

Chapter 50

The Green Man, 1993

Sandbach blinked and looked around the room to get his bearings. Shielding his eyes from the brightness, he could make out the others doing the same. Something wasn't right. Sandbach was hit with the smell of beer and cigarettes. The floor was carpeted, the lights were on and there were cushions on the seating areas.

'OK, how did you do that?' Carter asked suspiciously. 'Where are we?'

'A better question would be, when are we?' Hopkins replied, a satisfied smile on his face.

'Yeah right,' Carter said with a half-laugh.

A clock on the wall, that hadn't been there before, showed it was nearly half-past one. Without windows it was hard to tell whether that was early in the morning or afternoon. But Sandbach guessed that early morning would be less likely to meet any interruption.

'Bring me those pages, you witch!' Hopkins said, with an alarming look of excitement.

Fenella shook her head. Sandbach wasn't sure if her expression was one of panic or defiance. He watched Carter and Paige; they were just on the other side of Hopkins, but thankfully

Hopkins' attention was still fully on Fenella. Paige crept towards the doorway. Sandbach was puzzled at first; there was no door out of the pub, as far as he was aware, but Paige nodded to him, then over at Hopkins. Sandbach shrugged silently, trying not to draw attention to himself.

'For goodness' sake,' Terrence muttered, 'she wants you to distract Hopkins.'

'He seems fairly distracted already,' Sandbach replied.

Hopkins sighed. 'Look, you have no further use here, Detective Sandbach,' he said, sounding rather annoyed. 'I'll have to find some unpleasant way to dispose of you if you can't shut up.'

'Sorry,' Sandbach whispered, a little over dramatised for some reason. He wasn't sure why he'd done that. 'Don't mind me, I'll just sit here quietly.'

'Please do so,' Hopkins said, turning his attention back to Fenella.

'I won't say a word,' Sandbach added. 'Not a sausage.'

Terrence rolled his eyes, looking thoroughly embarrassed.

Hopkins turned to Sandbach, his jaw pushed forward and lips pursed in annoyance. Meanwhile, Paige had clearly wasted no time in taking the opportunity to make a move. She crept purposefully towards the door. Hopkins' angry expression changed to one of puzzlement as he stared back at Sandbach. Then a moment of realisation crossed his face before he spun round and stared at Paige.

'Not so fast, my dear. I need you to stay if you don't mind,' Hopkins said in an even but clearly agitated tone.

He whipped another leather tube out of his bag, pulled out the page within and let the empty tube fall to the floor. He tucked the topmost page he'd been holding under his arm and rested the new one on top of the remaining one, in a clearly practiced movement. He began to mutter and chant under his breath, not taking his eyes off Paige for a moment. Sandbach was about to stand up and think about whether now was a good time to be heroic; it had never suited him previously and he had to admit it was probably a large factor in why he was still alive today. Before he could move a muscle, Hopkins turned and glared at him, as if sensing his thinking. Sandbach thought better of acting now and decided to wait. He raised his hands slightly as if to say 'I'm not going to do anything'. Hopkins turned his attention back to Paige. In the time he'd looked away she'd reached the door at the foot of the old entrance and quickly pulled it open to allow warm daylight to pour into the room, clearly not from directly outside, as they were technically still in a basement. Blue light shone from between the pages Hopkins held. With a twist of the pages, there was a gust of hot air that pushed everyone backwards. Sandbach felt briefly disorientated and had to shake his head to re-focus on what was happening. The light from the doorway seemed to be moving away – not like the door closing, but as if it had been pushed backwards until it was gone, leaving a solid, featureless wall.

Sandbach watched as Paige regained her bearings and fumbled with the wall, clearly trying to find the missing door.

'Oh, now that's a cool trick,' Terrence exclaimed. 'Make her do it again.'

Sandbach nodded in appreciation of the architectural change Hopkins had just made to the pub. It did, however, prove that Hopkins was more dangerous than Sandbach had initially suspected. It was hard to tell how much of what he was seeing was illusion, or possibly magic. Whatever it was, Sandbach was not comfortable with Hopkins having these abilities. Who knows what he could do if he were to get hold of the other pages? The ones he was so eager to acquire.

Paige looked initially panicked by the disappearance of their means of escape, but was quickly forced to give up, so she shook her head and then turned and glared at Hopkins. Carter walked over to her and Hopkins turned his attention back to Fenella.

'The date is no longer an issue. You have nowhere to run to, nowhere to hide. I will kill you and those in this room here if you do not do as I ask,' Hopkins said. 'Give me the pages'

Fenella sighed. Her shoulders slumped in resignation, she walked towards the toilet door, but stopped just outside. Hopkins looked uneasy and seemed about to object but didn't. Fenella removed a lightweight scarf she wore around her neck, straightened it, then lifted one end to reveal an all-too-familiar-looking leather tube, which couldn't possibly have been hidden within the delicate scarf. Not in any normal way at least.

'Ooh, sneaky,' Terrence muttered. Sandbach nodded.

Fenella glanced back at Hopkins with a resentful glare, then removed the top of the tube and pulled out a page. She unfurled it then ran her fingers over the paper, tracing an unseen pattern.

'If this is a trick ...' Hopkins said, anxiously.

'Oh, shut up,' Fenella said and began to mutter something under her breath, while holding the page. A pale blue light shimmered from it, so that it looked like a small blue pond in her hands. It was hard to explain exactly what had happened, but Sandbach could swear something was different about the room they were in, something ethereal. Fenella stopped her muttering and reached her hand towards the wall next to the toilet door, but instead of hitting the solid surface, her hand passed straight through it. When she brought it back out again, she was holding yet another leather tube.

'Sandbach, make yourself useful and collect both pages from the witch, then bring them to me.'

Sandbach rolled his eyes. He would like to have told Hopkins where he could stick the pages but thought better of it, so he went to Fenella and she reluctantly handed him the pages, both of them returned to their respective leather tubes.

Sandbach hesitated before taking them, as if they were snakes about to bite. Although the idea seemed ridiculous to Sandbach, he was sure this would all be much simpler if they were nothing more than snakes. He took hold of the tubes gingerly and then turned to take them to Hopkins.

'And the rest, witch.' Hopkins demanded.

She reached into the wall again and pulled out another, then another, but on spotting a particular runic symbol on the end of one tube, she quickly slid that one into her scarf, which seemed to evaporate into thin air as she did so, before reaching back into the wall to pull out more. She glanced up at Sandbach quickly, but with enough severity to leave him in no doubt that this was a deliberate move and he ought to say nothing. She pulled out another three tubes and placed all of them in Sandbach's hands.

'Bring them all here,' Hopkins said, sounding impatient.

Sandbach saw Fenella put her hands behind her back, presumably to hide the other page. He handed the leather tubes to Hopkins, who took them with a greedy smile. As he held them his expression changed to one of strange calmness.

'You now have all the pages I know of.' Fenella looked resigned.

'Not quite,' Hopkins said, with a sly smile that conveyed menace. 'Hand over the one you have hidden behind you.' Sandbach took the last tube from Fenella and handed it to Hopkins, who then riffled through the leather tubes until he came to one that caught his attention. He quickly pulled out the page, then took one of the ones he'd been using earlier. The rest he stuffed back into his shoulder bag and threw it over his arm.

'What exactly are you going to do with all those?' Carter asked.

'Stay where you are. All of you,' Hopkins replied, looking more agitated.

He held two pages together, traced lines over patterns

and again muttered incomprehensible words. There was a fiery orange glow from between the pages. Hopkins wandered over to Paige and Carter.

'Move away, Constable,' Hopkins said, glaring at Carter.

Carter looked annoyed but did as she was asked. Paige began to follow her.

'Not you, my dear, you're going to stay exactly where you are.'

'No!' Fenella protested. 'You don't need her.'

'What are you doing?' Carter demanded.

'I ... I,' Hopkins stammered, angrily. 'I have true power at my fingertips, and I am a hair's breadth from ultimate power. This goes way beyond anything your tiny mind can possibly comprehend. Step back or I will remove you from existence. Is that clear enough for you to understand?'

'You have the pages, you do not need her,' Fenella repeated.

Carter took a step towards Hopkins, but he quickly pulled out a leather tube from the bag, presumably containing the page that would burn whoever it touched.

'I said get back!'

Florence gave an apologetic shrug to Paige as she did what she was told. Hopkins continued his muttering, which seemed to go on for some time, while the others in the room looked at each other uneasily. Finally, Hopkins stopped. He looked up from the pages with a wry smile. A small orange light appeared on the floor, which expanded to create a line; it continued in a wide arc, perhaps ten feet in diameter, eventually encircling Hopkins and Paige within. It remained lit and seemed to flicker slightly as if hot coals had burnt through from just under the surface.

'It's on the ceiling too,' Terrence muttered.

Sandbach had been vaguely aware of a glow from above, but looking up he saw an orange circle, the same diameter and position but directly above the other, suggesting that the two might be connected somehow.

'Don't do this,' Fenella pleaded softly to Hopkins.

'You cannot stop me now, witch!' he replied. 'Of course, I saw through your pathetic trick in no time. Flaunting her right in front of me, the final page, you must have thought you were so clever.'

'What's he talking about?' Carter asked.

'You have it all wrong,' Fenella pleaded.

'Do I? The book tells of one who can defy the laws of time, who is connected to magic and who will ultimately become one with the book. I know, now, that the book speaks of her, of Paige; the final missing page.'

He turned to Paige, who began to back away from him.

'I don't think so,' Paige replied, looking at him with disgust.

She backed into the edge of the circle and there was a flash of orange light. She screamed in pain, but Hopkins just laughed and returned to the leather tubes.

'Finally, I have them all.'

'OK, I'm confused,' Terrence said. He had remained sitting on the bar next to Sandbach. 'Why does he think Paige is the tenth page?'

'I really don't know, but I think we can be sure she isn't,' Sandbach replied.

'So what's he going to do?'

Sandbach shrugged. He didn't know where this was all going, but something was definitely wrong.

Hopkins sat himself on the ground eagerly, like a child about to tuck into a pile of sweets. He began ripping open the leather tubes and stacking the pages and discarding the tubes to his left without looking, or noticeably counting. On his right, Paige stood clutching her arm, with a terrified expression on her face. She was standing as far away from him as she could, which in the confines of the circle wasn't far. Hopkins removed all the pages, then began sifting through them, reordering them until they were in a neat stack.

'All but the last one, which of course is you, my dear,' Hopkins said with an unpleasant smile.

'Look, you mental bastard,' Paige said, looking wild with fear and anger. 'I'm not one of your weird pages. Let me out of here!' She shrieked the last words at him.

Hopkins smiled, then sifted through the sheets in front of him and pulled out one from near the bottom of the pile. He placed the other pages neatly on the ground on his other side, then began to mutter incoherent words, while tracing lines on the one he held. A yellow spark jumped out of it and into his finger. He then leant across and touched Paige on the leg. She yelped, as if he'd just poked her with something sharp, but then her face and posture relaxed. She didn't look afraid anymore, but she didn't look happy either. She simply looked vacant.

'Why don't you sit down,' Hopkins said, calmly.

Paige did as he suggested without a moment's hesitation.

'In fact, why don't you hold these pages for me. Then you will all be together.'

Paige held out her arms and Hopkins added the page to the stack and then placed them all into her upturned hands. She did nothing more than keep them from falling onto the floor. Hopkins began to chant more clearly. It looked as if he was concentrating hard. He placed both hands on top of the pages and was tracing different shapes and lines with each hand. At first nothing happened, but he repeated the words again and again, tracing the same patterns with meticulous precision. A glow came from somewhere within the stack of pages. It was like a kaleidoscope of colours that shone outwards. Sandbach felt mesmerised. He knew in the back of his mind that something bad must be taking place, but he couldn't take his eyes off the light. He couldn't move either. Hopkins finished his chant, then slapped both hands down onto the pages. There was a flash and lines began to draw themselves on the floor outside the circle, straight lines. They formed points, five points in fact. Then letters or symbols began to draw themselves in and around the lines.

'Ah, of course,' Sandbach said, feeling his stomach turn. 'The old pentagram on the floor thing.'

'Let her go!' Fenella pleaded again. 'Please.'

'I could take my time to work with these pages, but I have studied them for years, I feel like I know them so well already. So, I will skip to the good bit – immortality!'

Hopkins placed the stacked pages on the floor and knelt over them. He looked ready to give this his full attention. Paige remained motionless to the side of the circle.

'Once I begin this incantation, I cannot stop,' Hopkins said, to himself as much as anyone else. 'You will witness power like nothing you have ever seen.'

'It won't work!' Fenella shouted.

Hopkins rolled his eyes then pulled one of the pages out from the stack, performed an incantation, then pointed at Fenella.

'Silence,' he commanded.

Immediately Fenella fell quiet. Her mouth still moved, but the only sound she made was the hint of a whisper. Hopkins nodded in satisfaction, then stacked the pages as before. He took a deep breath and began to chant. Both hands moved purposefully across the pages, the motions looking practiced and confident. A light began to flicker from between the pages in multiple colours at first, but they quickly changed to a brilliant white. Hopkins' movements became quicker and more frantic looking, but he still seemed to be in control. The ground shook for a moment and there was a deep rumbling sound. Sandbach held on to the bar behind him for support. The pentagram glowed brighter and brighter. The circle within it glowed brighter too.

'What's he doing?' Carter asked.

'Performing some kind of incantation, something about immortality, he said,' Sandbach replied, feeling powerless to do anything about it. 'I have a feeling something's not right here, beyond the magic fire and stuff, obviously.'

'Well something's going to happen,' Terrence chipped in.

'I think you might be right,' Sandbach said, feeling worried.

'Can't we just get Paige out of there?' Carter asked.

'How? You saw how she got burnt when she tried to leave before,' Sandbach said. 'Anything more could kill her.'

Fenella turned to Sandbach and the others. 'Take care of her,' she mouthed. Making a supreme effort she managed to rasp 'The fool has started something that cannot be stopped. And now it must be seen through to the end,' just loud enough for Sandbach to catch her words.

She turned and walked towards Hopkins and Paige, trapped inside the pentagram. Hopkins seemed completely detached from what was going on.

Fenella began to mouth words that appeared to be a chant. She reached the pentagram and stopped, but continued chanting. Hopkins still paid her no attention.

There was a low rumbling sound all around them and the room shook slightly. It grew stronger as Fenella's chanting got louder; a grass-green glow seeped from the carpet bag she always seemed to have with her, and clung to her dark green dress surrounding her, protecting her, as she moved through the fire and into the pentagram. She pointed directly at Paige, then uttered the last few words of her spell. There was a viridescent shimmer to the room, which lasted a couple of seconds. Not much, just enough to indicate that something had happened. Sandbach thought he smelt the sharp tang of apples. He blinked to re-focus on the scene in front of him, checking to see if Paige was all right, but she was no longer next to Hopkins. She was now standing outside the ring of fire at the point where Fenella had entered. Paige turned around on the spot, as if to get her bearings, then stared at Fenella.

'Why?' she asked.

Fenella did not reply and turned to Hopkins, who had watched the recent developments with a distant look on his face. His amber eyes glowed with triumph as he spoke.

'It was you, all the time. You were the guardian of the pages, the one with power, the green woman aligned with the green man. You are the final page.'

Fenella simply glared at him, a look of generations of hatred in her eyes, concentrated into one moment. Hopkins took hold of Fenella's arm and placed his other hand on top of the stack in front of him. He closed his eyes. As he did this, a flash of white light blinded Sandbach, which was followed by a deafening thud that pushed him backwards and he fell and landed on the hard-concrete floor. Sandbach's ears rang from the noise, and he was completely disorientated. He felt suddenly alone and afraid. He quickly looked around. The circle of light was still where it had been, and the others in the room were where they had been, although they too were now either lying on the ground or getting up again. But something was very wrong; the walls were gone. They'd not been knocked down or broken, as far as he could see, they were simply not there. Nothing was. The floor around him went on in all directions around the circle. The ceiling was still where it had been, presumably at the same height, but now that the space around them was so vast, the ceiling felt oppressively close.

'What the hell just happened?' Carter asked.

'I don't know,' Sandbach replied.

'But the walls?'

'I ... I don't know.'

Hopkins held his arms in the air, a maniacal grin on his face. 'I've done it!' he shouted to the empty space around them.

'I've done what no one else has managed. Now grant me your gift.'

As Hopkins stood waiting for his answer, Sandbach was aware of the deafening silence in the empty darkness around them, pressing in on them despite the lack of walls.

There was a deep boom, so low and unnaturally powerful it gave Sandbach a headache instantly. Judging by people's reactions as he looked around, the others must have felt the same. Although perhaps worse for Fenella and Hopkins who looked to be in real pain. Fenella covered her ears and there was a thin dark line descending from her hand. As she moved, she smeared what looked like blood across the side of her cheek. Then the same could be seen from Hopkins, whose nose now also appeared to be bleeding. He seemed to tighten up suddenly, then looked around the room, past Sandbach and the others, clearly not looking at them.

'But I have brought the pages together, spoken the words and performed the rites as prescribed.' Hopkins spoke boldly but sounded like a frightened child. 'Please, I beg you, grant me immortality.'

His words sounded oddly phrased, as if he were speaking to someone present but unseen. Hopkins waited, his mouth hanging open.

'But I have studied your book for years,' Hopkins continued, 'the centuries of knowledge passed on for generations. Surely I —'

He stopped, as if cut off mid-sentence, but it seemed to be a fairly one-sided conversation to Sandbach.

'I command that you grant me immortality!' Hopkins shouted. 'I deserve this.'

Hopkins recoiled and cowered at what must have been his received answer.

'No, this is all wrong,' Hopkins seemed to be pleading, 'I understood that to mean —'

The pages stacked in his hands seemed to shake then flap as if in a breeze. One by one each page flew out of his hands and swirled around both Hopkins and Fenella, flying in circles, each following the previous one in some bizarre pre-set flight pattern. The pages picked up speed, travelling so fast they looked as if they would dice anything in their path.

'Fenella!' Paige called out, seemingly out of general concern as no one could be sure what was actually happening.

After only a few seconds the pages began to slow and then stopped dead. It wasn't until enough of them had stopped flying that Sandbach could see they were landing in a small pile in Fenella's outstretched hands. The last page landed, and it was only then that Sandbach realised Hopkins was no longer standing next to Fenella, in fact he was nowhere to be seen at all.

Sandbach glanced at the others in the room. Given the similar looks on their faces, clearly, they were all seeing the same thing.

'Okay, Fenella,' Sandbach called out tentatively. 'Can you move? Can you step away from the ...'

There was a sound of wind picking up all around them. The air pressure seemed to be increasing. Sandbach swallowed but it didn't help his headache. By now it was getting painful to his ears, so he covered them with the palms of his hands. The wind swelled to a gale force blast, then suddenly an orange flame appeared, momentarily, in front of them, he couldn't tell where exactly. Then everything stopped – silent and still. In an instant the pressure was gone, his ears popped – quite painfully – but his headache was gone. He let go of his ears and shook his head trying to make the room sound normal again, but they were in complete darkness. A bright light appeared from the side of the room, wobbling and moving erratically. It was the light from someone's mobile phone. It shone around the room and illuminated the fact that they were back in the Green Man pub, as it should look in present day. Damp and stained walls and furniture, that familiar musty smell, but there was now a burnt smell too. There was smoke in the air.

Sandbach took his mobile phone from his jacket and switched the torch facility on himself, which took longer than he would have liked given his unfamiliarity with this fancy technology. The smoke seemed to be coming from the point in the room where Hopkins and Fenella had been standing.

'Is everyone all right?' Carter asked, getting to her feet. 'Paige, are you okay? Are you hurt?'

'I'm fine,' she replied, waving Carter away. Paige ran over to Fenella who was lying on the ground, on top of a burnt area of floor, where the circle and pentagram shape had been previously.

'Are you all right, sir?' Carter asked Sandbach. 'You look like shit and you didn't even do anything.'

'Thank you, Carter,' Sandbach replied, getting slowly to his feet. 'So what exactly are we left with now? Where's Hopkins?'

Fenella stirred and began to lift herself up. Paige helped her.

Sandbach walked over holding his hands out, offering to help her up, but Fenella batted him away.

'Can you tell me where Hopkins has gone?' Sandbach asked.

'He's ... still here,' Fenella replied, sounding breathless and exhausted.

Paige looked panicked, her eyes darting around the room.

'Don't worry,' Fenella said with a tired smile. Possibly the first time Sandbach had seen her smile. 'He's right here.'

She held out a large flat, very old-looking book. It had a dark red, leather-bound cover. Its appearance very solid and important, but with not many pages inside.

'What? That's not that famous old book we've all been

hearing about is it?' Sandbach asked hopefully 'The Codex —'

'No,' Fenella snapped at him.

'Well the book wasn't here before,' Carter replied. 'So, it must be new,'

'This is clearly an ancient book of some sort, Carter, so it can't be new.'

'Florence is correct,' Fenella said, forcing the words out. 'The pages are indeed very old, Detective, apart from one, but the book itself did not exist before today.'

'OK, but where is Matthew Hopkins?' Sandbach repeated impatiently.

Fenella pulled open the cover of the book to reveal the first page. It looked like very old material; velum if that's what it was. It seemed to be a cover page rather than the other pages, with lots of text and illustrations on it. In fact, this one had no text at all, only a single illustration of some kind of demon.

'Matthew Hopkins will live forever – as the guardian of this book, and in this place, locked in time.'

Paige pushed her way past Sandbach and stared closely at the picture. She moved closer, turned the book sideways one way then the next, then moved her face in closer to examine it in detail. She'd been nose-to-nose with it for nearly ten seconds before she yelped. She almost jumped backwards across the room.

'That picture!' she exclaimed. 'The eyes moved – I saw it.' She dropped the book back down onto the floor.

'Shut up!' Carter exclaimed, then moved in close and picked up the book. She too stared closely at the picture. She recoiled, presumably having seen something similar. She held the book out for Sandbach to see. He leant in close. There was the grotesque looking demon illustration; something did indeed look familiar, but he couldn't quite put his finger on what. Then he noticed the eyes move. They darted quickly about, then blinked. 'Oh my God, that's disgusting.' Carter passed the book to

Sandbach, who then placed it on the bar and dusted off his hands.

'What's that?' Terrence asked, nodding towards a piece of paper near his feet. Sandbach leant down and picked it up. It looked like normal paper, not the yellowed velum of the book.

'It's the letter!' Paige was tapping her pockets. 'It must have fallen out when ...' Sandbach opened it and read it out.

My dear son,

Like my father, and his forefathers, we must rid the world of witches. The Codex Gigas is the only way to ensure this. I believe that ten pages have been removed and with each one a soul has to be traded for its return. We know that the scribe of this tome traded his soul to the Prince of Darkness so that he could complete the book in one night. You need to find the missing pages and trade them for the souls of the innocent. I tried in the past and succeeded in finding some, only to be thwarted by the she-devil with flaming hair who stole them all but one. I now entrust this task to you, Matthew. Find the Devil's Book, find all the pages, burn the witch and you will have the reward of immortality.

Your father,
Matthew Hopkins.

Epilogues

Hooke

Robert watched as his friend picked up the small cup of hot watery chocolate and poured it into a larger vessel full of steaming milk, as he had just done.

'Where did you get this idea from? The serving girl thought you had lost your senses,' Hall told him, copying the stirring actions that Robert had made. Robert smiled at the sight of the now light-chocolate coloured liquid. He brought it to his lips and sipped.

'It's almost as good as I remember,' he said. 'It's an idea I got on one of my visits to other parts. Everyone will be drinking it like this in the future. You'll see.'

'Well, it's very good.'

'I'd like to meet that Fox fellow. He seemed interesting. Do you know where I might find him?'

There had been a moment of disorientation when he'd got back. Hall had steadied him, and asked if he was taken ill, but his attention had still been on the passing charavaris. Robert hadn't been able to answer at first; he had been busy watching Fox as he spoke to a distraught young woman. It was Jayne, he realised. The girl who had been working with Ellen in Hall's house. Of course she had lost sight of her friend. Ellen had disappeared, hadn't she? And he now knew where to. Fox had obviously understood the situation more quickly than Robert had himself. Fox had leant down to her from the box he was standing on and Robert heard him say: 'God has taken care of her, but I know you will see her again.' Jayne had looked into Fox's compelling eyes and taken a deep breath. She'd nodded and moved away with what had seemed to Robert to be admirable composure.

'I thought science was your first love. I did not know you were taken with fanciful religious ideas, my boy,' Hall told him after a pause while he drained his cup. 'He's staying with that rake, Bromskill, if you are determined.'

'I am, Hall. I am. I'll call on him later. I'm open to all sorts of ideas. I think it's vital to keep an open mind. That's the path to the future.'

Ellen

Yes, she knew what the pink light meant. Paige had moved. And it was occurring to her that she had probably moved to the Green Man, because that's what she had requested. Now Ellen thought about it, every time she'd seen the pink light in the past, she'd moved to where she had wanted to go. The picture was the key. It had to be. She turned it over, removing the points of glass that were left hanging in the frame. She picked up the remaining pieces. Whatever this document was, it must have transferred its powers to her phone all those years ago when she photographed it. If it did what she supposed then she might be able to go where she wanted, when she wanted. An excitement was building in her, moving from the pit of her stomach and spreading out across her limbs.

'Oh. My. Days!' The words fell out of her mouth before both hands clamped themselves over it to shut out any more escaping sounds. Her whole body was trembling, but she knew she had to move. To make a decision.

Ellen picked up the manuscript, registering the tingly feeling as she touched it. She could feel the power emanating from it as she examined the frame. It wasn't too damaged. A little bit of sellotape would hold the corner together. She collected the glass shards and wrapped them in her jumper before stowing them in her backpack. She'd have to dispose of the bits in a bin away from the museum. Then she scuffed at the splinters left in the gravel to spread them and disguise what had happened. Ellen used her keys once more to open the Old Rectory Museum and quickly took the picture frame back upstairs. She used some Sellotape to affect a quick repair.

Placing the frame back on the wall, covering the blank space it had left, Ellen stood back. Yes, no one would know anything had occurred. But she knew where the power had come from to go back in time, and she knew that the photo of it on her phone was as good as the original. Back downstairs, she locked the door and walked down the path thinking of the people she'd met briefly and hoping they, too, would resolve their problems. She wondered if she'd ever know. Anyway, even though she was going to be late home the adventure had been worth it, because now who knew what the future, or the past might hold for her!

Paige and Wesley

Paige walked along Albert Place, the March wind propelling her and teasing her hair into knotted ribbons. She pulled the checkered throw more tightly around her shoulders and sniffed at the warming wool. It didn't smell of smoke, as she had thought it might, but of apples. She smiled and quickened her pace, hoping that Wesley had lit the fire – her hands and toes were numb with cold.

'I'm back,' she called, taking off her coat and shoes. No reply. She pushed open the oak door into their sitting room and was pleased to see flames licking the chimney-breast. She walked over and stood in front of the fire to warm her frozen fingers. Closing her eyes she soaked up the warmth and felt Wesley's arms wrap around her waist. He kissed the back of her neck and beneath her ear.

'I assume you took those two safely back to, when was it?'

'Yes, normal service is resumed in 1663 – and I did close the gate firmly behind me.' He kissed the back of her neck again. 'You smell nice, sort of apples and ...'

'And smoke? Fusty old basement? Stale beer?'

'No. Why would you smell like that?'

'Because I was in the Green Man; that page from the museum sent me there, but didn't end up there with me.'

'Go on.' Wesley rested his chin on her head.

'Well, Hopkins thought he had all the pages and that I was the tenth, but he hadn't as there's still the one at the Old Rectory. So his plan for immortality failed and he's trapped inside the book of nine pages that will remain in the Green Man forever.'

'Serves him right.' He kissed her under her left ear.

She spun round and was about to kiss him back when something caught her eye.

'What the hell is that?' Paige pointed to the far side of the room.

'That's my chair,' Wesley said, and moved to sit in it.

'Your chair? It's awful – ugly old thing.'

Wesley looked affronted.

'It's not staying,' she said, 'it's frightful.'

'But it's mine,' Wesley countered.

'What do you mean, it's yours?'

'It had my name on it.'

'You're talking nonsense. Show me where.'

'Well, it hasn't now; I took the label off.'

'Where's it from?'

'The Old Rectory Museum. It was upstairs in there and the label said: Wesley's Chair, so I took it as its rightful owner.'

Paige sighed. 'Idiot,' she said, 'it's Charles Wesley's chair, not yours.'

'It is rather magnificent though, isn't it?' He stroked the tapestried back and its polished wooden arms.

'No, it isn't. You must take it back before we leave.'

'Ah, about that.' Wesley had a fanciful look that she'd seen all too often. She pushed his sleeve up so that she could see his tattoo.

'It's quite ordinary,' she said, looking at it from all angles.

'Precisely,' Wesley said, and kissed the tip of her nose. 'I quite like it here; I think we should stick around for a while.'

Florence

Florence waited for the white Mini Clubman in front of her to leave the box junction before turning right and then taking the first left into Gaskell Close. After five hundred yards she slowed, selected second gear and turned right through the open gates and parked on the drive.

Grabbing her bag, she stepped out of the car and stretched her arms wide.

'Honey, I'm home,' she yelled.

The front door swung open and Caitlin strode out. 'About bloody time too,' she said as she passed the large tabby cat she had in her arms to Florence, 'he's been pacing the hallway since I mentioned you were on your way back.'

'Hello, my darling,' Florence crooned into the silky fur on the cat's neck. 'God, I've missed you – has Auntie Cat been looking after you? I know she's fed you tuna – I do hope you rewarded her with a fabulous scented display in the cat tray!'

'You are so delightful, and yes I am well thanks, and so is Thomas. He has literally eaten me out of house and home and I've not seen one deadline owing to his fixation with that Scandinavian detective programme – who knew cats could speak Danish? – but we've both slept really well and ...'

'Oh do shut up,' Florence interrupted, 'and get the kettle on. If you make me a huge cup of coffee I will regale you with a highly unlikely story full of witches, magic pages and time-travelling detectives. Oh, and missing people that continue to be missing but presumed sent to a happier place and time that did not involve dying first.'

'Sounds wonderful. Does it have a happy ending?'

'Well, I'm alive, but the factual ending certainly won't be making it onto the super's desk!'

Sandbach

'Remind me again how Sergeant Harriet Boyle comes out of this as the hero?' Terrence asked, trotting along next to Sandbach on their way back to the car.

'The debriefing back at the station didn't go too smoothly,' Sandbach replied, 'Sergeant Boyle wasn't convinced by my report.'

'Well, it was unlikely that a gas leak exploding would have caused all that damage, especially since there are no active gas mains anywhere near the Green Man.'

'Yes, but can you imagine trying to explain what really happened?'

Terrence shrugged as they reached the car. Sandbach opened his door and climbed in.

'Exactly,' Terrence continued from the passenger seat, 'she had no choice but to go with your report, so why make it look like she did all the work?'

'I don't know, she was actually more helpful than I expected. Presumably she had faith in us solving this case one way or another. Although perhaps more faith in Carter.'

Sandbach searched his pockets for the car keys, next time he would really try to keep them in one place.

'Besides,' Sandbach said, 'focusing on her heroic actions last night took the spotlight away from us. People might wonder what we were doing down there in the first place.'

'Fair enough. Back home then?' Terrence said.

'Yes, there's always another case and we need to be back at the London office by four. But you know what?' Sandbach said, turning to his four-legged companion, 'I fancy a bacon sandwich on the way.'

Thank you!

If you have enjoyed this book, the authors would appreciate it if you could leave a review.

Also available from Ruler's Wit are four seasonal anthologies of short stories, each available in paperback and Kindle format.

Spring Tales

UK paperback - http://amzn.to/28YNOwT

UK Kindle - http://amzn.to/293BawW

US paperback - http://amzn.to/299L4e0

US Kindle - http://amzn.to/299L0uX

Summer Tales

UK paperback - https://amzn.to/2eDZvs4

UK Kindle - https://amzn.to/2dH2jmC

US paperback - https://amzn.to/2eOCe5U

US Kindle - https://amzn.to/2ePVcu9

Autumn Tales

UK paperback - https://amzn.to/2imnpgA

UK Kindle - https://amzn.to/2hRS30f

US paperback - https://amzn.to/2hRWhp0

US Kindle - https://amzn.to/2ipfqLX

Winter Tales

UK paperback - https://amzn.to/3mTcM2y

UK Kindle - https://amzn.to/3qG59io

US paperback - https://amzn.to/2Is1wv4

US Kindle - https://amzn.to/37MmJZh

Reviews

Reviews for Spring Tales

In reading this compendium, I remembered why I used to love short stories. They whet your appetite for more from the authors (and perhaps introducing you to new writers) and set you thinking about the issues that they discuss. The authors are all members of a UK based writing group and it is good to see such a group publish their work - it should encourage others to give it a go. I highly recommend this to you and will watch out for the Summer Tales next!

Biker Bird, 11 May 2016

This is an excellent collection of well-written short stories - all very different but all good. I've really enjoyed reading all the stories and am looking forward to Summer Tales.

S S, 9 August 2016

Super easy bite sized reads. A real variety of unpredictable tasty tales.

Caroline Norton, 28 July 2016

Lovely little book to accompany previous winter tales. I will certainly be purchasing more for gifts.

Amazon Customer, 17 May 2016

Reviews for Summer Tales

Beautifully written with a combination of stories to satisfy most readers this anthology follows on well from the previous two. Highly recommended.

D. Edwards, 21 July 2016

Great read for the beach and summer holidays. Ordered this to pass the time at the airport and couldn't put it down. I enjoy short stories, and these kept my attention. I thought the one set in New Zealand was really interesting, now I'm intrigued about Maori culture and history.

Amazon Customer, 16 July 2016

An excellent collection of intriguing short stories.

Amazon Customer, 25 Aug 2016

Reviews for Autumn Tales

Excellent light-hearted reading material you can pick up and put down anytime you have 10/15 minutes in the day. Would certainly recommend it.

Jillie F, 18 December 2016

Reviews for Winter Tales: First Edition

I wouldn't usually read short stories, but decided to give this one a go. I am so glad I did, lovely little book. Each uplifting story is perfect to savour during a coffee break. Would highly recommend it and hope they keep them coming.

K Hellwig, 7 April 2016

I'm not an avid reader so enjoyed these lovely short stories which were enough for me. I have already purchased Spring Tales and am looking forward to the next adventures. Clever authors all!

Amazon Customer, 17 May 2016

Ruler's Wit

Ruler's Wit is a team of Leicestershire writers who meet fortnightly enabling constructive, critical evaluation of written work for publication. Meet the team on the following pages.

www.rulerswit.co.uk

Stephen Ashurst

www.ash28.co.uk

Stephen has a BA Hons degree in Art and Design from Suffolk College and currently works as Senior Web Designer at Loughborough University. He has however been a keen writer and storyteller since he was old enough to write. With an odd and sometimes surreal sense of humour, he enjoys writing stories of most genres and styles.

He has three novels on the go at present and is a member of two writing groups – Bell's Shower and, of course, Ruler's Wit.

Stephen's characters

Detective Inspector Sandbach

Sandbach is a detective who, perhaps not through choice, specialises in the more unusual cases. Sometimes these may be particularly impossible to solve, perhaps unusually macabre, or even just that no other detective in their right mind would want to go near these cases. Sandbach has a dry, off-beat sense of humour that doesn't always sit well with other people. Which is just as well, as he works alone apart from the help or hindrance, he gets from a small imaginary dog who keeps him company. Sandbach has appeared in two short stories from the Ruler's Wit seasonal collection.

Terrence

Terrence is Sandbach's imaginary dog. Given that he can talk he acts as Sandbach's alter ego, helping to solve cases with him, Terrence would definitely not class himself as a pet. He sees himself at least as Sandbach's equal. But as an imaginary being, seen only by Sandbach, this raises complex existentialist questions. He does, however, like bacon. Terrence goes wherever Sandbach goes, and so has also appeared in the same two stories in the Ruler's Wit seasonal collection.

Fenella

Fenella is one of the traders on Loughborough Market. She has the appearance of a mid-late-middle-aged hippy, with wild, flowing ginger hair and long, floaty ethnic dresses. She runs a barely sustainable stall selling incense sticks, dream catchers and other new-age paraphernalia. No one knows where she lives or where she comes from, but behind her mild and innocent appearance, she can be sharp and short tempered, and she may be far older and wiser than appearances suggest.

Karen Ette

www.the-writers-secret-helper.com
www.Battlefieldsandbeyond.com
www.FancyPansCafe.com

Karen completed her PhD at Loughborough University, where she also gained her MA in English, Creative Writing. She has since taught there on the MA Creative Writing course and on the third-year undergraduate Publishing module.

Karen's recent novel, Don't Be Late in the Morning, published by Goldcrest Books, is the first and only novel to have been written about the Leicestershire Regiment in the First World War and whilst it is fiction, it is written from unpublished letters and diaries, and solid historical facts. She has also written: A Second Christmas Truce? – Christmas on the Western Front, 1915, The Advent Calendar Recipe Book, and Your UCAS Application: a step-by-step guide.

She has written introductions and chapters for three books, published by Igloo, (Comfort Food, Chocolate and Harold Shipman) and published magazine articles include: Your Cat, The Racing Pigeon and the magazine of the Leicestershire and Rutland Western Front Association, The Tiger. She is also a member of the Association of Christian Writers and Leicester Writers' Club.

Karen is also a professional member of the Chartered Institute for Editors and Proofreaders.

Karen's characters

Paige and Wesley

Paige and Wesley are historical time travellers. Their means of travel to the past is through gates. They first appeared in Winter Tales, published by Ruler's Wit, when they were the main characters in the re-telling of the Good King Wenceslas story. They have helped William Wordsworth in Spring Tales, were on the Western Front in 1916 in Summer Tales and at the signing of the Armistice in 1918, in Autumn Tales. They are very much in love and can't travel into the future.

Matthew Hopkins

Matthew Hopkins is a direct descendant of the Witchfinder General, Matthew Hopkins, of the 1640s. His ancestors have tried, but failed, to gain immortal life by trading the souls of innocent people with the devil. He believes that he has almost finally gained everything he needs to give him eternal life and embarks on the last phase of his quest in Loughborough today.

Melinda Ingram

Melinda gained an MA in English – Creative Writing at Loughborough University. She is a qualified teacher and has taught people aged two to sixty in a variety of settings. Melinda retired from the University of Leicester and now teaches psychology and English part-time at a nearby FE College. She is also a trustee of her local Community Library.

Melinda has edited and contributed chapters to books on Education for Sage and Learning Matters (under Min Wilkie) including Supporting Learning in Primary Schools and Doing Action Research. She has self-published Fictionalising Iraq in British and American Literature (Children's and YA) and is working on two stories for YA readers. Melinda's creative writing often reflects her interest in Life Writing and Time Slip stories.

Melinda's characters

Ellen

Ellen appears in three stories in the Ruler's Wit seasonal collections, which are all extracts from one of Melinda's novels-in-progress. In those stories she is about thirteen and is staying at Caravelli's with her family in order to celebrate her grandmother's ninetieth birthday. Whilst on a visit to the Old Rectory Museum with her history-loving parents Ellen time-slips to the 1660s. In this story, some years later, she is studying at Loughborough University and working part-time at Caravelli's.

Robert Hooke

Hooke graduated from Oxford. He was a man of many talents and enthusiasms: architect, surveyor, mathematician. As Surveyor to the City of London he contributed to the first modern plan-form maps. From 1662 he was curator of experiments at the Royal Society, presenting scientific ideas to gatherings of scientists. He was a contemporary of Boyle and Newton and worked on telescopes and theories to do with refraction of light. He had a fascination with and a zest for life, investigating geology, astrology and the microscopic world. He published a book on the latter subject, an interest reflected in this story.

George Fox

Fox was the leader of the movement known now as Quakers, and in the 1660s as the Society of Friends. Fox was born in Leicestershire but travelled extensively across England and Wales and even to America (but never in time as far as we know), often preaching in public. He was jailed several times, more than once in Leicester, and at least once because he would not remove his hat in court. He valued simplicity and truth; many of his speeches and his own writings still exist, so some of the words he speaks in this story are his actual words. In the short stories with the young Ellen, Fox is preaching in Loughborough Market.

Donna Shepherd

www.wordsbyredkite.co.uk

Donna gained her BA and MA in English as a mature student at Loughborough University and runs her own business, Red Kite Copywriting Services. She also works as a development editor.

Donna lives in North Warwickshire with her husband, daughter, Harry the rescue terrier and two rescue cats. A frequent character of Donna's stories is Tom the cat who in reality died six years ago and is still missed every day.

Donna's characters

Florence Carter
Florence appears in three stories in the Ruler's Wit seasonal collections. In those stories she is not one to suffer fools, protective of her independence and freely admits that the closest she's ever come to falling in love was when she first laid eyes on her rescue cat, Tom. In this story, very little has changed for Florence with the exception that she is now on the firearms team and in her early forties.

Florence and Caitlin met on an Army assault course near Lichfield and their subsequent friendship has been a life-line to both women.

Caitlin Blake
Caitlin has also appeared in three of Donna's previous short stories as Florence's kind of sidekick. Her background is in the military, but after the death of her husband she left the Army and started writing articles and blogs based on and around war- from a female perspective. Caitlin is the only other human-being that Florence trusts with Tom and is therefore on 'aunt' duty whenever Florence is called away.

Printed in Great Britain
by Amazon